POPULAR PUBLICATIONS ⸺ FACSIMILE EDITIONS

Dime Detective Magazine #5 (March 1932)

Dime Detective magazine was the flagship detective pulp in the Popular Publications stable, running for almost 300 issues over twenty years. The fifth issue contains stories by Oscar Schisgall, Frederick Nebel, Carroll John Daly, Edward Parrish Ware, and J. Allan Dunn, and includes appearances by series character such as Cardigan, Tug Norton, and Vee "Crime Machine" Brown.

Authors:

Oscar Schisgall, Edward Parrish Ware, Carroll John Daly, J. Allan Dunn, Frederick Nebel, Maxwell Hawkins

Illustrators:

William Reusswig, John Fleming Gould

1

10¢ DIME DETECTIVE MAGAZINE

EVERY STORY COMPLETE   EVERY STORY NEW

Vol. 2   **CONTENTS for MARCH, 1932**   No. 1

FOUR GREAT MYSTERY-ACTION NOVELETTES

TENSE SHORT STORIES OF CRIMELAND

Watch for the April Issue   On the Newsstands March 20th

Published every month by Popular Publications, Inc., 2256 Grove Street, Chicago, Illinois. Editorial and executive offices 205 East Forty-second Street, New York City. Harry Steeger, President and Secretary, Harold S. Goldsmith, Vice President and Treasurer. Entered as second class matter Aug. 6th, 1930, at the Post Office at Chicago, Ill., under the Act of March 3, 1879. Title registration pending at U. S. Patent Office. Copyrighted 1932 by Popular Publications, Inc. Single copy price 10c. Yearly subscriptions in U. S. A. $1.00. For advertising rates address H. D. Cushing, 67 West 44th Street, New York, N. Y. When submitting manuscripts, kindly enclose sufficient postage for their return if found unavailable. The publishers cannot accept responsibility for return of unsolicited manuscripts, although all care will be exercised in handling them.

Who else wants to learn to play....

at home without a teacher, in ½ the usual time and ⅓ the usual cost?

Over 600,000 men and women have learned to play their favorite instruments the U. S. School of Music way!

That's a record of which we're mighty proud! A record that proves, better than any words, how *thorough*, how *easy*, how *modern* this famous method is.

Just think! You can quickly learn to play any instrument—directly from the notes—and at an average cost of only a few cents a day.

You study in your own home, practice as much or as little as you please. Yet almost before you realize it you are playing real tunes and melodies — not dull scales, as with old-fashioned methods.

Like Playing a Game

The lessons come to you by mail. They consist of complete printed instructions, diagrams, and all the music you need. You simply can't go wrong. First you are *told* what to do. Then a picture *shows* you how to do it. Then you do it yourself and *hear* it. No private teacher could make it any clearer.

As the lessons continue they become easier and easier. For instead of just scales you learn to play by *actual notes* the favorites that formerly you've only *listened* to. You can't imag-

ine what fun it is, until you've started!

Truly, the U. S. School method has removed all the difficulty, boredom, and extravagance from music lessons.

Fun — Popularity

You'll never know what real fun and good times are until you've learned to play some musical instrument. For music is a joy-building tonic—a sure cure for the "blues." If you can play, you are always in demand, sought after, sure of a good time. Many invitations come to you. Amateur orchestras offer you wonderful afternoons and evenings. And you meet the kind of people you have always wanted to know.

Never before have you had such a chance as this to become a musician—a really good player on your favorite instrument—without the deadly drudging and prohibitive expense that were such drawbacks before. At last you can start right in and *get somewhere*, quickly, cheaply, thoroughly.

Here's Proof!

"I am making excellent progress on the 'cello—*and owe it all to your easy lessons*," writes George C. Lauer of Belfast, Maine.

"I am now on my 12th lesson and can already play simple pieces," says Ethel Harnishfeger, Fort Wayne, Ind. "I knew nothing about music when I started."

"I have completed only 20 lessons and can play almost any kind of music I wish. My friends are astonished," writes Turner B. Blake, of Harrisburg, Ill.

And C. C. Mittlestadt, of Mora, Minn., says, "I have been playing in the brass band for several months now. I learned to play from

your *easy lessons*."

You, too, can learn to master the piano, violin, 'cello, saxophone—any instrument you prefer—this quick, easy way! For every single thing you need to know is explained in detail. And the explanation is always *practical*. Little theory—plenty of *accomplishments*. That's why students of the U. S. School course get ahead *twice as fast* as those who study by old-fashioned, plodding methods.

Booklet and Demonstration Lesson — FREE!

The whole interesting story about the U. S. School course cannot be told on this page. A booklet has been printed, "Music Lessons in Your Own Home," that explains this famous method in detail, and is yours free for the asking. With it will be sent a Free Demonstration Lesson, which *proves* how delightfully quick and easy—how *thorough*—this modern method is.

If you really want to learn to play at home—without a teacher—in one-half the usual time—and at one-third the usual cost—by all means send for the Free Booklet and Free Demonstration Lesson AT ONCE. No obligation. (Instruments supplied if desired—cash or credit.) U. S. SCHOOL OF MUSIC, 862 Brunswick Bldg., New York.

Thirty-Fourth Year (Estab. 1898)

Pick Your Instrument

Piano	Violin
Organ	Clarinet
Ukulele	Flute
Cornet	Saxophone
Trombone	Harp
Piccolo	Mandolin
Guitar	'Cello

Hawaiian Steel Guitar
Sight Singing
Piano Accordion
Italian and German Accordion
Voice and Speech Culture
Harmony and Composition
Drums and Traps
Automatic Finger Control
Banjo (Plectrum, 5-String or Tenor)
Juniors' Piano Course

U. S. SCHOOL OF MUSIC,
862 Brunswick Bldg., New York City

Please send me your free book, "Music Lessons in Your Own Home," with introduction by Dr. Frank Crane, Free Demonstration Lesson and particulars of your easy payment plan. I am interested in the following course:

Have You Instrument? ......

Name ....

Address ....

City ....State.......

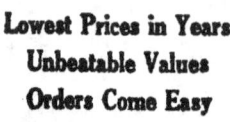

Those who laughed loudest

when I started to play

...were the most curious
when I finished

"HAIL! HAIL! THE GANG'S ALL HERE"

"Sure the gang's all here," moaned Iris, "but Ken Davis forgot to bring his music and he can't play a note without it."

"I'm dreadfully sorry, Iris," said Ken. "It was just stupidness on my part."

"Ah, what's the difference," I intruded. "If we're lucky we'll get some good dance music on the radio."

"The radio," said Iris dejectedly, "that's out too, Tom. Father ordered a new set and it's already two days overdue. There goes all my visions of a good party up in smoke."

"Cheer up," I said. "I'll play the old school songs and a few dance numbers."

"I know you don't know one note from another," said Iris, "but please try and keep the party in good humor."

I started to open the piano. Before I even had a chance to sit down, the wise cracks began. "Hey! What are you going to do — tune the piano?" said one of the boys.

"No, Brother, I'm going to play if you have no objections."

By this time the room rocked with laughter . . . giggles . . . hoots. "You play! That's rich," roared Ken.

A Dramatic Surprise

Solemnly a voice interrupted, "Sir, we do hereby appoint you musical director of this gathering. While you go through the motions of playing, we'll sing our famous Marching Song."

Go through the motions! What a ripe time for my little surprise. With much gusto I struck the introductory chords of the famous "Stein Song."

Suddenly the laugh bombardment was silenced. One by one they moved closer to the piano—curiosity written all over their faces. Funny, too, the ones who had laughed loudest were the most inquisitive. "So, Tom, you've been taking lessons on the sly from one of the teachers at the conservatory," said Ken.

"You're wrong—I learned to play by mail," I said proudly.

"Without a teacher, you mean?" asked Iris.

"Certainly—why not? You see you don't need a teacher when you learn the U. S. School of Music way—the lessons are mailed right to your home."

Then I told them all about this famous course—how I set my own study periods and played real tunes *by note* right from the very start—how the clear and simple print and picture instructions kept me from making mistakes—how in almost no time, I could play any kind of selections—jazz or classical.

Want To Be Popular?

This story is typical. The sooner you get started musically, the sooner you'll be popular. No matter which instrument you select, the cost of learning the U. S. School way averages just a few cents a day. Previous musical talent is never required. We've already proved that to more than 600,000 people. Every single thing you need to know is explained in detail. Little theory—plenty of *accomplishment*. That's why students of this course get ahead *twice as fast*—*three times as fast*—as those who study by old time, plodding methods.

Free Book and Demonstration Lesson

Our illustrated Free Book and Free Demonstration Lesson explain all about this remarkable method. The booklet will also tell you about the amazing new Automatic Finger Control. Sign the coupon below. Instruments supplied if desired, cash or credit. U. S. SCHOOL OF MUSIC, 863 BRUNSWICK BUILDING, New York City.

Pick Your Instrument	
Piano	Violin
Organ	Clarinet
Ukulele	Flute
Cornet	Saxophone
Trombone	Harp
Piccolo	Mandolin
Guitar	'Cello
Hawaiian Steel Guitar	
Sight Singing	
Piano Accordion	
Italian and German Accordion	
Voice and Speech Culture	
Harmony and Composition	
Drums and Traps	
Automatic Finger Control	
Banjo (Plectrum, 5-String or Tenor)	
Juniors' Piano Course	

Compare these Drawings

Both the above drawings are the work of Art Nelson. (1) He made before Federal training. (2) He completed recently. Today he is making a good income in Art. He says, "The Federal Schools made this possible as I had only average ability before enrolling as a student."

Opportunities for artists have never been better. Publishers pay millions of dollars every year for illustrations. If you like to draw, let your talent make your living. It's easy to learn the "Federal Home-Study Way." Over fifty famous artists teach you.

The Federal Course includes illustrating, cartooning, lettering, poster designing and window card illustrating. Why plod along? Send your name, address, age and occupation for our free book, "A Road to Bigger Things."

Federal School of Illustrating

3442 Federal School Bldg., Minneapolis, Minn.

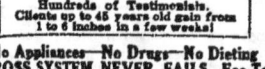

The DESTROYER of MALE HEALTH

FREE To Men Past 40

Amazing New Facts
About the Misunderstood Subject of
Rejuvenation!

An extraordinary new book, based on certain discoveries about old age reveals facts which, to many men, will be amazing. Did you know that two-thirds of all men past middle age are said to have a certain seldom-mentioned disorder? Do you know the frequent cause of this decline in health?

Common Old-Age Symptoms

Medical men know this condition as hypertrophy of the prostate gland. Science now reveals that this swollen gland—painless in itself—not only often cheats men of health, but also bears on the bladder and often directly responsible for sciatica, backache, pains in the legs and feet, frequent nightly rising, and dizziness, denoting high blood pressure. When allowed to run on it frequently the cause of the dreaded disease cystitis, a very severe bladder inflammation.

65% Have This Gland Disorder

Prostate trouble is now reached immediately by a new kind of home treatment—a new safe hygiene that goes directly to the gland itself, without drugs, medicines, massage, lessons, diet or the application of electricity. It is absolutely safe. 100,000 men have used it for restoring the prostate gland to normal functioning. The principle involved in this treatment is recommended by practically all physicians in America. Amazing recoveries are made in seven days. Another

grateful effect is usually the immediate disappearance of chronic constipation. Usually the entire body is toned up. Either you feel ten years younger in seven days or the treatment costs you nothing.

Send for FREE Book

If you have this gland trouble or if you have any of the symptoms mentioned above, you should not lose a day in writing for the scientist's free Book, "The Destroyer of Male Health." It will enable you to ask yourself certain frank questions that may reveal your true condition. Every man past 40 should make this test, as insidious prostate disorder often leads to surgery. This book is absolutely free, but mail coupon immediately, as the edition is limited. Address

THE ELECTRO THERMAL CO.

5551 Morris Avenue   Steubenville, Ohio

The Death Scream

by
Oscar Schisgall

Author of "Once a Crook," etc.

Out of the New England fog it came—the midnight murder wail of the desert tribes. What could it mean? Whose awful throat had sent it shrieking through the black? For Egypt was across the world and here were only cased and mummied dead to guard the secrets of the East.

CHAPTER ONE

"Ayeee!"

S HE awoke with a gasp; sat up rigid, shocked, her eyes round in fear. For some time she could not be certain she had actually heard the sound. It might easily have been a nightmarish delusion; the echo, in a dream, of a dreadful shriek she had heard those other nights.

But she realized soon enough that the sound had been real. Apparently everyone in the house had been roused by it. Doors were opening, and she caught the clamor of frightened voices in the hall the thumps of running feet. There was something of panic in the sudden excitement, as if a fire had been discovered.

Katherine Lacombe swung out of bed As she reached for her negligée, electri tinglings, like chills, were quivering through her tense body. And her dark eyes flamed.

The Arab screamed in insane terror. "I won't tell you! You can't shoot it out of me!"

She knew exactly what she was going to do. She was going to telephone Police Chief Cory—or rather, his son, Hal. Yes, Hal Cory! Regardless of how anyone in this crazy household opposed her, she was going to have the local authorities investigate this frightful affair! After all, she was twenty-two and nominally the mistress of her uncle's home; and she didn't intend to endure such nights as these in passive terror.

She started wrapping the negligée about her slim figure but stopped. Stopped abruptly, stiffly, with her head jerked up and her breath crushed.

For the sound came again!

"Ayee! . . . . "

Strident, harsh, piercing. It was unlike any scream she had ever heard before. There was nothing of pain in it. Only a kind of exultation and savagery. A cry of insane glee.

"Ayee! . . . . "

The breath exploded from her lungs. With an impulsive lurch Katherine Lacombe darted across the room to a window. The shriek came from out there, in the night. From somewhere among the trees, she thought; or from the rocks by the shore, where waves were crashing. If she could see—

But she couldn't.

FOG—the dense, gray fog that overwhelms the Maine coast in winter—hung before her in an impenetrable mass. It pressed against the pane. She could peer hardly ten feet into its rolling thickness. And a little groan of despair escaped her. That fog seemed to be laughing at her frustration, wickedly.

The essential thing to do, at once, was to notify the police; and so she ran out of the room. In the corridor the lights had been switched on. She saw her gaunt, bald-headed Uncle Philip at the top of the stairs, listening in a sort of agony to the agitated whispers of Dr. Kyne and Mr. Merriton. All of them, with dressing gowns thrown over their pajamas, looked addled, like men snatched out of sleep to meet calamity. And Dr. Kyne was hoarsely arguing.

"I tell you it can't be anything else! There's no other cry in the world like it! It's the death scream!"

"But—but how can it be?" her uncle protested in dazed bewilderment. He was always dazed in moments of stress. Primarily a scholar absorbed in the study of a remote past, he invariably seemed baffled and a little helpless when the present jolted him out of his detachment. "It—it's absurd," he stammered, "to suppose that here, in America—"

"I'm not trying to explain how it can be," Dr. Kyne rapped out, his eyes blazing through his glasses. "I only know I've heard that scream often enough to recognize it now. And so have you. It's the death scream! Nobody but one of those desert devils, charging across the Sahara into battle, could utter a scream like that. And he'd utter it only when he meant death!"

"Oh, nonsense!" snapped Mr. Merriton. He was a big, practical man with no taste for the bizarre. His deep voice brought a welcome note of sanity. "Bedouins," he scoffed, "don't go screaming into battle on the coast of Maine."

"Nevertheless—" heatedly began Dr. Kyne.

Then he saw Katherine. They all saw Katherine. In their abrupt silence she recognized consternation; they were visibly dismayed by her presence and by the realization that she must have overheard their talk.

Their attitude, however, did not surprise her. For days she had suspected that they were all concealing some secret knowledge concerning those demoniacal screams. Now she felt sure of it. Very deliberately she turned away from them and started toward the rear stairs.

"Kit!"

Her uncle's quick, anxious call halted her, and she looked back with an uncompromising, "Yes?"

"Where—where are you going?"

"I'm going," she told him firmly, "to telephone the police."

"Oh, but I—I say! You mustn't do that, Kit!" His dismay became almost ludicrous. He moved toward her with hesitant, uneven steps, his nervous fingers knotting the cord of his dressing gown. Though Professor Lacombe was as gaunt and homely as a beardless Abe Lincoln, he lacked all semblance of Lincolnian resolution. "You really mustn't," he stammered. "I mean—"

"Uncle Phil, it's the only thing to do! I've had enough of this mystery!" And she moved again, determinedly, toward the back stairs.

"Wait!"

This time it was Dr. Kyne who stopped her. The single word cracked from him harshly, like a shot; and its very suddenness caused her to stare at him in astonishment. For ordinarily Dr. Henry Aldrich Kyne was the most suave, courteous, and soft-spoken of men.

HE STRODE toward the girl grimly— a short figure, thick-set and vigorous. He had a gray Vandyke, sharply trimmed, and waves of flowing silver hair that contributed enormously to his really handsome appearance. Katherine knew her uncle esteemed him as a man of profound culture. But at that moment he seemed to her just an irascible old nuisance.

"Miss Lacombe," he said, "it would be most unwise to summon the police!"

"Why?" she challenged.

"For many reasons. In the first place, it would mean a sort of public mystery, with reporters and curiosity seekers swarming in upon us. You must see that talk of ghostly screams, when linked with anyone of your uncle's prominence, is bound to stir a great deal of interest. We don't want such notoriety. We're all too busy here to be annoyed by outsiders."

"I'd rather submit to a bit of such annoyance," retorted Katherine Lacombe, "than to be awakened night after night by those horrible screams! Heaven knows this house, with all the Egyptian relics you've heaped into it, is creepy enough. Those shrieks are just about the last straw."

"But there's no cause to call the police," Dr. Kyne insisted. "After all, no crime has been committed."

"Oh, come, Miss Lacombe—" The ponderous Mr. Merriton, having followed the others along the corridor, now smiled at her reassuringly, while his fine, deep voice joined the attempt at dissuasion. "Surely you understand that none of us care for public sensation. I'm certain you yourself have no desire to become the center of—"

"It seems to me," she interrupted coldly, "that you are all hiding your real reason for not wanting the police here!"

At that she saw Mr. Merriton and Dr. Kyne exchange a swift, startled glance. Then she looked at her uncle, inviting him to speak. But Professor Philip Lacombe, moistening his lips, shook his gaunt head in ineffectual distress. She fancied he would have given much just then to be in the safe seclusion of his studies.

"You—you had better do as these gentlemen advise, Kit," he muttered. "I think that would be best for all of us. We're doing everything possible to clear this mystery ourselves. Young Berkely and Haj are outside this very minute, trying to locate the source of those cries."

"In this fog," said Katherine, "they'll find nothing!"

"Still—"

"No, I can't take it so easily, Uncle Phil. I feel there's something awful—something terrible and menacing and insane—in those screams! I told Chief of Police Cory about them the other day, and—"

"You—you told?" gasped Dr. Kyne, wide-eyed.

"Of course. Why shouldn't I? Chief Cory himself is in bed with a twisted ankle. But his son promised to come out immediately if we heard the screams again. And I'm going to call him!"

Without uttering another word she spun around and darted swiftly down the stairs. Her abrupt departure disconcerted the men, alarmed them, too. She heard both her uncle and Mr. Merriton shout after her. But she no longer listened. Those outlandish shrieks in the night had been more eloquent than all these protestations!

By the time she reached the lower floor she knew that Dr. Kyne was coming in pursuit of her. But she did not even trouble to look back at him; ran, instead, into the library. And there, to prevent further dispute, she did something quite incompatible with her rôle as hostess to her uncle's guests.

Katherine closed and locked the door.

When she heard Dr. Kyne rattling the knob and calling out angrily, she gave the man no attention. Resolutely she crossed the dark room toward the telephone. Her nerves were twanging queerly. She paused only to switch on the light of a reading lamp. And as its glow darted into shadowy corners, she thought of Hal Cory, the police chief's son. It would be a distinct relief to have someone like him —young, capable, sensible—around this eerie house!

She reached for the telephone. And at that very instant, as she lifted it, a wild shudder raced through her, and she stood rigid.

For out of the distant fog it came again —long-drawn, piercing.

"*Ayeee! . . . .* "

CHAPTER TWO

Dagger Death

IT WAS four o'clock in the morning when Hal Cory's flivver, groping its way through the fog, finally brought him to Evergreen Point—that long, wooded promontory dominated by the Lacombe house.

For the twentieth time in the past half hour he had to stop, with an irritated grunt, to wipe the heavy mist from the car's windshield.

Then, though he was still a considerable distance from his destination, Cory decided to walk. Walking, he told himself, would be much easier and perhaps just as fast as trying to steer through this blinding fog. So he parked the coupé under roadside trees and set off afoot, moving with brisk, rapid strides that exercised every muscle in his hard young body.

There was no wind about him. Not even a breeze from the sea. Yet the night was penetratingly cold. He kept his overcoat collar turned high and pushed his clenched hands deep into the warmth of his pockets, where they touched a police badge and a revolver—twin symbols of his mission.

Hal Cory felt as if he were trudging through wilderness; as if he were the only creature alive in a world of fog and darkness. His steps crunched loudly in the silence. And yet it was not silence at all, for the night was uproarious with the crash and pounding of waves on the rocky shore somewhere to his right.

As he followed the road, Cory thought of the girl whose telephone call had snatched him out of sleep. He had seen Katherine Lacombe just once—two days ago, when she had come to tell his father of the amazing screams. But he remembered her vividly, remembered that he had been unable to tear his gaze away from her lustrous, excited eyes, from the loveliness of her tense face.

He was still thinking of her when, some ten minutes later, he found himself at a gate in a tall hedge. Cory paused, then turned into the Lacombe grounds.

The house, he knew, was some three hundred yards ahead. Three hundred yards through black fog in which a weird mystery wrought its spell. . . .

Cory frowned as he walked.

He knew the Lacombe house well enough—from the outside. Often, while sailing around Evergreen Point in his old catboat, he had gazed at it and marvelled at its stately isolation. A splendid white Colonial mansion, it stood near the tip of the point, alone, facing the sea, as lonely as a lighthouse. Usually scores of gulls were winging about its chimneys. He had always regarded it as a sort of remote, legendary castle—for certainly there was something of Old World majesty in its aloofness.

"The perfect spot," he thought with grim irony, "for a spook hunt like this. And at this hour—"

But he could not complete the phrase. For Cory heard something that halted him—a rigid figure crushed in fog—something that tautened his nerves and set his heart to thudding. Mechanically his fingers curled around the revolver in his pocket. He remained utterly motionless, listening, waiting.

Out of the darkness ahead of him came the distinct sounds of rapid footfalls!

They were hurrying toward him. As they became louder, he grew more tense. And his eyes gleamed. Was he going to encounter, at the very outset, the one who had been haunting the estate with his screams?

In the few seconds he stood there, squinting into the fog, Cory felt queer chills crawl over his body. He spread his feet slightly, as if steadying himself to sustain a blow. His grip on the revolver in his pocket became hard.

Then—

Like a wraith a figure materialized in front of him. A lean figure, its shoulders hunched. At the sight of Cory the man stopped with a gasp. He was a young man with a dark, narrow face in which burned frightened eyes. He wore a stiff felt hat and a black coat. And instantly, with explosive force, he cried: "D-don't move! I've got you covered!"

CORY, staring in amazement, did indeed see a revolver in the fellow's shaking hand. But his own gun, still in his pocket, was levelled at the other's chest. In contrast with the man's hoarse agitation, he himself felt strangely calm.

"What's the idea?" he asked quietly.

"N-never mind the idea! Who are you?"

"You'd better answer that one yourself," snapped Cory. "I happen to be a policeman!"

He wasn't a policeman, of course. He was just a young lawyer, two months out of college, who had been deputized by his father—Shag Harbor's chief and only police official—to investigate an emergency call. A sort of detective for the night. But Cory found a certain comfort in legalizing his position by calling himself a policeman.

The thin man gaped at him incredulously. "A—a what?" he ejaculated.

"I think you heard me." For emphasis Cory offered a brief glimpse of the badge in his left pocket, then thrust it down out of sight.

"But—wh-what are you doing here?" the man floundered in bewilderment.

"Miss Lacombe phoned for me," said Cory. "And now I'll ask the questions!"

He narrowed his eyes. "Who are you?"

"Why—" The man in the fog faltered, hesitantly lowering his revolver. Obviously he was disconcerted and puzzled, hardly knowing what to do. "I—I'm Harrison Berkely!"

"Oh, yes," muttered Cory. "Miss Lacombe mentioned you the other day. Professor Lacombe's assistant, aren't you?"

"Yes."

"What are you doing out here?"

"—I've been out almost an hour!" Berkely rasped with sudden harshness. He glared about into the night. "Trying to find the—the damned—"

"The man who screamed?"

"Yes. If it was a man. Lord, the thing sounded inhuman to me! I've never heard anything else like it!"

"How long is it since you heard the last scream?"

"Oh, more than half an hour! I've been hunting everywhere in this damned fog. When I heard you walking down here, I thought I'd finally struck something. So I came running."

Cory was silent a moment, peering intently at the other's lean, handsome face. A pointed mustache lent Berkely a peculiarly Continental air; one would have judged him to be either French or Spanish.

"Well," suddenly said Hal Cory, "I don't think you'll find your screamer by groping about blindly like this. Suppose you come along and show me the way to the house."

To this Harrison Berkely readily agreed. In truth, he seemed relieved by the suggestion that he end his search, or perhaps by the fact that the police were at last assuming some responsibility in the uncanny affair. As they trudged through the fog, he shivered, and Cory eyed him curiously. It struck him as odd that so nervous a man, whose hand had trembled as it held a gun, had the courage to hunt an unknown menace.

"You out here alone?" he asked.

"No," said Berkely. "Haj is around somewhere. But we separated a little while ago."

"Haj?"

"Haj Ibn Mayyud."

"Oh, yes," Cory recalled, as if speaking to himself. "Miss Lacombe did say the professor had an Arab servant."

"He's more than a servant," Berkely corrected. "Haj has charge of the Egyptian room—you know, the professor's museum."

CORY nodded. He had, of course, heard of the private museum with its famed collection of Egyptian antiques, knew that it had drawn many a noted archeologist to Evergreen Point. Recently, when Professor Lacombe had brought new treasures home from the Nile country, it had achieved considerable newspaper publicity.

But Cory did not give much thought to the museum now. As they pressed on into the fog, he reverted to the core of the fantastic mystery by asking: "Just what do you know about these screams?"

"Not a thing," muttered Berkely, "except that they're horrible!"

"Miss Lacombe said they began a week ago."

"And we've been hearing them almost every night since then. It—it's like having a ghost around the place. Tonight Haj and I decided not to undress. We remained ready to rush out as soon as the cries came. There were two revolvers in the house—guns the professor had used on some of his trips—and we each took one of them. But it didn't do much good. We haven't been able to find anything."

"Has anyone in the house any explanation to offer?"

"Not that I've heard of, no."

"No one can guess what they mean, eh?"

Berkely shook his narrow head, scowling. "That's the maddening part of it," he rapped out roughly. "There doesn't seem to be any reason for the screams! They're getting everybody's nerves on edge. Why, one of the professor's guests —Mr. Burrill—couldn't stand them any longer. He'd lie awake all night, listening. And so he left us yesterday. Went to stay at the hotel in town. The other two—Dr. Kyne and Mr. Merriton—are sticking it out, but they're frightfully upset, too."

Cory asked, after a pause: "By the way, how long have these men been here?"

"Two weeks," said Berkely.

"Just visiting the professor?"

"Oh, no! They were in Egypt with Professor Lacombe on this last trip, when he made those excavations near Nirri ed Basa. Now they're helping him catalogue and study the relics he brought back with him. . . . Well, here we are!"

Like a white curtain in the mist, the front of the house suddenly loomed before them. A few windows emitted pale light that painted yellow daubs in the fog. Cory followed Berkely up the veranda steps and waited, with his hands in his pockets, while the lean man jabbed at the bell button.

It seemed Berkely had scarcely touched that button when the door was pulled open—almost violently. Katherine Lacombe, dressed now, stood there staring at them. And at the sight of her Cory snatched his hands out of his pockets, stiffened in alarm.

For the girl was pallid. Her eyes flamed with a mixture of horror and fear. The hand she impulsively thrust out to seize Cory's arm trembled.

"I—I thought you'd never get here!" she cried huskily.

"What's happened?" he demanded.

"Mr. Merriton—Stewart Merriton! He—he's been stabbed to death!"

For a stunned second Hal Cory could not stir.

He heard Harrison Berkely gasp in a hoarse, incredulous outcry: "Good God! . . . . How? . . . . Wh-who did it?"

"We—we don't know who did it," whispered Katherine Lacombe in an unrecognizable voice. "Dr. Kyne found him there—in his room upstairs—on the floor—"

THEN Cory recaptured his senses. Without a word he plunged past the girl and went up the steps, three at a bound. The others followed him. As he ran he thought confusedly of the strange screams and this tragic aftermath, and wondered if the two had any kind of connection.

His nerves were quivering.

On the upper floor he saw the gaunt Professor Lacombe and the bearded Dr. Kyne staring into an open door. Both were fully dressed and both appeared paralyzed by horror. Behind them, gaping over their shoulders, terrified, were two kimono-clad women—the cook and the housekeeper. They turned and retreated a little, fearfully, when Cory came striding down the hall.

"Dead!" Professor Lacombe was dazedly mumbling, again and again, as if he could not conceive so monstrous a thing. "Dead! He's—dead!"

Cory's first glance into the room froze him. Left him feeling a little sick and dizzy.

He saw the half-dressed body of Stewart Merriton sprawling on its back. The arms were outflung; one knee was raised. The man had not worn a shirt, and his underwear was soaked hideously with blood that had spilled over on the floor. His eyes were wide open, glazed, staring with horrible fixity at the ceiling.

"Dead!" Professor Lacombe continued to mumble in that stupefied way. "Merriton is dead!"

Cory stepped past him into the room. White of face, he quite forgot his closely buttoned overcoat and his tugged-down hat. He knelt beside the body, and his heart was thundering, pounding, with crazy violence. He had to force himself to peer straight at the wound. To this sort of thing he was not at all accustomed. He had come to investigate ghostly screams, not brutal murder.

His fingers were stiff as he lifted Merriton's undershirt far enough to disclose the wound. It was a thin gash, like a knife-cut, perhaps an inch and a quarter long. And directly over the heart.

Cory dropped the shirt. Without otherwise moving he peered about the floor, under chairs, under the bed, under a bureau, everywhere. Of a weapon, however, there was no sign. The killer had evidently taken it away with him.

Grimly Cory rose and faced the group in the door.

"Will you please telephone Dr. Westervelt for me?" he said to Harrison Berkely, in a hard, quiet voice. Dr. Westervelt was the local coroner. "The number is Shag Harbor 107. Ask him to come immediately!"

And as the stunned Berkely hurried away, he turned to Professor Lacombe. "I'm Hal Cory," he said. "My father, the police chief, has deputized me to represent him here. So I guess it's up to me to take charge of this."

Professor Lacombe nodded dully, as if he had not quite heard, his gaze still fastened on the body.

"Suppose you tell me," Cory began, "just what you know about this thing."

"It—it's unbelievable!" muttered the professor. "We don't know how it happened at all. There was no sound of any kind. No cry. Nothing!"

Cory glanced at the pale face of Dr. Henry Aldrich Kyne. "You were the one who found the body?" he inquired.

"Yes!" whispered the bearded man, huskily. "Yes. I was the one who found him!"

"As he is now?"

"Exactly as he is, yes!"

"You mean you came here, to this room?"

"I did! To—to call for him."

"For what?"

"Why," faltered Dr. Kyne, "he didn't come down to the library, and we were wondering what was delaying him. And so I—"

"We'd better explain everything to Mr. Cory!" suddenly put in Katherine Lacombe, her eyes unnaturally bright and determined. She spoke to Cory himself now, quickly, as if to supercede the others. "After I telephoned you," she said, "we all agreed to wait up to tell you what we knew about the screams. Nobody could sleep, anyhow, with those devilish shrieks out there! It was cold, and Uncle Phil decided to get dressed. The rest of us did, too. We all went to our rooms. About fifteen minutes later we met again in the library. That is, Dr. Kyne, Uncle Phil, and I. Mr. Merriton didn't come down. We began to wonder about him. And finally, after another ten minutes, Dr. Kyne volunteered to see what was detaining him. You see, we'd had coffee served by the housekeeper, and we wanted Mr. Merriton to join us. Dr. Kyne went upstairs, and—and then we heard him cry out. Uncle Phil and I ran up at once and saw—saw this!"

She finished with an anguished little wave of her hand toward the room.

CORY nodded. He drew off his hat to reveal a mass of disheveled brown hair. Then began to unbutton his coat with the air of a man who has a difficult task to perform and intends to remain until the thing is done.

"No weapon around?" he asked.

"I didn't see any," said Dr. Kyne.

"Nor did I," added Professor Lacombe, roused at last from his daze.

"You say," Cory pressed, "there was no sound in the house to indicate when Merriton was killed?"

"None at all!" from Dr. Kyne.

Cory glanced back at the body on the floor. Unfortunately, he realized, he had no personal experience in the investigation of murder mysteries. To find Merriton's slayer he would have to rely solely on his judgment, not on police ritual. He tightened his lips grimly and peered again about the room.

Did it contain obvious clues which he was overlooking?

The chamber, he saw, had two windows, and both were closed against the thick fog. Not only closed, but locked. Unless they had been closed after the murder, it was evident the killer had entered and left this bedroom by way of the door. Did that, Cory asked himself with an uncomfortable frown, mean the murderer was one of these people in the house?

He checked the idea. "No use jumping at conclusions!" he thought sharply. An opinion or a prejudice formed now might blind him to subsequent possibilities.

Another thing he saw was this: the big Stewart Merriton had been dressing at the time of his death. He had already drawn on trousers and shoes, and had apparently been ready to slip into a shirt. And at that moment someone had appeared to drive a knife into his heart.

Cory drew a deep breath. Once more he turned toward Dr. Henry Aldrich Kyne. "When you came up," he asked, "did you find this door closed?"

"Yes, of course."

"Then you opened it yourself?"

"After knocking several times, yes," the bearded man admitted, somewhat stiffly. "I couldn't understand why Merriton didn't answer. So I pushed the door open, and—and there he lay."

"Were the windows as they are now, shut?"

"Certainly. No one has touched them. No one has touched anything!"

"Except," coldly corrected Katherine Lacombe, "the body."

At that Dr. Kyne shot a distinctly resentful glance at her; he argued: "Naturally I touched the body! I had to. When first I saw him there, I couldn't be sure he was dead. I jumped in and picked up his head and felt his pulse. But I put him right down again as soon as—as I knew!"

There was a moment of silence while Hal Cory stepped out into the corridor and closed the door of the tragic room behind him. No use carrying on this inquisition in sight of the body, he decided; to strain the nerves of these people was to confuse them. And he wanted no further confusion now.

He perceived that a very definite hostility existed between Katherine Lacombe and Dr. Kyne. And without pausing to analyze his reaction to this, he felt his sympathy surge toward the girl. For one thing, her dark-haired loveliness lured his eyes even in this crisis. For another, he saw that her manner toward the bearded man was merely aloof; while his toward her, on the other hand, was angry and harsh.

As Cory read these indications of emotional undercurrents, young Harrison Berkely hastily returned to say that Dr. Westervelt, the coroner, would come at once. The investigator nodded. But Berkely's reappearance reminded him of someone else; and he asked Professor Lacombe: "By the way, where is your Arab?"

"Haj Ibn Mayyud?" The professor looked slightly surprised by the query. "Why, he was here a few moments ago. I—I sent him down to the museum."

"The museum?"

"We have many valuable objects—"

"With a desperate criminal around," quickly interrupted Dr. Kyne (too quickly, thought Cory), "we decided we'd better be sure the museum was locked and untouched. After all—"

He got no further.

His words were suddenly, eerily, shattered by a piercing scream that leaped from somewhere far out in the fog! Crazy, gleefully exultant.

"*Ayeee! . . . .*"

Dan Cory caught his breath in amazement.

And Professor Philip Lacombe, whirling around with his gaunt face as yellow as butter, gasped a hoarse and terrified: "God! . . . . Then it—it *is* the death scream!"

CHAPTER THREE

He Came by Boat!

HAL CORY did not pause to ask questions.

Though a wild shiver raced through him as he heard that frightful screech, he spun around and dashed to the stairs. He plunged down at reckless speed, his eyes aflame, his white face rock-hard.

That scream, he judged, had been uttered perhaps a hundred yards from the front of the house. Somewhere close to the shore. If he could get there in time to. . . .

But he did not attempt to think now. He dashed out of the door to fling himself into the fog. Harrison Berkely, he was vaguely aware, had followed and was racing along behind him. Cory drew his revolver.

To see where he was running was im-

possible. He had only the crash of waves on rocks to guide him. There were no more screams. Yet his ears were desperately strained in an effort to hear someone, something, in that thick mist!

Suddenly he had to slacken his speed. He was stumbling among wet, slippery boulders. And fine showers of spray swept upon him through the fog.

"We're just about thirty feet from the water!" panted Berkely, reaching him. "He can't very well be up there!"

"Listen!"

Cory's word broke from him like a shot. His eyes flared. He half raised his hand, and both men stood tense, unstirring. Very distinctly, above the roar and splash of waves, they heard the *put-put-put-put* of a motorboat. Clearly, it was slipping off through the fog, for its sound was becoming ever more faint, more uncertain.

Berkely gasped: "He got away!"

Who?

That was the question that blazed in Cory's mind. Who? The one who had screamed, no doubt. The killer of Stewart Merriton, at a guess. But—who?

"He's crazy!" Berkely blurted in a whisper. "To take a boat out in this fog!"

"Where the devil could he have landed?" Cory wanted to know. For no one would have dared to bring a craft in among those wave-pounded rocks.

"There's a strip of sheltered beach," Berkely said, "down below."

"Oh, yes? Where?"

"To the left. A path leads down to it."

At Cory's quick request Harrison Berkely led him toward the path. They found it only after considerable groping—a stony, slippery declivity that demanded caution at every step. As they descended, the lean man asked: "What do you expect to find?"

"The mark where the boat was drawn

up," grimly replied Cory. "And footprints around it!"

Two minutes later they were trudging across the sand of the small beach. It was in a cove, cozily protected by long arms of rock that warded off breakers. The waves that did reach the shore here were small, listless. Cory felt rather than saw the calm around him. For the fog still obscured everything more than a dozen feet away.

They carried no flashlights—an omission for which Cory furiously berated himself. But because there was little wind, they could light matches under cupped hands and study the beach in the feeble diffused glow. Presently, with the aid of the brief flares, they discovered the unmistakable groove left by the keel of a small boat.

"He must have had X-ray eyes," exclaimed Berkely, "to have found this beach in the fog!"

"The fog didn't settle heavily until midnight. He probably came before that time and waited."

"Still," muttered the lean man, "this doesn't tell us why he comes here with those hellish shrieks, or who he is."

"But it does tell us," snapped Cory, lighting another match, "that he is someone who knows this point well enough to strike a landing place in the dark! Also, that he's someone who has a motorboat." Mentally, he added that this discovery cancelled the first notion of the murderer's being someone in and of the house. At any rate, it strongly militated against the conclusiveness of such an idea.

He turned now to seek footprints.

BOTH men struck matches, and the yellow auras revealed faces that were tense and eager and strained. They bent to study the sand; and when they found the marks they sought, Cory widened his eyes in amazement.

For the footprints were not footprints at all! They were large, shapeless smudges that might have been left by an elephant sliding his huge feet through the sand!

"Wh-what on earth are these?" stammered Berkely.

"The old trick!" retorted Cory, scowling. "He had rags or sacks bound around his shoes."

"Then—you mean these marks are valueless?"

"Valueless as a means of identification, yes. But at least they show we're hunting somebody with plenty of shrewd foresight and common sense!"

They followed the line of smudge back to the rocks and up to the hard level ground above. There, among stones, they lost all sign of the tracks.

"Well," asked Berkely with an air of futility, "what now?"

"We're going back," grimly announced Cory, "to ask a few mighty important questions. Come on!"

On the way through the fog they encountered Katherine Lacombe and the Arab caretaker of the museum, Haj Ibn Mayyud. Both of them, bundled in heavy coats, were running toward the rocks; going, the girl explained, to see what had happened. Cory shocked her with a crisp mention of the motorboat, then led the whole group back toward the house.

As they walked, he obliquely studied the Arab.

An exceedingly slight, small, almost effeminite creature, Haj Ibn Mayyud could not have weighed much more than a hundred pounds. His dark face was sharp and shrewd and intelligent, with a pair of startlingly brilliant black eyes. He scarcely spoke. From the few things he did utter, however, Cory gathered that the man had a peculiar accent. He stressed all sibilants, so that he seemed always to be hissing the things he said.

Within the house, Hal Cory threw off his hat and coat and went at once into the library. The others all stood behind him, silent, while he telephoned a report of the astounding murder to his father. For a moment the chief was dumbstruck; then he demanded: "Think you can handle it all right, Hal?"

"I'll do my best."

"Got any ideas?"

"Lots of them. Too many, I'm afraid. But there's no use discussing them until I get some definite information. I'll call you again in the morning."

"Right," muttered the chief. "And—good luck to you, boy!"

Cory put down the telephone and turned grimly to confront the group in the library.

"The situation is this," Cory began, his eyes darting keenly from one stunned face to another. "According to the evidence we have, Stewart Merriton was murdered by someone who could enter his room without causing the man to cry out in alarm or surprise. In other words, it seems he was killed by somebody he knew well enough to trust in his chamber. Then, in all probability, he was stabbed suddenly, unexpectedly, before he had time to make a sound."

On this significant statement of the case he paused, watched the expressions of those who so tensely stared at him. He was never to forget that inquisition. The very atmosphere that hung over it was to linger with him as an uncanny memory.

THE library was illuminated only by reading lamps which threw localized patches of light. The housekeeper had kindled a fire in the hearth, and its leaping flames painted the room with daubs of quivering red. Professor Lacombe and Katherine sat very close to the fire, drenched in its glow. Dr. Kyne shared a settee with Harrison Berkely, on the op-posite side of the chamber. The dark-clad, dark-skinned Arab, Haj Ibn May-yud, stood alone near the door, as rigid as a statue. Even the cook and the house-keeper were there, shuddering together in a shadowy corner. It was five o'clock in the morning—an eerie enough hour in which to seek a murderer!

"Professor Lacombe," asked Cory tersely, "do you know of any explanation for Merriton's death? Do you know any-one who could have wanted to kill him?"

"No," huskily said the gaunt man, shaking his bony head. "I don't. I—I can't understand it. We all liked Stewart Merriton. Everybody liked him. He was a rich and generous friend."

Nor could anybody else offer a possible reason for the slaying, though Cory gave each of them a chance to speak. So, finally, he abandoned the question and moved to another.

"Merriton," he said, "must surely have made some sound, at least in falling. A sound loud enough to be heard, say, in the adjoining rooms. Whose rooms are next to his?"

"Mine, for one!" quickly replied Harrison Berkely, thrusting out his lean, handsome face in anxiety. "Mine was at his left. But I was out in the fog at the time of the murder. Hunting the—the devil who screamed! You know that, Mr. Cory."

"Yes, I know it," Cory said, a little wrily. He did not like the defensive note in Berkely's tones. "And who occupied the room at Merriton's right?"

"Why—" Professor Lacombe frowned into the fireplace as he answered. "Until yesterday it belonged to another of my guests—Mr. Charles Burrill. Unfortun-ately Mr. Burrill was so badly tormented by the screams we've been hearing that night after night he could not sleep. He was beginning to be actually ill. He left us yesterday and went to stay at the

American House in Shag Harbor. He had to be near us, you see, because we are all working together here. Tonight, of course, his room was unoccupied."

Cory started. "How long," he demanded quickly, "has Mr. Burrill been your guest?"

"Just two weeks."

At that a curious agitation stirred the investigator. Was there any significance in the fact that Stewart Merriton had been murdered on the very night Charles Burrill was absent from the house? After all, Cory was now seeking a man who could have entered Merriton's room without frightening him; one, perhaps, who knew the topography of Evergreen Point well enough to bring a boat to the small beach.

Did Mr. Burrill fit such a description?

Well, his connection with the killing was easy enough to ascertain! For the sake of thoroughness it must be ascertained. If the man was at his hotel now, he could not have been at the beach fifteen minutes ago. Hardly!

Cory glanced sharply at the housekeeper who stood beside the telephone. He asked her to call the American House and have Mr. Burrill summoned.

"Oh, but I say!" promptly protested Dr. Kyne, half rising. "Is that necessary?"

"Quite," Cory assured him.

"But poor Burrill hasn't slept in days! Why wake him now? I'm sure you can talk to him in the morning."

CORY, however, remained obdurate; and because he represented the inexorable law, the bearded Dr. Kyne settled back with a displeased but yielding grunt, while the housekeeper picked up the telephone.

"Now," firmly said the investigator, "while we wait, I'd like to have a better understanding of what work you gentlemen are all doing here. Will one of you please explain?"

It was, however, Katherine Lacombe who answered his request. She eyed him frankly, capably, and she spoke in a low, confident tone that captured his ears just as her gaze enslaved his eyes.

"You know, of course," she said, "that Uncle Phil has led several archeological expeditions into the Nile country. Two weeks ago he returned from some new excavations he had been superintending near Nirri ed Basa, in central Egypt.... You mind my telling this, uncle?" she asked, turning to the gaunt man.

"No, no. Not at all. Go on, Kit."

"On that expedition," Katherine resumed, "Uncle Phil was accompanied by Dr. Kyne, Mr. Burrill, and Mr. Merriton. When they returned, really loaded with invaluable relics, everything was brought here. And Uncle Phil invited the other gentlemen to help him study and catalogue the items. So, of course, they've been staying with us."

"I see," said Cory. He heard the housekeeper, at the telephone, asking for Mr. Burrill. While she waited, a vague figure in the shadows, he turned to Professor Lacombe to observe: "All these gentlemen in the house, then, were with you in Egypt during your last trip?"

"Not all," the gaunt man corrected, his face weirdly licked by firelight. "Haj was right here at the house during my absence, in charge of my museum. And Mr. Berkely, of course, has been associated with me only since my return."

Cory glanced curiously at the Arab. There was something enigmatic about that small, stiff man at the door. Something disturbing. An illusion? Perhaps. Yet it was an illusion hard to escape.

"By the way," Cory asked him, "where were you at the time of the murder?"

"S-searching," replied Haj Ibn Mayyud, with his peculiarly sibilant accent.

"S-searching for the s-screamer in the fog, like Mr. Berkely."

"Then you—"

But Cory checked the comment and flashed a sharp, startled look at the housekeeper. She was talking again. Talking with sudden surprise and agitation. He started toward her. And she turned, round-eyed, to exclaim amazedly—

"Mr. Burrill isn't there! He isn't in his room at the hotel!"

CHAPTER FOUR

The Hand of Egypt

CORY snatched the telephone from the housekeeper. He knew the manager of the hotel well, as did everyone in Shag Harbor. The group behind him gaped in stunned bewilderment as he began to talk. "Hal Cory speaking! Fred, are you certain Burrill is not in his room?"

"I just been up there myself," came the manager's voice. "What's the matter, anyhow?"

"Plenty!" snapped Cory. "Don't ask me to explain now. Do you know when Burrill left the hotel?"

"Sure. About nine o'clock last night."

"Just walked out without saying anything about being gone all night?"

"Well, it was this way," the manager said. "He was sitting around the lobby, reading a newspaper, when he got a phone call. Right after that he got his hat and coat and left; far as I know, he hasn't been back since."

Cory bit his lip. This matter of the phone call for Burrill somehow didn't fit into the pattern of evidence surrounding the man. Was this to be a new mystery? Lord, there were enough confusing puzzles without that!

He asked: "Do you know who called him, Fred?"

"Why, no. But it was a man's voice."

"Did you happen to hear anything Burrill said over the phone?"

"I couldn't. He talked from the booth."

Cory felt more and more baffled. Who could have summoned Burrill to leave the hotel? Why was a man who had not slept for the better part of a week spending the night out? This night of all nights!

"Listen, Fred," Hal Cory said grimly, "I'd like you to do something for me."

"What?"

"As soon as Burrill comes back, phone me here. The number is Shag Harbor 223."

"223. O. K. But Hal, I wish you'd tell me what the devil all this is about."

Cory briefly told him of the murder, then hung up the receiver. His heart hammered oddly. For a moment he stood frowning into the dark corner.

Charles Burrill! Here was a man he did not yet know, completely filling his mind. Not that he had incriminating evidence against Burrill. Or, for that matter, any tangible evidence at all. Circumstances, however, were assuredly weaving a fantastic network around the man!

Finally Cory turned, his face hard. In that dimly lit library he confronted a group who appeared wholly confounded. They were whispering in animated, uneasy astonishment. From what he gathered, none of them could explain Mr. Burrill's absence from the hotel; nor did they understand who might have telephoned him, because, as Dr. Kyne so vehemently declared: "He doesn't know anybody in Shag Harbor!"

Cory concluded it would be futile to question these people about Burrill's disappearance. Clearly, they were all baffled by it. And yet, to his surprise, Katherine Lacombe rose, eyed him levelly across the murky room, and said with absolute confidence: "I know, Mr. Cory, you think

Charles Burrill may be responsible for Mr. Merriton's death. But you mustn't suspect that. It can't be."

"Why can't it?" he asked.

"Because they were the best of friends. In fact, they've been close friends, admiring and liking each other, for— Just how long is it, Uncle Phil?"

Professor Lacombe shrugged dismally. "Since their school days," he muttered. "Probably twenty-five or thirty years. Kit is quite right, Mr. Cory. You can't possibly think of Burrill as—as Merriton's slayer."

TO this Hal Cory said nothing. He was frowning intently. In silence he crossed the library toward the fireplace and helped himself, rather absently, to a cigarette from an ornately lacquered box. As he lit it his mind reverted to a former consideration. It was not a thought directly connected with Burrill; yet he could not prevent his speculations from darting back to it. He cast his match into the fire and eyed Professor Lacombe narrowly through a billow of blue smoke.

"You said something before," he began, "concerning a 'death scream.' Just what did you mean by that, professor?"

"Eh?" There was a startled pause. Professor Lacombe jerked up his head and stared. Perhaps he did not realize that he had mentioned the "death scream" earlier in the night, in Cory's hearing. Now, half surprised, half frightened, he glanced at Dr. Kyne, wet his lips; then rose and began to stride back and forth, irresolutely, like a man in a tormenting quandary.

"Oh, you may as well tell him!" snapped Dr. Kyne, running an unsteady hand through his silver hair. "With Merriton gone, it doesn't matter—now—"

"No, I—I suppose it doesn't," agreed Professor Lacombe, in a thick voice. He stopped and faced Cory. There was a new and curious tension about his gaunt figure. "This death scream," he said, "is —well, it's a name we ourselves have given to the war cry of a certain band of Bedouin thieves near Nirri ed Basa. They live by preying on passing caravans. And usually their attacks mean several killings. They come dashing into battle on flying horses, screaming like crazy—"

"The kind of screams," Katherine Lacombe ejaculated, "we've been hearing?"

"Yes!" said the professor. He spoke softly, in a tone divided between awe and wonder. "Those screams we have been hearing are exactly like those we heard on the desert!"

"Go on," Cory urged grimly, quite forgetting the cigarette between his fingers. "Why do you think a Bedouin war yell is being heard here, near your house?"

"Oh, it—it's all so fantastic and weird and implausible that I—I can't believe it!" exclaimed Professor Lacombe. The firelight played devilish pranks on his countenance. And his eyes flamed as he spoke, his voice becoming increasingly hoarse. "It's like a sort of ghostly retribution! As if. . . . Oh, with Merriton dead, it doesn't matter if I do tell you everything! You see, he killed one of those Bedouins!"

"Merriton?" Cory exclaimed, his eyes widening. "Murdered one of them?"

"Ye-es. But he didn't realize what he was doing. He had drunk a bit too much. We were excavating seven miles from Nirri ed Basa when one of these Bedouins came to ask, in a friendly enough fashion, if we'd let him have some quinine for a sick member of his tribe. Somehow Merriton fell into an argument with the fellow, and being drunk, he lost his temper and shot the Arab. We all knew, of course, that we'd have the entire band down on our heads before morning, screaming and killing for vengeance. So we got military protection from Nirri ed Basa."

"But you didn't tell the authorities," Cory put in drily, "how the Bedouin had died?"

Professor Lacombe sent an uncomfortable glance at Dr. Kyne, then cleared his throat.

"To be honest with you, Mr. Cory," he admitted, "we didn't. Had we done so, we'd all have been in trouble, and the fruits of our expedition would have been ruined. So, to save old Merriton and ourselves—I'm telling you this frankly, because I want you to understand our position—"

"I do understand. Go ahead."

"We told the authorities the Bedouin had attempted to steal something from our camp. And since that band is notorious for its depredations, we were readily believed. We said the Arab had been shot while fighting to get away with his plunder. Naturally, when the Bedouins arrived to wreak their vengeance, they found us strongly protected by soldiers, and they could do nothing. But their *sheik* sent us bitter assurance that some day we'd be made to pay for the killing of their man. A week later we left for America. That was the last we heard of the threat—until the screams began here last week. Now, with poor Merriton dead, I—I'm beginning to believe that Egypt is reaching out to us—" Professor Lacombe stopped and gaped emptily into the fire.

And Hal Cory stood astounded.

Bedouin vengeance? . . . . Fantastic! And yet, certainly, another possibility to cope with!

HIS suspicions were being snatched from one idea to another with maddening, confusing speed. First he had told himself the murderer of Stewart Merriton must be one of these people in the house; their very nearness to the dead man implicated them. But this theory had the weakness of not accounting for the screams. Then, a moment ago, he had transferred all his thoughts to Charles Burrill, whom he had never even seen; for surely there was ample cause to focus a searching look upon the man. Again, however, no explanation for the screams accompanied the suspicion. And now—bizarre as the idea might sound—he found himself compelled to consider the notion of a mystical, ghostlike Bedouin avenger! In this case the screams might be regarded, plausibly enough, as a means of terrorization.

Still—

Hal Cory was a practical young man. The hint of an uncanny Egyptian Nemesis might have fascinated him in a bit of lurid fiction. But here, in the reality of Shag Harbor, in the rugged woods of the Maine coast, such a conception somehow seemed unconvincing. It struck him a little like a story of goblins and spectres and bogeys.

"Do you really believe," he demanded skeptically of Professor Lacombe, "that a Bedouin murdered Stewart Merriton?"

The gaunt man shook his head hopelessly, lifted his hands. "What else can I believe?" he asked.

"And how do we know," huskily cried Dr. Kyne, rising, "that their vengeance will stop with the death of Merriton? How do we know they won't strike at the *rest* of us?"

Five minutes later Hal Cory reached a decision. If the killer was not one of the people in the house, he must somehow, somewhere, have broken into the place. That, now, was the first thing to investigate.

He asked crisply, of the group in general: "Were all the doors and windows locked tonight?"

"Oh, yes," Katherine Lacombe assured

him. "We've been locking them every night since the screams began."

"Has any outsider a key?"

"Certainly not."

"Mr. Burrill—"

"No. He never had a key."

Cory nodded, as if satisfied. He knew, however, that Charles Burrill had had plenty of time—two weeks—in which to make a wax impression of a key, had he desired one. Aloud he said quickly: "Professor, if you'll come along with me, I'd like to look over the doors and windows. I wish the rest of you would wait right here."

The search was thorough, including the chamber of horror in which Merriton's big, bloody body sprawled. But it yielded only the baffling fact that no lock, either of door or window, had been forced! If an outsider had killed Stewart Merriton, how, then, had he entered?

At last they reached the wing, built only a few years ago, which contained the Egyptian museum. It extended from the south side of the house.

Professor Lacombe had just opened its door and switched on its lights when the housekeeper pattered up behind them, excitedly, to announce that the coroner had arrived.

"He wants everybody upstairs!" she added breathlessly.

Cory said, in answer to the professor's questioning glance: "You'd better go. I'll look through the museum here and join you in a few minutes."

And so he was left alone.

AS HE entered that long, silent chamber, filled with surprises and monstrosities, a curious little shiver rippled through him. It was like stepping into an Oriental nightmare. He paused and stared about, wide-eyed.

Six mummies gaped down at him from their positions against the walls; six

hideous cadavers, old as the Pyramids, regarding him out of eternity. All about them, like offerings strewn at their feet, were Egyptian relics that might have enhanced any of the great museums. Pieces of weird sculpture, of wood carvings, of pottery, of jewelry. Cases displaying slabs of hieroglyphics and writings on papyrus of more recent dynasties. A wall devoted exclusively to weapons—daggers, hatchets, cruelly twisted scimitars with wondrously fashioned hilts. A bronze aegis on a tall pole. And in the center of the room, standing there like an altar, was a tremendous, intricately carved sarcophagus.

At all this Hal Cory gazed in a kind of trance. He felt that the eerie crime he was investigating fitted perfectly into an atmosphere of this sort.

Slowly he moved about the vast room. There were many windows, but he found no indication that any of them had been forced. Still, unless an occupant of the house had murdered Merriton, an outsider did get in. Where?

It seemed to him that the six mummies watched his quest with baleful intensity.

At the far end of the museum he came to a small door. When he opened it, he looked into an anteroom which appeared to be an office. It contained a desk, several chairs, filing cabinets, and wide bookcases. The light of the museum poured into it, and Cory saw something that narrowed his eyes.

A trash basket had been upset, and its papers were scattered over the floor.

At that he stared darkly. No one, he imagined, would willfully have left the basket like that. Had it, then, been kicked over by someone hurrying across the office? Or had it been emptied by somebody who had sought a discarded paper?

Cory glanced first at the single window in the room. It was locked. Moreover, it showed no evidence of having been forced. It was quite clear now that if an outsider had entered the house to stab Merriton, he had possessed a key. Cory frowned and bent to the floor.

The first paper he picked up out of that scattered mass bore some reference to Egyptian lore. Carefully written across it, in a tiny script, were a few words.

> The treasures of Amakhin II were interred with the body of his son, Prahm, in the Holy Garden of—

That was all.

Hal Cory contracted his brows. Offhand, he could discern no connection between the phrase and the mystery he was struggling to shatter. But he picked up another paper. This, curiously enough, bore merely an elaboration, in a different handwriting, of the words on the first slip.

> The jewels of Amakkin were buried with the body of his son, Pramm, in the Holy Garden of Amek, behind the Temple of Suk Tabal.

Cory, sinking deeper into a strange fascination he could not have explained, tried a third sheet. Again he found allusions to Amakhin, or Amakkin, and treasure, and a body buried in the Holy Garden of Amek. . . . He started picking up other papers, more quickly. But— he had no chance to read any of them.

For at that instant something happened that brought him to his feet with a gasp, made him whirl around in amazement, his hand leaping for his revolver.

Quite suddenly, without the slightest warning, the lights in the museum were extinguished!

Blackness, then. . . . Blinding blackness. . . .

He stood rigid. His nerves began to twang, and a prickling sensation crawled over his scalp like a chill. He saw noth-

ing, heard nothing. Yet he knew, he sensed, that through the darkness of the museum something was creeping toward him!

CHAPTER FIVE

The Jewels of Amakhin

HAL CORY'S voice shot out harshly: "Who's that?" He stood unstirring, his heart pounding crazily. His eyes blazed in an effort to penetrate that wall of blackness. But he could not see. Nor did his words evoke a reply.

"Who's there?"

Again he flung out the challenge. His revolver was pointing straight into the museum. And his left hand rose to grope for an electric switch on the wall of the office. It slipped up, down, left, right, in a swift search, but encountered nothing.

Then his straining ears caught a sound. A queer sound. The scraping of a foot, perhaps. Or—

Cory did not see the thing that flew at him out of the darkness. He knew only that something heavy, like a rock, crashed viciously against the side of his head, just over the left ear, and plunged on to smash the glass of one of the cases.

It was not a direct blow. Yet it staggered him. For an instant the blackness seemed filled with explosive lights. He reeled back against the desk. Groaned. A thousand daggers were stabbing agony through his head. He tottered on the brink of oblivion, his arms reaching out as if to seize something for support.

And as he swayed there, sick and dizzy and stunned, somebody leaped upon him with the ferocity of a tiger!

A spurt of hot breath struck his face. Savage breath. He opened his eyes to catch a momentary impression of a raised arm holding something, poised to strike.

Hal Cory squeezed the trigger of his revolver.

A crack—a flash of flame—

Then a shriek ripped through the blackness. Whoever had sprung upon Cory went down in a writhing, wormlike spasm of pain. He must have thrown himself about the floor in sheer agony, for the office was filled with the sounds he made among the scattered papers. His moans became guttural, griping, terrible.

Cory stumbled away blindly until he struck a wall. He doubted that he had the strength to cross the museum to the electric light switch. So, leaning there limply, with warm rivulets of blood twisting down his cheek and the world spinning about his head, he sent trembling fingers into his pocket for matches.

Why this thing had happened, or who had attacked him, he could not attempt to guess now. Not while his knees sagged under him; not while his brain struggled desperately to cling to consciousness; not while he had to exert all his strength and will merely to remain on his feet.

He found a match and struck it. A burst of weird yellow light filled the office. It was dim enough, yet momentarily it blinded him. Cory had to blink painfully as he gaped down at the figure on the floor. He recognized the wounded man at once. And gasped.

It was Haj! Haj Ibn Mayyud!

The Arab lay writhing like a serpent, both his hands pressed to his stomach. Cory stared at him as though he were looking upon a miracle.

Then, as the match flame neared his fingertips, he shot a wild look at the desk. It held a lamp. Cory staggered to it and pulled its little chain just as the match lost its fire. Now a steady golden radiance filled the room, and he dropped to his knees beside the man he had shot. A spattering of his own blood splashed on Haj Ibn Mayyud's forehead.

Cory could not reason now. Nor could he temporize. He could only leap to a wild conclusion.

"You!" he rasped thickly. "You killed Merriton!"

"No!" groaned Haj Ibn Mayyud. "No-o!"

"Don't lie to me now!"

"I didn't! I didn't kill him!" the Arab gasped. "I didn't!"

Cory jammed the muzzle of his gun against the man's heart. He had no intention of shooting. But he was madly determined to get facts.

"You tell me the truth!" he smashed through his teeth. "This is no time to—"

"I tell you I didn't kill him!"

"Then who did?"

"I don't know!" Haj Ibn Mayyud felt another hard jab of the revolver and suddenly screamed in an insane mixture of terror and pain and defiance: "I won't tell! You can't shoot it out of me! I won't tell!"

Then the museum was ablaze with lights.

Cory raised his head. He saw the whole crowd—Katherine Lacombe, the professor, Dr. Kyne, Harrison Berkely, Dr. Westervelt, the servants—all rushing toward him in horror. They must have heard the shot, of course.

He grinned crookedly, tried to rise. His left hand rested for support on the missile that had struck his head—a grotesque piece of Egyptian sculpture. He managed to lift one leg.

But that was all.

A sudden flood of darkness overwhelmed his senses, and Hal Cory toppled forward into oblivion.

THERE came an anxious whisper from Katherine Lacombe. "You—you feel better now, don't you?"

"Much," Cory assured her, trying to smile.

He was stretched on the settee in the

library. The girl sat beside him, adjusting with deft, yet nervous fingers, the bandage that encircled his head like a turban. It was some ten minutes since he had regained consciousness; and though his bruise still throbbed cruelly, he could think lucidly enough.

He glanced at the window to discover, in surprise, that it was daylight. Outside the fog was beginning to lift, so that he could see trees quite clearly. He turned his eyes toward a clock in a corner. It was half-past eight.

"Whew!" he muttered. "I've been out longer than I thought! It's three hours since— Why, what's the matter?"

The quick change in tone occurred as he looked back at Katherine Lacombe's face. Her expression widened his eyes. She seemed strained, pallid, gripped by something between terror and despair. At the sight of her he tried to rise on his elbow, but she pushed him back with gentle insistence.

"Don't," she pleaded. "Dr. Westervelt wants you to remain quiet a while."

"Oh, I'm all right!" impatiently. "It's you who look like a ghost. Don't tell me something else has happened in this crazy affair!"

"It—it has," she whispered huskily, looking away at the fireplace. "Something terrible—"

"You mean Haj Ibn Mayyud is dead?"

"No, oh, no! Haj is upstairs, unconscious. Dr. Westervelt is with him. He's in a dangerous condition. But it—it isn't Haj. It's—Charles Burrill!" She gaped into Cory's eyes miserably. "He's been murdered!"

"Wha-at!"

"Last night. He was stabbed—just like Merriton! His body was found at six o'clock this morning, at the roadside within a few minutes' walk of his hotel."

"Good God!" gasped Cory, and nothing could prevent him now from jerking himself up to his elbow. His face was white as he demanded, "Who—who told you about this?"

"Your father. He phoned for Dr. Westervelt. The doctor has been in to see the body, and now he's back."

"Has anyone any information about it?"

"No." The girl shook her dark head wretchedly. "All we know is Burrill received that phone call at nine o'clock, then went out and was killed!"

And after a pause Cory asked abruptly: "Did Dr. Westervelt say how long Burrill had been dead?"

"He thinks Burrill must have died some time before midnight yesterday."

Before midnight! . . . . And Stewart Merriton had not been killed until 3 A. M.

Cory closed his eyes—a curtain lowered over mental chaos. He lay very still, thinking, struggling to gather all that had happened into a coherent sequence.

Charles Burrill, at any rate, had been definitely eliminated as a suspect—by death itself. True, his tragedy created a mystery of its own. But Cory did not want to confuse himself by considering too many riddles at once. For the moment only one problem held his thoughts.

Who had stabbed Stewart Merriton?

SOMEWHERE perversely, he still found it difficult to believe, with conviction, in a vague, jinni-like, Bedouin avenger. The guilt of so ghostly a figure would not account for the savage attack of Haj Ibn Mayyud in the museum.

Haj?

Was he guilty of the killings? If so, how explain the motorboat which had carried someone away in the fog?

Cory finally opened his eyes to find the girl watching him worriedly. He realized, with a little start, that she was holding his hand, had, indeed, been holding it for several minutes. He looked at her; and somehow, despite all this tragedy and horror, he wanted to smile. But he didn't. He remained quite grave and asked, in a surprisingly crisp voice: "Has anyone been able to explain why Haj flew at me?"

Katherine Lacombe cast a swift nod toward a chair. "Those bags over there," she said quickly. "Harrison Berkely thinks it was because Haj feared you would find them—or had already found them."

Cory glanced at the chair she indicated —and with one wild heave swung his body out of the settee. He crossed the room shakily but resolutely, despite Katherine's efforts to stop him. In the excitement of this new discovery his dizziness was ignored. And his eyes were exceedingly bright.

For the chair held several burlap bags bound into two bundles. When he picked them up, in eager hands, he found they were moist, and grains of sand spilled out of their folds. He stood there like a turbaned Hindu, weak yet heedless of his weakness, all his senses focussed in agitation on the bags.

"Where were these picked up?" he demanded.

"Harrison Berkely found them behind a bookcase in the museum office. A piece of the burlap was sticking out. Are they really so important?"

"Important?" cried Cory, swinging toward her with flaming eyes. "Why, these are the bags that made the prints on the beach! They're still wet and sandy!"

She gaped at him. "You think Haj—"

"I think the fact he knew they were in the office and feared I'd find them indicates he was the one who put them behind the bookcase! And if he put them there, he was probably the one who made the marks on the beach!"

"But good heavens!" ejaculated Katherine, her own countenance white. "That's impossible! Haj certainly didn't go off in that motorboat! You know that. He was on shore with us. It was somebody else!"

"Yes, I know. . . . Wait." Cory sat down, grimly. He clasped his hands between his knees and stared with burning eyes into the hearth. "This thing has to make sense," he declared, almost savagely. "There must be a way of explaining the screams, the killings, the motorboat, the prints in the sand—everything! Let's try to figure this thing out."

He sat unstirring for many minutes. Katherine Lacombe watched him in despairing silence. Of the puzzles that had accumulated around the murder of Stewart Merriton she herself could make nothing. Rather hopelessly she sank to the settee and waited for Hal Cory to speak.

When he did speak, suddenly, it was to utter a most unexpected question. He looked at her sharply.

"What time," he asked, "did you all go to bed last night?"

"Why—" She was startled. "Early. Very early. We had all been losing so much sleep this past week that we were glad to retire almost immediately after supper."

"What time was it?"

"About eight, I think."

"And you all went to your rooms?"

"Yes."

CORY jumped up as if he had struck the most important feature of the entire case. His eyes actually glowed upon the girl, held her hypnotized.

"It's beginning to clear!" he whispered excitedly. "I wonder if you can tell me something else!"

"Wh-what?"

"In the museum office I found some scribblings about the treasure of Amakhia II. Do you know anything about that?"

"Oh!" Katherine rose quickly, seized the back of a chair. "Yes, of course. I've often heard them discuss it, though it was a secret among them. But I don't see what connection—

"Tell me what you know!" he urged fervently.

"Why, it's all based on some hieroglyphics they dug up near Nirri ed Basa. The four of them—that is, Uncle Phil, Dr. Kyne, Mr. Merriton, and Mr. Burrill—have been working to decipher the writings. As soon as they discovered a reference to the jewels of Amakhin II, they all became dreadfully excited. It seems those jewels, though often mentioned in other hieroglyphics, have been lost for thousands of years. And they're worth an imperial fortune. Uncle Phil and the others were certain they'd at last struck a clue to the whereabouts of the treasure. There was talk of the Egyptian Government's claiming it if it was found. But Uncle Phil and the rest didn't seem to mind that much. They didn't want the treasure itself—just the triumph of locating it. And they—"

"Oh, hello, Cory! So you're up again, eh?"

The deep, harsh voice of Dr. Westervelt interrupted as the heavy coroner hurried into the library. He was a portly man of fifty, and he appeared very tired this morning, with purplish puffs under his eyes.

"How's the head?" he asked.

"Better," Cory assured him. "How is Haj?"

"Not so good, not so good." Dr. Westervelt shook his head ominously. "It's a nasty wound."

"Any chance of talking to him soon?"

"Talking to him! Dont' make me laugh." But there was no sign of humor in the doctor's face as he lowered himself wearily into a chair. "I haven't let anybody even see him for hours, and I

don't intend to—except the nurse I've sent for. I expect we'll have a neat case of delirium when he comes out of his coma—if he does come out. I say, Miss Lacombe, any chance of getting a cup of hot black coffee?"

She nodded quickly and went to ring for the housekeeper, and the coroner eyed Cory narrowly.

"Say," he asked, "are you getting anywhere with this blasted mystery?"

"Yes!" Cory swept a swift glance at Katherine as he answered, in a whisper.. "I think I am—at last!"

"Really? H'm." Dr. Westervelt, however, looked skeptical as he leaned forward to take a cigarette from a little box. "Well, that's encouraging. I suppose you heard about Al Mammoth's motorboat?"

Cory stiffened. "Heard what?"

"It was missing this morning. You know, the boat he kept moored at the old wharf. Somebody stole it. I heard about it when I went in to see the Burrill body. Seems—"

"Good Lord!" hoarsely cried Cory. "Why didn't you tell me this before?"

"Before?" drily. "Last time I saw you, young fellow, you were unconscious."

Hal Cory scarcely heard the words. His face was suddenly flushed, the eyes gleaming. A motorboat stolen last night! His mind pounced upon the fact as if it had reached its goal.

Cory saw things now—dazzling things. A few seconds he stood still, organizing the wild thoughts in his head, planning. Then, impetuously, he seized the coroner's arm.

"You and Professor Lacombe," he said tensely, "are the only ones who can help me! Will you come with me?"

"Where?" in surprise.

"I'll explain as we go. Come on, doc!"

His ardor amazed yet swayed Dr. Westervelt. He rose, forgetting his coffee, an expression of wonder on his round countenance. From Katherine, in equal bewilderment, came: "Uncle Phil went into the museum with Dr. Kyne and Harrison Berkely. You'll find him there. What is all this, Mr. Cory? Do you mean you—"

She paused, and Cory eyed her curiously, hesitantly, his teeth pressing his lip. Then, of a sudden, he said: "I'll tell you everything in a little while. No, don't come. Please. Just wait here. I'll be back with an explanation as soon as—as we have the killer!"

And, grasping Dr. Westervelt's arm, he actually pulled the startled man out of the room.

CHAPTER SIX

The Last Scream

DR. HENRY ALDRICH KYNE, silver-haired and handsome, stood in a corner of the fantastic museum, arguing in low tones with the gaunt Professor Lacombe and young Harrison Berkely. But when Cory and the coroner appeared in the door, all three men turned in astonishment.

"Well, Mr. Cory!" exclaimed Dr. Kyne. "I didn't know you were up again!"

Hal Cory did not reply. Frowning, his head still encircled by the bandage, he and Dr. Westervelt crossed the museum until, before two staring mummies, they confronted the other men. He was grim and uncompromising. He did not intend to waste time. Having finally evolved an astounding theory which would explain the mystery of Evergreen Point, he wanted to test it immediately. His idea was founded on everything he had discovered since coming to this house. And he felt strangely confident of its accuracy.

On the way from the library he had briefly confided in the coroner and had enlisted the man's aid. And now Dr.

Westervelt played his rôle with the gravity of an experienced actor.

"We have just heard," he snapped, scowling from one face to another, "a very ugly and amazing story!"

Silence. . . . Breathless silence.

First the three scientists stared at the coroner; and then, because he did not augment his statement, they looked dazedly at Hal Cory.

"It's a horrible story," he said in a low, hard voice. "I may as well tell it to you at once."

And he did. He spoke in curt, staccato syllables that were utterly certain of the things they pronounced. His narrow eyes blazed first upon one face, then upon another. It was his weird theory he propounded; but he outlined it as if it were already an established fact.

"The explanation for the murders of Merriton and Burrill is this: you gentlemen had discovered the location of an ancient Egyptian treasure—the treasure of Amakhin II. It was a discovery you kept secret among you."

He saw a startled glance dart from Dr. Kyne to Professor Lacombe, but he did not pause.

"One of you decided to make it a one-man secret! To have the entire treasure at his own command! But in order to do that, the others who knew of Amakhin's jewels must be silenced permanently. It was a dangerous thing to attempt. But the fortune at stake was so tremendous, so fabulous, that any risk was worth taking for the sake of—"

"Look here!" gasped Harrison Berkely, his young face gray, his voice choked. "Are you trying to accuse one of these two gentlemen of—"

"Please let me go on," quietly snapped Cory. His narrow gaze met Berkely's in a sort of deadlock. And after a moment he won silence.

"Once the murders were decided upon,"

Cory resumed in that same implacable tone, "a very ingenious plan for diverting suspicion occurred to the killer. At any rate, he considered it ingenious. He knew his friends were under the shadow of a Bedouin threat. And he decided to profit by that circumstance. To do it, he sought and obtained the help of Haj Ibn Mayyud. Haj, when he learned of the plan, expected himself to profit enormously when the treasure of Amakhin was unearthed. So he greedily complied. The screams were Haj's contribution to the scheme. He, himself an Arab, slipped out at night to emit those cries and create the impression that a Bedouin avenger—fantastic as the idea might be—was somewhere around."

"Now listen!" again gasped Berkely. "You can't make such accusations without—"

"Let me finish!"

Once more there was a moment of dumbstruck silence. Cory had an objective in delivering his words in this manner. By outlining his theory in such detail, he gave himself time to study those pallid faces before him, to judge whether his shots were striking bull's eyes. And what he saw encouraged him. He knew he was right. He went on succinctly.

"Last night the killer, instead of going to sleep, slipped out of the house and went to Shag Harbor. There he telephoned Burrill, and when Burrill came to meet him, he committed his first murder. This was shortly after nine. When the killer returned to Evergreen Point, it was in a stolen motorboat—a boat stolen for a purpose. A very clever purpose. For later, when Merriton had been killed, Haj Ibn Mayyud used that boat to shrewd advantage. He screamed to attract attention to the beach. Then he started the motor and sent the boat out into the sea alone—without anyone in it!"

A second Cory paused; then: "That was clever of the killer, who planned the trick. The boat, puttering out to sea, was intended to create the impression of some unknown murderer—the Bedouin, no doubt—making his escape. Haj himself ran back to hide the bags he had bound around his feet; then he met Miss Lacombe and returned to the beach."

And now Dr. Henry Aldrich Kyne could no longer crush his savage impatience. His eyes were blazing. In a hoarse, stifled voice he demanded: "Who —whom are you accusing, anyway?"

Hal Cory grimly turned to fix his eyes on Professor Philip Lacombe.

"You, professor," he said quietly.

A HUSH. A frightful, appalling hush. Professor Lacombe, gaunt and pallid, did not move. He looked straight into Cory's eyes. And after a moment he said thickly: "So—so Haj told you this—"

Neither Cory nor Dr. Westervelt replied. This was the thing they had hoped to make the professor believe. They waited, waited until a bitter, hopeless smile twisted the professor's cadaverous face.

He was utterly colorless. He must have been certain that the Arab had betrayed him, for he did not attempt a denial. But his desperate calm was belied by the drops of perspiration that oozed out of his forehead.

He turned his head to meet the horrified gape of Dr. Kyne. To him he said, dazedly: "You're shocked, Henry. . . . Of course. . . . So am I, when I look back at the plan now. But—but I'd given everything I had to—to archeology. My life and my money. I thought it was time to seek my—reward."

"God!" whispered Dr. Kyne, shakily. "But by murder?"

"By obtaining the treasure of Amakhin!"

They went on talking, in broken phrases. Cory did not try to interrupt.

Every word the professor uttered, he realized, was more deeply incriminating him.

And Cory knew his theory had been sound.

From the instant he had bent over the wounded Haj, in the museum office, the idea had begun to grow in him. Haj, when asked who had committed the murders, had screamed: "I won't tell! You can't shoot it out of me! I won't tell!"

That had made him wonder. Whom was Haj protecting? Whom would he shield in that household? Most likely, of course, the man with whom he had so long been associated, Professor Lacombe!

Building on that idea, Cory had discovered, to his own amazement, that a plausible, though horrifying theory could be evolved. The theory of the professor's guilt! That was the only theory which explained all the rapidly accruing evidence—the locked windows and doors, the fact that Merriton had made no sound when the killer entered his room. With such a theory accepted, even the screams and the mystery of the motorboat could be understood—or guessed.

Yes, Cory had guessed, as detectives so often must guess. But he had guessed right.

The burlap bags found in the museum office had assured him of Haj's complicity. The report of the stolen motorboat had fitted perfectly with this discovery, for it suggested how a man who had apparently escaped in the boat had left his footwear in the Egyptian museum. The answer was that no man had escaped. That instead, Haj Ibn Mayyud had—

And then Hal Cory was snatched out of his thoughts with a gasp. For an amazing thing happened.

Professor Lacombe darted into the office!

Cory and Dr. Kyne sprang after him, but they were half a second too late. The door was slammed before them, locked. And Professor Lacombe's voice—harsh and wild and defiant—burst out to them.

"I was prepared for this!"

They could not stop what they all knew must be the next act. They battered the door, kicked it, yelled. Cory threw himself against the wood. But it was useless.

A single shot cracked behind that door.

Then a thud—as of a falling body—and silence.

Those in the museum stood rigid, pallid. Cory, wild-eyed, heard quick steps behind him. He swung around to gape, in despair, at Katherine Lacombe. He started toward her—but halted with a jerk, while a terrible shudder raced through him.

For at that instant an astounding thing—almost an incredible thing—happened.

Haj Ibn Mayyud, upstairs, must have slipped into delirium. And suddenly the house was filled with a cry—piercing, horrible.

"Ayeee! . . ."

The Skull of Judgment

by
Edward Parrish Ware

Author of "The Masked Moccasin," etc.

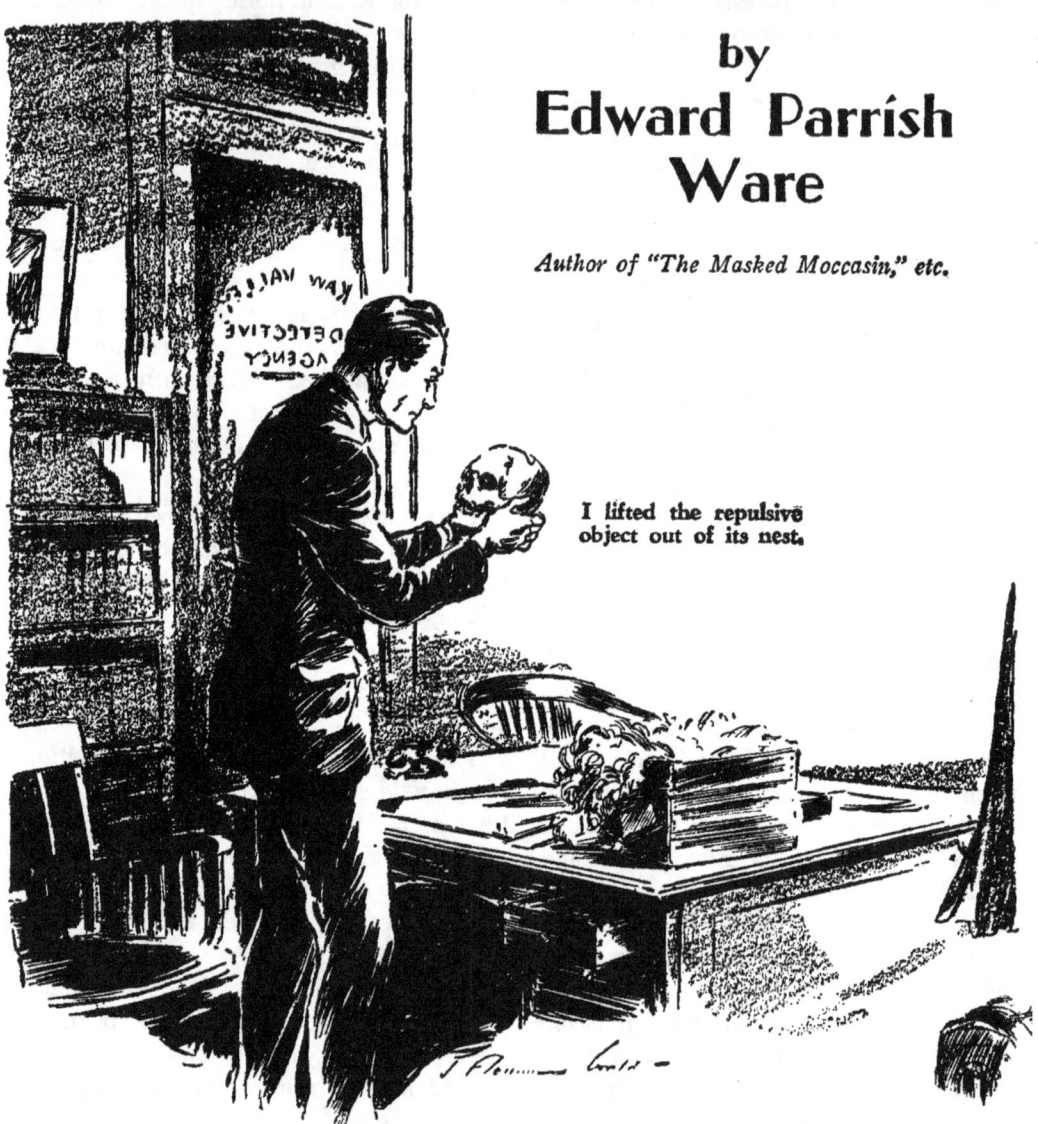

I lifted the repulsive object out of its nest.

Ghastly it was—this polished putty-colored dome—trepanned in silver with a lead slug rattling in its maw. Fearsome freight to come to any man, but to Tug Norton its eyeless sockets were gaping doors to murder, and a dead man's secret.

CHAPTER ONE

Boxed Mystery

ONE by one, our ancient wisecracks have exploded. A dozen years ago, this one went off with a bang: *As you sow, so shall you reap.*

Prove it?

Sure.

How about the farmers who sowed rye and barley, and reaped the Eighteenth Amendment?

The case-books of the Kaw Valley Detective Bureau, of which I, "Tug" Norton, am owner and chief operative, if closely studied would shed revealing light upon every possible human emotion and activity. Comedy, melodrama, tragedy, success, failure, righteousness, cussedness —anything, in fine, you may be looking for, and some things you never dreamed of. One of the most interesting records deals with a man who spent practically all his life sowing one kind of crop and reaping something entirely different. I'm going to tell you about it.

The thing had a grisly beginning and one I didn't relish. Not that I'm in the habit of worrying a lot over unexplained happenings, but this one was absolutely unique in my experience, and I'll wager that it never occurs again—to me or anybody else.

"Specs," the office-boy, brought it into my room. A plain, white, wooden box; such a box as might have contained a one-gallon jug, in the days when jugs were not respectable. It bore my address, printed in ink, but no marks to indicate who sent it or whence it had come.

I placed a suspicious ear against the package, heard nothing to support the half-formed theory that some unfriendly person had presented me with a bundle of potential annihilation, and concluded to open it. When the lid was plied off there was exposed a thick layer of excelsior, and under the layer was something so startling and unbelievable as to hold me rooted where I stood, eyes staring incredulously.

Nested in wads of excelsior was a human skull!

The polished, putty-colored dome alone was visible, but I needed no more to be able to tag it for what it was. With the conviction suddenly in my mind that the repulsive object in the box was a forerunner of something tragic, menacing, I lifted it out of its nest and placed it on the desk.

It was unmistakably the skull of a man, and, unmistakably also, the life which once had animated it had escaped through a hole made by a bullet. Two inches above the left eye-socket was a splintery crack through which the lead had passed.

My interest had by then vanquished the natural repulsion I had felt at first, and I took up the skull and examined it. One bullet hole was all that showed, and I gave the skull a shake. Something rattled inside, and a moment later I had the thing that had rattled out on my blotter.

It was a slug of lead, flattened and battered, which must have come from the muzzle of a large-caliber revolver. Probably a forty-five.

There was something else about the skull that interested me, and far more than did the hole and the bullet. It was a silver plate, set in the back on the right side, which testified to the fact that a very skilful job of trepanning had once been done to the head. If the surgeon who patched that fracture still lived, then there would be a good chance of identifying the grisly thing—in case the mysterious sender chose to leave me in the dark.

The teeth, too, several of which remained, might give up something. They would bear looking at.

There was nothing else about it that enlisted my interest. No note in the box, no hint concerning the identity of the man whose skull it had been, nor of that of the person who had sent the slug of lead on its mission of death. Nothing at all but the bare cranium, the suggestive hole in the forehead and the bullet that doubtless had made it.

Murder? Naturally, that thought occurred. But why unload the evidence on me? Or was some ghoul-minded person attempting a joke?

The door opened and Jim Steel, my chief assistant, sauntered in. He stopped dead for an instant, stared at me fingering the dome, then permitted himself a wide grin. Nothing ever fazes Steel, even human skulls.

" 'Alas, poor Yorick!' " he quoted in deep, melancholy tones.

"Hamlet *knew his* skulls," I came back. "Had the advantage of me, there. This doesn't happen to be the dome of one of my acquaintances, Jim—"

"Nor of a victim, either," Jim cut in. "The hole is a bit too far off center, Tug. You didn't drill it. But you've got it. What are you going to do with it?"

I didn't answer, but buzzed for Spec. He was able to give me the name of the local city-express agency whose man had left the box. I got the agency on the phone immediately.

NOTHING gained there. One of their delivery trucks had been flagged down on Gladstone Boulevard, and a man had given the box to the driver, along with a bill large enough to cover expressage. The agency had checked the box in and delivered it to me.

"What did the man look like?" I asked.

The manager didn't know, and the expressman who received the package was out on a trip. Would I call up later?

All I learned was that the box had been sent by somebody in the city, but even that did not mean that the sender belonged there, or that the skull had not come from some other place.

Spec came in with the mail, and I opened the letters hurriedly in the hope of getting a line on the box. There was nothing, however. Then the phone rang.

"Kaw Valley Detective Agency, Norton speaking."

No one responded, and I repeated. Then, very faintly: "You are a private agency? You are not connected with the police?"

It was the voice of a woman.

"Our investigations are private affairs between us and our clients," I assured her.

"We do not, however, bind ourselves to conceal crimes, or to withhold evidence of crime. You may consult us about anything you wish, though, and know that your confidences will not be abused, whether we take your case or not."

There was a moment of hesitancy, then she spoke again.

"It is, I think, a crime to be investigated," she said. "But I am not certain. In case it is, then it must be handled with absolute secrecy until you are quite certain of your ground. Where can I see you for a consultation?"

"Here at my office would be best," I told her. "Or I can send one of my assistants to your residence—"

"No, no!" There was sudden alarm in the voice. "I cannot have anyone at my residence, nor is it advisable that I call at your office. May I suggest a place for you to meet me? And I do not want to consult with an assistant. It is Mr. Tug Norton I wish to see, and no other."

"Certainly. Just designate any place you wish, and I'll see you there. What name, please?"

She dodged that one.

"If you take the case, then you shall know my name. Unless you do there would be no need of it, would there? The Lone Jack Inn, where the Lone Jack Road crosses Highway Forty? Would that suit you?"

"Perfectly. At what time, and how shall I recognize you?"

"Ten o'clock tonight. You will wait until I approach you. At exactly ten o'clock, you will get up from your table —please have one as private as possible —walk to the front door, look at your watch, nod your head three times, then return to your table. I'll join you there immediately. Is that clear?"

"It is. I'll follow instructions. But, if you have no objections, I'd like at least to know something of the nature of the matter—"

She dodged that one too by bidding me good-by and hanging up.

"The lady of the skull," Steel said as I turned from the phone. "I'll bet a month's salary on that."

"What makes you so certain?" I asked.

"Who but a woman would send a thing like that to a man, with no word or letter to prepare him for it? Tell me that, will you?"

"Granting you're right," I said, "it's no cinch that the lady who just called me up is the one who sent the box."

"You'll find out that they are the same." Jim was positive. "And I'm advising you to watch your step, Tug, because when a woman gets plumb mysterious she's dangerous—to others."

JIM has fixed ideas about women, and likes to air them. I was saved by the phone.

"Kaw Valley. Norton speaking."

"Sorry to trouble you, Mr. Norton," came a cultured voice to my ear, "but a mistake has occurred in the delivery of an express package, and I'm trying to correct it. A small, white box was sent out bearing the wrong address. Did you receive such a box? One for which you cannot account?"

"I didn't get your name," I came back. "Would you mind repeating it?"

"Pardon me, I did forget to mention my name. I am Professor James Donnovan, late of the Central College of Medicine and Surgery, Chicago. As for the box, my secretary intended sending it to Jacob Minturn, Taxidermist who also mounts anatomical specimens, with offices and workroom in the same biulding with you. The number was 624, Sandstone Building. After the box had gone he recalled that he had addressed it to 424, which is the number of your suite. Did you receive such a box?"

"Didn't your secretary know that Jake Minturn moved out of his quarters here a month ago?" I countered, while Jim was busy tracing the call.

"He found that out a trifle late." The voice had become edged with heat, charged with growing impatience. "Surely, sir, you can answer my question without so much evasion? A simple mistake has been made, and to rectify it should also be simple. Have you such a box?"

I began jiggling the receiver hook up and down, talking all the while. The professor began shouting at the top of his voice, and what he said came in fragments —just as my remarks were reaching him.

"Shake up your receiver!" I bawled. "Can't get you!"

"Aw—gaw—guggle—damn—it—to—gugg—gwawk——"

I hung up. Two minutes passed, and the bell rang again. I repeated my jiggling of the receiver, got a lot of gibberish over the wire, sent out some myself, and hung up again. Five minutes passed, but the phone did not ring a third time. I turned to Jim.

"If I'm not badly off," I said, grinning, "the professor or a representative will be with us presently. Just step into the back room, Jim, and take the skull with you. Lock it in the vault, then tail the professor when he goes out."

"What kind of line are you going to hand him?" Jim wanted to know.

"I'm going to hand him his box, all neatly nailed up—but with a couple of old books in it to add weight," I returned. "It occurs to me that we are about to engage in something extremely interesting, Jim— and that whoever possesses that trepanned skull has an ace in the hole. So lock our ace up safely, old man, until we need it.

Steel took the skull out with him, and I carefully renailed the lid on the box. A couple of books on criminology, utterly useless in the detecting business, gave it the required weight. Then I parked back of my desk to await the coming of

Professor James Donnovan or his messenger.

It's claimed that heaven's angels are never recognized until they wing away from us, but I recognized the devil's emissary who came in an hour later without even a second glance.

CHAPTER TWO

Mystery on the Wire

SPEC opened the door, and "Frog" Scanlon crowded in past him. Frog is another private dick operating in Kansas City, but he wouldn't be if crooks got their dues. His liking for me and the Kaw Valley is absolutely zero, and mine for him and his snoopery is less than that.

"Fine morning, Tug!" he exclaimed, with a grin that exposed his wisdom teeth.

"It was," I told him. "But you've spoiled it. Under what false pretense did you manage to break in here?"

"Ha, ha, ha! You will have your little joke, eh, Tug?" he breezed. "Fair question, though, deserves a fair answer. I didn't get in on false pretenses, oldtimer. I just walked through to your door, with a good grip on the collar of Spec's coat, and here I am."

"But won't be shortly," I told him. "Let's have it. What do you want?"

I already knew. His bulging eyes had discovered the white box, and a look of satisfaction on his face at sight of it gave his game away.

"I have a client, Tug," he said pompously.

"Most unusual," I cut in. "Who misdirected him to your joint?"

"Aw, go to hell!" he snapped, the red of anger dying his fat face. "I want that box! Talking about false pretense, you're holding it that way. Got no right to it, because it was sent here by mistake. I've come to get it.

"Oh," I said indifferently, "the box. Well, take it along, Frog. It came a short while ago, and I wasn't expecting anything like it. Meant to open it, however, but haven't got around to it yet. You won't mind, I'm sure, identifying your client's property—if it his—by describing the contents? We'll open it after you do, and make sure there is not another mistake. Just name the contents, Frog, and take it."

Scanlon shot me a venomous glance, and his teeth showed in a snarl. "Some day, Norton," he grated menacingly, "you and me are going to hook up good and proper—and then I'll pay you off for a lot! What you so particular about the box for?"

"I'm hoping it will provide the occasion for that hook-up between you and me," I told him. "Maybe it will. But we're wasting time, and time is important in my young life. Name the contents—or get out."

"I can't, and damned well do you know it!" he bleated. "And I see your game, too. You want a piece of jack for turning the box over, and you mean to get it! All right. How much?"

"How much have you got?"

"A fifty-case note."

"Too much. It makes me suspicious. If you'd mentioned a fiver, now, I'd have thought nothing of it. Fifty bucks though—that tells me the box is rather valuable. You keep the fifty, Frog, and I'll keep the box."

Scanlon glared his rage, but past experience served to help him restrain himself. We had come up against each other before.

"A hundred!" he offered like it hurt him.

"Now that does queer the game!" I declared. "Gosh, but that box must be filled with jack—or maybe it contains the Rajah's favorite emerald? Couldn't think of parting with it, Frog—unless you can name what it holds. Can you?"

"Go to hell!" Frog bleated, and stormed out.

But I knew that he was not done. Not by a long shot. A cunning hombre, Frog Scanlon—and one that doesn't give up easily. I knew I'd hear more from him.

Frog could hardly have cleared the front office when my phone bell jangled again. This time the voice was that of a man, and he labored under considerable excitement.

"Mr. Tug Norton?" he asked, striving to hide his agitation.

"Yes."

"You received a small, white, wooden box by express this morning," he stated.

"How did you know I did?" I came back.

"I do know it," he said. "It was handed to an expressman on Gladstone Boulevard at exactly nine minutes after eight o'clock this morning, sir, and the address was plain on it. The express agency informed the sender, not more than ten minutes ago, that delivery was made to your office. Sir, I assure you that it is important that you keep the box."

ONE wanted to take the box from me. Another urged me to keep it!

"Which I intend to do," I told him. "And the skull that came in it. Come through, hombre, if you want to do business with me. You sent the box. Why?"

"No, no! I didn't send it!"

"You're lying. So I'll hang up—"

"For God's sake!" came pleadingly. "Don't hang up yet! I'll admit that I sent the box—only, hear what I want to say!"

"Then say it—briefly."

"It is this: keep that box and its contents, no matter who tries to get it from you! Tonight, at the Lone Jack Inn, things will be cleared up for you, sir. Please guard the box closely—because life and death could be no more important!"

"Listen!" I snapped. "You people are only clouding matters by shrouding this thing in so much mystery! Why don't you come out in the open and let me get busy?"

"We don't, because to do that would mean death, sir," came agitatedly. "And we do not want to die, naturally. At least, I do not until justice is done. After it is, if it ever is, I don't so much care, sir. We are depending on you, sir, to see that it is!"

All those "sirs" identified the speaker as of the serving class. His accent, too, was fairly British, and I tagged him as being somebody's butler. Maybe a valet. Anyhow, a servant.

"I'll hold the deal, Hopkins," I told him. "But no longer than ten o'clock tonight. If somebody doesn't wise me up by then, or very shortly afterward, the box goes to the city cops. And that's that!"

"For God's sake, sir, don't do that!" he cried agonizedly. "You will know about it when you see her at the inn! Can we count on your discretion, sir?"

"Absolutely—until ten o'clock tonight. Good-by!"

Things were getting hot. I looked up to find Jim Steel at my elbow.

"No need for me to tag Frog Scanlon," he said, grimacing his distaste. "You still expecting Professor So-and-so?"

"I'm expecting most anybody, or nobody at all," I told him. "From the way this case is developing, Jim, most any old thing may happen. Can you imagine anything more futile than sending Frog after something in this office?"

"That's a laugh, and no mistake," Jim agreed.

The phone again.

"Norton," said a voice I recognized as belonging to the professor, "Scanlon has just reported your refusal to deliver my box to him. What do you want, anyhow?"

"To be let alone, more than anything else I can mention off-hand," I told him.

"You won't be," he assured me threateningly, "unless you listen to reason. That box does not belong to you, but regardless of that I'll pay you well to return it to me—and to keep your mouth shut about it. Would five hundred meet your price?"

"For what?" I asked.

"For the box, damn it!"

"Oh, the box. Well hardly. You see, professor, the more that's bid for the box, the more unwilling I become to part with it. Tell you what I'll do, however. I'll turn it over to you in person, and without taking a cent of your money—but it must be to you direct. What say?"

I KNEW from the time expiring between Frog's exit and the call on the phone that the professor must have been parked close at hand. While I stalled, Jim Steel was on his way down to the street. Jim would locate the professor, provided he still had Frog with him. Otherwise, he probably wouldn't.

"Your idea being to have a man tail me from your office, eh?" came back to me. "That informs me that you have opened the box—and no wonder you're holding it high. But let me assure you, Norton, that the skull in that box is of absolutely no importance except to me. It is part of a skeleton I wish to have mounted, and I came by it legitimately—"

"Tell that to Scanlon," I broke in. "Maybe he'll believe it. I don't. Are you coming after the skull, or not?"

Silence. Then: "I will call at one o'clock this afternoon—"

"Then you won't get it," I interrupted. "At one o'clock this afternoon you mean to send somebody after the skull. As I do not know you, professor, it would be easy to send a sub. But it won't work. Come now, or forever after hold your peace."

"My final offer!" the professor, now in a cold rage, spat at me. "One thousand dollars—and you keep mum. If you don't come through, then there is no place in this city where you will be safe! I'm weary of trying to overcome your stubbornness, and shall adopt measures better calculated to impress you! One thousand dollars, and safety, if you comply. A slab in a mortuary if you refuse. It should not be hard for you to make your choice!"

"Now you're speaking my language, professor!" I declared. "But why do it by phone? Why not in person? I'm not hard to see!"

I began, with that, to jiggle the hook again, bawling incoherently into the transmitter as I did so. If that failed to start him on a rampage, then it was hopeless. It failed. He hung up.

Five minutes later Jim Steel returned. He had not been able to spot the professor.

"He probably knew better than to tag himself by being in company with Frog," was Steel's opinion. "For which I don't blame him. Argues, doesn't it, that the prof does a bit of shrewd thinking, now and then?"

"It does. Nothing to do, now, I suppose, but wait for my date at the inn. Maybe, though, the professor isn't through yet."

Jim's face became serious. "I'm thinking that there's going to be something hot happen at that inn tonight," he said. "Better have me along, eh?"

I nodded, for the same thought had crossed my mind.

"You'll be outside, Jim," I told him, "and when I come to the front door you'll make certain that I don't get a slug from somewhere. That stunt of exposing my person in a manner that will positively identify me looks all to the bad. I wonder, now, if the sweet-voiced lady of the phone call is framing me for the spot?"

"Once in a while you do use your head, oldtimer," Jim applauded. "And I know it's sensible stuff—because I've been reasoning that way myself!"

Jim was born an egotist, and has never been reformed.

THERE was nothing more about the skull during the rest of the day, and when I left my office for the night I left two good tailors on the spot. If anybody should try a little job of burglary, it was all right with me.

I'd be pleased to say that I entered the Lone Jack Inn that evening with genuine nonchalance, but I didn't. As a matter of fact, the skull business had begun to take on a sinister aspect, and it might well be in the cards that I would be called upon to sit in a mighty stiff game before I was many hours older.

It was nine-thirty, and I had gone early in order to look the gathering over. The tables in the big dining room were plentiful and the place was well filled with diners. I secured a place near the kitchen entrance, sat down and scanned the crowd. Nowhere did I locate a lone woman diner. They were there in parties, by twos, threes and fours. All had male escorts. If my prospective client had arrived, then she certainly had not come alone. I ordered something to eat and drink, and kept my eyes open.

Steel was outside in a darkened motor-car, and at exactly one minute of ten he would be hanging around the front door. If anybody tried to pot me when I appeared, it would be just too bad for the potter. In that respect I felt safe. And I rather thought somebody would try it. Thought that in nodding my head three times I would be in reality kow-towing to death. But, as I have said, with Steel on the job I felt safe.

As I sat there waiting, I ran over the strange case in my mind, but could make nothing of it. That the box containing the skull had been knowingly addressed to me was never doubted in my calculations. The chap calling himself Professor James Donovan had not sent it, of course, but knew it had been sent and was hot to get it in his hands. It was in my mind that the skull constituted positive evidence of a murder, and it was possible also that it could be made to point conclusively to the murderer. And that was as far as I could get.

People came and went, but no lone woman showed up, nor could I see anybody, male or female, who seemed interested in sifting the gathering for any particular individual. But I was pretty certain that the woman was somewhere in the room.

Ten o'clock approached. At that hour precisely I arose, walked to the door, glanced at my watch, nodded my head three times—and nothing happened. I might have been a mechanical toy doing a stunt there in the doorway, for all the attention I attracted. But as I started to return to my table I was stopped.

"A telephone call has just come in for a gentleman whom I believe to be you, sir," a waiter captain informed me courteously. "Is your name Norton, may I ask?"

"Were you told to watch for a man who walked to the door, looked at his watch, nodded three times and then returned toward his table?" I countered, my interest keening to say the least.

"Yes, sir. And it is a lady calling. Will you follow me, please?"

You bet I'd follow him! The booth was right at hand, and I went in and closed the door.

"Well?" I called, not choosing to commit myself further.

"Mr. Tug Norton?" was the query.

Was it the same voice that had called me that morning? I couldn't be certain, although it sounded the same. I took a chance.

"Norton, yes," I replied. "You wish to speak to me?"

"Yes indeed!" she exclaimed. "Something has arisen to prevent my seeing you at the Lone Jack Inn, and it is important that our conference take place tonight. Will you come to me instead?"

"Certainly," I replied. "You are buying my time, you know. Where shall I come?"

"I am at the residence of an acquaintance, so there can be no risk. Come to 3329 Independence Boulevard. It is a large house, and back from the street in extensive grounds. I will answer the door. And please hurry!"

"Hurry it is," I assured her, and hung up.

I left the booth in a puzzled state of mind. Was I being stalled? Was the woman just on the phone the same who had made the appointment for Lone Jack Inn? The voices certainly were similar, if not identical—but I was suspicious, nevertheless. I decided to return to my table, sit down and see what happened.

CHAPTER THREE

At the Lone Jack Inn

NO sooner had I taken my seat than I became aware of somebody at my elbow. I glanced back and up—and looked into the face of a cigarette girl. A lovely face in which was set a pair of brown eyes —eyes holding a look of fear.

"Cigarettes, sir?" she asked, extending her tray.

"I believe so," I said, feeling for a coin with one hand and choosing a pack with the other.

"Drive your car to the cross-road!" she whispered, bending over toward me. "I'll join you there in five minutes!"

She was gone, working her way toward the entrance at the rear. I got up and went out to where my car was parked, meeting Steel there in the darkness.

"Follow my car," I whispered. "If you lose me, drive to 3329 Independence Boulevard and wait outside."

The Lone Jack Road and Highway Forty crossed about one hundred yards

east of the inn, and I pulled up there and stopped. Not another car was nearer to me than the inn, and nobody was in sight. I shut off my lights, opened a door and waited. A pair of minutes later, the cigarette girl, her scant costume covered with a light cloak, slid in beside me.

"Drive toward town!" she whispered excitedly. "I think I am being followed!"

She was. As I stepped on the starter a big sedan started up back at the inn, and a spotlight covered my machine. The car came toward us—and at that instant Jim Steel swung his boat across the road and killed his engine.

"Get th' hell out of th' way!" bellowed a voice angrily.

"Go to the devil!" was Jim's prompt reply.

"You're blocking the road!"

"Tell me something I don't know— Frog!"

Yeah, the hombre in the sedan was Frog Scanlon, and he had struck a snag in Steel. I stepped on the gas and left the matter with them.

"Someone tried to follow us!" the girl exclaimed anxiously.

"Sure. But don't worry about that. He didn't have any luck, and he won't," I assured her. "Where to, now?"

"Any place," she replied. "Drive out where we can talk."

I headed my car down a by-road that would take us up to Independence Boulevard by the shortest route, and gave it the gas.

"So you're a cigarette girl at the Lone Jack?" I queried.

"No," was the answer. "I paid the regular girl to let me take her place tonight. You see, I had no one I could trust as an escort, and unescorted women are not admitted there. It worked nicely."

"And fooled me nicely," I told her. "Suppose you shed a little light on that skull matter while we drive? Something tells me that we're going to have to do some fast stepping if we win this race, and we'd just as well get down to business. Do you know, to start with, the identity of the man whose skull was in the box?"

"I do not," was the answer—and you can bet that it surprised me. "I know only that it was sent to the house of my uncle by an unknown person. A card was in the box containing it, and on the card was printed in ink: The Skull of Judgment."

"Addressed to whom?" I asked.

"Andrew Larrimore, my uncle."

"How did he react to it?"

"He has never seen the ghastly thing!" she exclaimed. "Knows nothing whatever about it—and, I hope, never will!"

"Who besides yourself knows?" I asked.

"Briggs, the butler. He received the box and opened it. When he discovered what it contained he concealed it in his room, and after a week had passed he told me about it, cautioning me to say nothing to Uncle Andrew. Briggs has been with my family for many years—since before we came here—and I have every confidence in him. I obeyed his suggestion, and kept still."

"Funny that he should take that attitude in the matter," I commented. "Did he offer any explanation?"

THE girl was silent for a moment, then replied: "He told me that the sight of the skull had roused in him a suspicion that astounded him even to think of. That if what the skull suggested proved true, our lives, his and mine, depended upon our silence. The skull meant certain death to the possessor, once its possession was known. That, Mr. Norton, may sound melodramatic and foolish—but, knowing Briggs, I believe it to be true!"

"And," I agreed with her silently, "knowing a few things about the skull which you do not, I also believe it to be true!"

We turned into Independence Boulevard then, and fifteen minutes later I was driving slowly past number 3329. It was, as I had been told, a large house well back in extensive grounds. All the windows were dark, but through the fanlight above the entrance door a faint yellow showed.

A block farther on I parked against the curb. I had a hunch that there was something to be learned in that house, and I meant to find out whether the hunch was false or true.

My companion had been so occupied with her own thoughts that she had not moved or spoken for some time, but when I parked she sat up and surveyed her surroundings. A look of perplexity shadowed her face when she turned to me.

"Why," she exclaimed, "this is our neighborhood! Why did you come here?"

"What is your number?" I demanded quickly.

She hesitated, then answered: "It is 3329 Independence Boulevard, a large place in the middle of the block just above here. But you must not go there!"

"On the contrary," I corrected, concealing my surprise, "I must go there. Is there another woman in your household?"

"Yes. Uncle Andrew has a secretary —or did you mean a relative?"

"No. And you've answered my question. Going to leave you here for the present, while I keep an appointment with you at Number 3329 Independence—"

"With me!" she broke in, looking at me like she thought I had gone batty. "What do you mean?"

"That a woman called me up, in your name, broke the date at the Lone Jack and asked me to come to the Independence number," I explained. "And I wouldn't for the world miss seeing her."

At that moment a car showed up in the block above, prowled along slowly and when abreast of us, was brought to a stop.

"What's doing, Tug?" Steel asked, as he got out and came around to my side.

"Park ahead, Jim, and then keep this young lady company," I instructed. "I've got to keep a date."

Jim got in beside the girl, taking my place under the wheel.

"But you are only wasting time, Mr. Norton!" the girl declared. "The solution of this mystery could not possibly be in our home! Briggs knows only what I have told you, and Uncle Andrew, poor man, knows nothing at all!"

"Sorry to differ with you," I told her. "But I'm going in just the same. Anyhow, you remain with Mr. Steel, and leave the rest to me. That's what you are paying me for, you know."

I walked down the street, turned into 36th, slipped into an alley and backtracked until I reached the rear of Number 3329 Independence. I was going to keep my appointment with the unknown who had made it—but not exactly in accordance with polite custom. I was going to keep it by way of the back door.

There was no light in the rear of the house, and as I stole across the grounds from the garage no dog challenged me. Very likely the woman then waiting inside for me to show up would have no suspicion that I had tumbled to her attempted imposture, but I used just as much caution as if there might be alert eyes watching from every window.

THE door of the latticed back porch was not locked, but the one to the kitchen was. It gave me no trouble, however, as the second key on my ring shot the tumbler back. Inside the kitchen, having left the rear door unlocked as a precaution, I felt my way into the butler's pantry, thence to the dining room. A cop must be something of a house-prowler, at least a private cop should be, and I had no collisions on my way. In the dining room I stopped and listened.

The house was quiet. Very dimly came a sheen of light from the front hallway, visible through the partly opened door giving into what I surmised was the drawing room. Passing into the drawing room I risked a shot from my flash and saw that the room was deserted. Then I went into the hall, finding nobody there.

So carefully that not even a squeak ensued, I opened the front door, jabbed a thumb against a button, heard a bell ring upstairs, then closed the door and darted back into the drawing room. There, concealed by a voluminous drapery over the hallway arch, I waited.

A floor board squeaked above me; a door opened. Silence. Then I heard a soft tread on the stairway, the swish of a garment, and a woman in a flame-colored dinner-gown appeared abruptly in the dim light of the hall. I had only a bare glimpse of her as she hastened to the front door and opened it.

Silence, followed by an exclamation denoting surprise. A long moment, and the door was very softly closed. The bolt clicked home. I prepared to step out and announce myself, assured, now, that no trap had been set for me—downstairs, at least. Disclosure of my presence, however, was to be made much more dramatically than I had planned it. Much more.

As I laid a hand on the drapery to draw it aside, the woman then being on her way back toward the stairs, a deafening report from above filled the house with stunning suddenness, rattling the windows. An inarticulate cry broke from the lips of the woman in the hall—and, so blended with the report of the revolver as almost to seem a part of it, something heavy thudded upon the floor above. I leaped forward, plunged into the abruptly darkened hall, then stopped dead while a shiver played up and down my spine.

From the blackness above the stairhead

a cry came shivering down. It began as a low, gurgling plaint, and ended in shrill agony!

At that instant, and before I had taken a step toward the upper regions, a soft, perfumed body hurled itself against mine, and the woman's frightened scream cut into the diminishing wail from above. That wail with the grim note of death in it!

There was no time for gallantry, even if there had been an inclination. My arms went about the woman's waist, pinioning her arms at her sides. She screamed again, and I heard a door open upstairs, saw a shaft of light cross the blackness.

"Who—who are you?" my captive gasped shakily. "Take your arms away!"

"Steady," I cautioned her. "If you resist you may be hurt. What's the trouble here, anyhow—"

"I don't know!" she denied fiercely. "Take your arms off me!"

"You snapped off the hall light when that shot was fired," I said. "You were covering up for somebody. No need to lie!"

"You're doing the lying!" she shot back. "Release me—and run, you fool! Do you want to stay here and be killed?"

A slow, dragging noise above caught my attention, and I shot a glance upward. The opening of the door had let out enough illumination to render things vaguely visible—and I saw something on the stair. A dark huddle of something that moved, slowly and evidently at great cost, downward, tread by tread. A groan, deep, agonized, came from the crawling man, and he ceased to move.

Clasping the woman with my left arm, I clapped a hand against her right knee —and felt what I suspected might be there. With a flirt of her silken skirt I exposed the garter holster she wore— and slid a little automatic out of it.

"You—you beast!"

She hadn't time to say more. I thrust her into the drawing rom, yanked down the heavy drapes from the arch, rolled her in them and then rolled her across the floor. Then I sprang up the stairway toward that dark huddle on the landing.

CHAPTER FOUR

Death on the Stairs

AS I reached him the dying man groaned hollowly and strove to pull himself up by clutching the balustrade with his hands. He failed, and dropped back to the landing again. I reached for my flash with my left hand, the right being otherwise employed.

Before my flash was going, a switch snapped above, light flooded the hall and clove a bright path down the stairs. I looked up to see a man standing just above me. A tall man in dressing gown and pyjamas, graying hair mussed and tangled—an automatic in his right hand.

"Hold it!" I warned him, and had him covered before he could raise his gun. "Drop the rod—carefully!"

"Who are you? What has happened? Who is that on the landing?" he demanded, standing there like a frozen image.

"Drop that rod!" I snapped at him. "Else you'll be down too!"

At that he seemed to awake to the fact that his situation was not without a considerable element of danger, and he allowed the automatic to fall to the thickly carpeted tread at his feet.

"That's better," I approved. "Just come down here to the landing, and tell me who the injured man is. And move like you had life in you!" I said sharply, seeing him hesitate. "This is a case of life and death!"

He started as though he had been prodded from behind, and came half stumbling down toward me. Before he reached the landing, however, heavy footsteps beat upon the front porch, and a gun butt began a loud, peremptory tattoo on the door.

"Go down and open it!" I ordered.

"Good God!" he muttered, obeying me at the same time. "What is all this?"

He swung the door open, and Jim Steel stepped inside. Back of him was the girl.

"Heard a shot in here, Tug," Jim called. "What's happened?"

"Plenty," I answered. "Unwrap a bundle you'll find in the drawing room, and hold tight to what you find. You, Mister Man in the robe, get a doctor here as quick as you can—"

The girl was no longer behind Jim. With a sharp cry she darted past him and up the stairs, fell to her knees beside the injured man and cried: "Briggs! Oh, Briggs—what has happened? Quick, tell me!"

"Miss— Anne— I— I—"

The effort proved too great. He ceased trying to talk. His right hand raised feebly toward a pocket of his vest, faltered, lowered, then his palsied fingers rose again and clutched at the pocket. Anne thrust her hand into it—and drew out a small brass key.

"This, Briggs?" she whispered. "You wanted me to have this?"

"Yes!" came a whisper. "Give—it—to—Norton! Tell him—tell him—"

He shuddered, gasped—and death stifled the whisper in his throat!

"Briggs! Briggs! You—you can't go this way! Tell me what you meant—"

She ceased, turned her tear-stained face up to me.

"He is dead!" she cried, her voice filled with grief and awe. It was as though she had looked at the truth, but couldn't, wouldn't believe it.

"What is all this, anyhow?"

The man in the dressing gown, standing at the foot of the stairs, asked the question just as Steel appeared from the drawing room with the woman I had wrapped in the drape. She walked beside him, strangely composed, considering what her state had been when I was roughing her up, and added her demand to that of the man.

"Somebody had better do some quick explaining," she said coldly. "Or shall I call the police? What is all this about? What has happened?"

"Well," I answered, "judging from what I have seen and heard, I'd say a pretty fair job of murder has happened —and, if I'm not badly off, it is about a skull. A certain trepanned skull. The Skull of Judgment, in short. Ever hear of it?"

The face of the man in the gown, clearly revealed in the light which Steel had switched on, presented an utter blank. He turned inquiring eyes toward the woman, then, with a startled gasp, leaped toward her.

Steel was quicker, however. He caught her slender body as it sagged to the floor!

STEEL carried the woman into the drawing room and placed her on a divan, and Anne hastened to her.

"Uncle Andrew, call a doctor," she said. "Isobel is ill from fright! No wonder, poor girl!"

The man in the dressing robe blinked his eyes rapidly, hesitated, then glanced at me.

"You seem to have taken charge here," he said. "I don't know who you are, but my niece seems to be acquainted with you—"

"Slightly," I interrupted. "As for calling a doctor, I think that won't be necessary. Isobel has merely swooned, and it won't be long until she comes out of it. Get some water, Jim, and sprinkle her face."

Jim departed for the kitchen, and Uncle Andrew turned to me again.

"Will you explain what you are doing here, and what you meant when you spoke of a skull?" he demanded, beginning to show heat. "You must admit that your presence in my house at such a time is suspicious to say the least. How did you get here, and what do you know about the killing of poor Briggs?"

"I came by appointment, and knowing nothing about Briggs—except that he was shot by somebody above stairs," I answered, noting that Isobel was coming out of her faint. "You will have all your questions answered, but not just yet."

Steel came with the water, and Isobel opened her long-fringed lids before a drop touched her.

"What has h a p p e n e d?" she asked moaningly. "I feel very ill! Something terrible has happened! Oh, I remember!"

"I thought you would," I commented. "Jim," I instructed, "keep Uncle Andrew and Isobel here with you, while I have a look through the rooms upstairs—"

"If you go up those stairs," Andrew broke in sharply, "I go with you—and that is that!"

"You'll sit down and stay there," Jim snapped, walking toward him. "And that is something else that is more thatter than that!"

"Come with me, Anne," I bade my employer. "I'll want to ask you a question or two."

"But, Mr. Norton!" the girl exclaimed. "You should not allow your man to treat uncle so! I don't understand!"

"I merely do not want him with me when I go up stairs," I told her. "I do want you. Come, please."

Anne followed me up the stairs, and at the top I paused to query her. "How many servants?" I asked.

"Only poor Briggs lived here," she answered. "A cook and maid come in by the day."

"Any other members of your household except those I have seen?"

"None. Just Uncle, Isobel and myself."

"How did you come to send that skull to me?"

"I didn't. Briggs did that. He felt that he could not handle the matter himself, so consulted with me. We agreed to send it to a detective, and found your name in the telephone book—"

"Why send it?" I broke in. "Why didn't he come with it in person?"

"I do not know, only he said he believed he had best get it away quickly. That it would be safe with you, and he would call you up and arrange an appointment. Then, when uncle became ill—which he did yesterday—and Briggs could not get off, he told me to arrange an appointment for myself. But he insisted that the place of meeting be somewhere outside of this house. I do not know why, except that he wanted the matter kept from Uncle Andrew, as it would worry him needlessly. Uncle is something of a recluse, I should tell you, and devoted to literary work. That is why Isobel—Miss Hollis—came as secretary. I made the appointment, and now all this has happened! Poor Briggs, I'm sure he knew something of great value!"

"Two of us are sure about that," I told her. "What did Briggs tell you to say to me when we should meet?"

"I was to give you a note from him, sealed in an envelope, after I was certain I could trust you fully, was the surprising answer. "And here is the note—"

She reached into a pocket in the scant skirt she wore, and stopped speaking, a look of surprise in her eyes.

"The note!" she exclaimed. "It is gone!"

I grinned. "Don't worry about the note," I told her. "Isobel, dead to the world though she was, took it out of your pocket while you were bending over her on the divan. A smooth article, Isobel— but she was a trifle slow on the job. We'll go down, now, and Mr. Steel will persuade her to give up the note. Come."

WE reentered the drawing room, and I said to Steel: "Isobel hooked an envelope out of Anne's pocket a bit ago, Jim. See if you can get her to produce it. I'm going up to have a look for the bird that killed Briggs—knowing beforehand that I won't find him. Still, the usual thing must be done. I'll hurry the job, and be back with you before long."

Isobel smiled sweetly at me—which aroused my suspicions. Andrew gave me a sour look that might mean anything or nothing. I didn't try to analyze the look, but went back up the stairs. There were four bedrooms which appeared to be in use. Three on the second floor and one on the third. The one on the third was unmistakably that of the butler.

On my way up to the butler's room I observed an open window at the end of the second-story hall, and, thrusting my head out, found a sloping roof beneath it. Clearly, the killer had escaped that way—or, perhaps, it was intended that an investigator should think he had.

The butler's room, where I had expected to find something vital, proved to be disappointing. His trunk gave up nothing, and the rest of the room was as barren. One thing I came across lying upon a table, and which did not strike me as important, was a Kansas City Southern time-table, quite new. Then I began to wonder what Briggs would be doing with a railway time-table in his room, and that speculation led me to look the thing over. What I found might be important, and might not be, but at any rate the butler had either made a trip on the K. C. S. lately, or contemplated making one.

The time of departure of the Red Bird, crack passenger train, was checked in pencil, and, turning to the map, I found a circle drawn around the name of a town. Hanging Rock. Briggs had been to Hanging Rock, Arkansas, or had planned to go. I put the time-table in my pocket and went down to the lower floor.

At the front of the house I found Andrew's room, but found nothing there to interest me—except a concealed telephone set. For some reason or other, Andrew had hooked up a special set for himself, and had hidden it back of a row of books on a shelf. It might mean much—or little.

Anne's room gave up nothing, which was not disappointing, as I had expected nothing. I then entered a bedroom directly across the corridor from Andrew's. The bedroom of the handsome secretary, Isobel Hollis.

All the time, I had been searching for something to explain the little brass key which Briggs had wanted me to have. Nowhere had there appeared a box, casket or other locked receptacle that the key would fit.

But there was a lock in existence which that key would open—and it held the solution of the mystery of the trepanned skull. I was certain of that. Maybe it would be in the attic, possibly in the basement—but I knew that it must be somewhere on the premises.

I was right. At least, the box was on the premises. In the handsome Isobel's room I located it. Had she not been a bit careless, due perhaps to haste, I should not have found the hiding place so easily. Maybe not at all. It was a very cunningly conceived and executed hiding place, and one new to me.

I had known of hiding places being arranged beneath the hearth-bricks of a fireplace, but never before had I found one set into a hearth of tile. Not under the tile, if you please, but forming a section of the surface itself. Isobel, however, had betrayed herself by failing to see that the all-important section was pushed down far enough to correspond with the level of the rest of the hearth. She had been in a hurry, no doubt.

The hiding place proved to be a shallow metal box, the lid overlaid with tile. Nothing could have been handier, nor so certain of escaping detection as that contrivance. But haste spilled the beans.

The little brass key fitted the box, and when I raised the lid I saw that the shallow receptacle was filled with papers. That they would lay the whole case bare I could not doubt—else why had Briggs wanted me to have the key?

"She stole the papers from Briggs and hid 'em here. Briggs then stole the key, or secured a duplicate—" I started checking up, unconsciously speaking out loud.

"And you can hand over both the key and the box to me—pronto!"

The man who interrupted my speculations was Frog Scanlon—and he had the drop on me from the doorway!

CHAPTER FIVE

Hangman's Harvest

I FACED Scanlon—but he was a different Scanlon than I had ever seen before. His face presented a mask of hate, cunning, avarice, and his eyes glittered evilly. He was primed to kill, and no mistake about it.

"As usual, Frog," I said, "I'm not glad to see you. Put that gat in your pocket, before it goes off and frightens the neighbors. What are you made up for, anyhow? Jesse James, or Diamond Dick, Junior?"

"Put that box down on the table!" he snarled. "Put it down, damn you Norton, or I'll slug you!"

"Every time I get hold of a box, Frog," I complained, "you try to take it away from me! This morning it was a wooden box—"

"On the table!" he broke in. "Cut the chatter!"

I placed the casket on the table as directed. Frog took a step or two into the room.

"Elevate!" he ordered.

I obeyed, and his gasp of relief when he had both my gats in his possession was quite flattering to me. It was flattery I could have easily foregone, I'll add.

He backed to the door, poked his head into the hall and called down the stairs: "O. K. Got him dead to rights! Everybody stay where you are until I call you! Stay where you are—and I mean just that!"

"Gotcha, boss," "Skimp" Needham, Frogs right-hand man, called up from below.

"Reckon you and Skimp sprung a little surprise on Steel, eh?" I queried when Frog drew his head back and closed the door.

"You reckon right," he crowed. "Steel blocked my game once tonight, damn him, but I returned the compliment—with the honors all mine. Thanks to whoever left the back door open, Skimp and me was able to get the drop on Mr. Steel. He won't give us any trouble, either, because he's got a pair of cuffs on his wrists and a pair around his ankles. But that's not here nor there. You're going to do what I tell you to, else you won't ever see sweet mamma again. Get me?"

"Sure. Fire when ready, Grid, old chap. I know when my hand is beat."

"All right. Sit down in the chair by the table," Frog directed, "and take out the first paper in that box. Read it out loud."

"Why, Frog!" I exclaimed, obeying the order. "I thought you knew how to read!"

"Cut the comedy!" he gritted. "I don't trust you, Norton—not by a damned sight. You read to me, while I watch you—and remember, you big sap, that I've got my gat handy!"

He had drawn a chair up to the door and was then sitting in it, his sixgun lying in his lap. No question but what he had me faded.

"Read that first paper," he ordered again.

A long envelope, lying on top of the pile, contained the paper Frog wanted read to him. I first read the direction penned thereon: "To whom it may Concern."

"Never mind that!" Frog snapped. "Read what's inside!"

I WITHDREW some sheets of letterhead-size bond, all covered with neat penmanship, and began reading aloud.

"My name is Arthur Goss, although I have been using that of Briggs for a number of years. I was once a butler in England, but couldn't keep straight, so I came to America and entered the service of Mr. Ronald Larrimore, a fine gentleman of great wealth. Five years ago he moved from New York City to Kansas City, bringing me with him. He had a brother whom he had not seen for fifteen years, his only living relative, save his daughter. The brother held mining interests in the southwest part of Missouri. One week after Mr. Larrimore reached the city and located at 3329 Independence Avenue, he died. Death was unquestionably due to heart disease. He left one child, Miss Anne, then thirteen years old, she being his heir. The brother, Andrew Larrimore, was appointed guardian of Miss Anne, and executor of the estate, without bond.

"Mr. Andrew Larrimore was notified, and came on to take charge. I do not know when it was I became suspicious of him, but do recall that my suspicions were confirmed about a year ago. I happened to mention an old injury to Mr. Andrew which Mr. Ronald had spoken of to me. Something in the paper about a trepanning operation called it to my mind. He looked at me blankly, asked me to what I referred, and I told him I had reference to the wound he had received in the back of his head, years before, and which had been covered with a silver plate. He then told me that he had never had any trouble because of the wound, and that the trepanning

was a complete success. But it was too late for that.

"The man calling himself Andrew Larrimore is an imposter, and was, until I mentioned it, unaware that the real Andrew Larrimore had had such an operation performed.

"I puzzled over the matter a great deal, and came to see how easily the imposture had been effected. There was nobody else in the family except Miss Anne, who had never seen Mr. Andrew, and there were no friends of the family who knew him. The purpose of the fraud was clear. Ronald Larrimore left an estate valued at two million dollars—a stake well worth playing for.

"Having become satisfied that the man posing as Andrew was an imposter, I began making investigations. He had, two years before, brought a young woman into the house as his secretary, never informing anyone that she had been known to him in the past. But their familiarity with each other when they thought themselves unobserved soon told a different tale. The Hollis woman is either his mistress or his wife. By listening to their talk when unobserved, I gathered that Andrew had been slowly converting the estate into ready cash and negotiable securities, and that he meant to have the estate for his own. Either he would abscond with the bulk of it—else heir it as next of kin.

"I take my oath that I have heard the killing of Miss Anne discussed as coldbloodedly as a couple of butchers would have discussed the slaughter of a calf!

"It is not my purpose to attempt to cover up myself in the least. When I started investigating this matter it was with the intention of profiting richly by what I discovered. By reading old letters from Mr. Andrew to Mr. Ronald, I learned that the trepanning operation had been done at a place called New Madrid, in southwest Missouri. The doctor's name was Woods. I got in communication with him, and got him to send me a sworn copy of his records—and that sworn copy relates in detail about the performance of the trepanning operation. The name of the man treated was Andrew Larrimore, and he had given the address of his brother, Ronald Larrimore in New York, in case anything happened and he failed to survive. The sworn copy is attached hereto.

"I will not describe all the moves made, but tell only the important points. Andrew had lived on his mining land near Hanging Rock, and I went down there while pretending to be in St. Louis to see a sick sister. I was satisfied that Andrew had been slain somewhere on the land, and I was right. After two days search, I found a skeleton at the bottom of a shallow prospect-hole, dug it up—and saw, by the skull, that it was that of Andrew Larrimore.

"I took the head—that tell-tale plate of silver being enough for my purpose—and returned to the village. There I learned that a man had been working with Andrew —a man named Kinsley. He had not been seen since Andrew left the section, however.

"I had the skull, but was unwilling to carry it with me to the train, so I packed it in a box and expressed it to myself at the Kansas City address. I knew that nobody would open the box, since it was mine. It was my purpose to charge this man Kinsley, for I was sure it was he, with the imposture—and sell him the damning skull for a big sum of money. How I had underestimated the man and his resourcefulness!

"Since the day on which I had mentioned the trepanning to him, he had been deeply suspicious of me. Through the woman, Isobel, he had established espionage upon my movements—and there was little I had done that remained unknown to him. And he had acted while I, too, had been busy. He traced me back to England—and, when I approached him about the skull and what I knew, he laid certain evidence before me which would, should he choose to use it, send me back to England to answer for a serious crime! He had me helpless!

"But I was determined that he must pay. He did not know that I really possessed the skull, since I had it well hidden, and when I told him that I had been stalling about it he appeared satisfied. Whether or not he really is I do not know.

"I decided, after much thought, to take Miss Anne partly into my confidence, place the skull along with all the evidence, in the hands of a competent detective—and then disappear. If I could not get a slice of that big fortune, I'd save it for Miss Anne. For that reason I am writing this true account, and attaching the documentary evidence to it.

(Signed)

Arthur Goss, alias

Arthur Briggs."

I FOLDED the document and looked up at Scanlon. He was sitting forward in his chair, drinking in my words like they had been draughts of wine. His face fairly beamed.

"Looks like rain—for somebody, eh, Frog?" I queried.

"Yes!" he exclaimed hoarsely. "I hoped I'd find something good—but this is more than I dreamed of! Two million! Good God!"

"How does that affect your fortunes, Frog? From your looks, a fellow would think it was water on your wheel."

"It is!" he snapped. "That crook downstairs is going to pay through his nose. Pay big! And I'm the boy he's due to pay!"

"What will I be doing, Frog, while you're collecting your blackmail?"

"You!" He laughed—and I didn't like the sound of it. "I hate you and Steel like poison already. Do you think I'd let the lives of a pair of skunks like you stand between me and a million? Hell, no! You two are going bye-bye—and tonight! Read the other papers, damn you!"

There was nothing for it but to obey, and I lifted another long envelope from the box. Lifted it—and stared down at something that made my heart leap into my throat. Something that caused me to bless Isobel most sincerely, crook though she was.

A small automatic, little sister to the one I had taken from her garter holster, was what the removal of the paper disclosed! It lay there, a deadly invitation to get busy. Deadly to Frog, I mean!

"You're a nut, Scanlon," I told him, "to think you can get away with a thing like that— There's not a chance in the world of—"

"Never mind!" he growled. "Read the paper!"

I had taken the box on my lap when I took the second envelope out of it, and my right hand lay upon its edge. I began reading. The thing was not germain to the murder, but that made no difference. I went right on, making up what I pretended to read—until I saw Frog's concentration was again causing him to become careless. It was my move.

Was the little gun loaded?

Damn it, I'd soon find out!

"It's time to reach for the ceiling, Frog!" I snapped into his state of abstraction—and let him look into the muzzle of the gun.

Scanlon leaped in his chair as though he had been shot—but he froze immediately thereafter. For I was walking toward him, and maybe he didn't like what he saw in my eyes.

"Move so much as a finger, speak above a whisper, make any play that I don't like —and I'll shoot both of your eyes out!" I told him—and meant it.

Frog wilted. A pair of minutes sufficed to snap cuffs on his wrists, bind him with a strip of bed-sheet, and gag him good and proper. He was the sickest looking man I ever saw—and I've seen some mighty sick ones.

With my old reliables once more in their holsters, I closed the door on Scanlon and crept softly down the stairs.

When I stepped into the drawing room, with those same old dependables prominently displayed, the atmosphere became instantly charged with a variety of emotions. Astonishment, fear, panic, relief —Jim Steel contributing the latter current.

"Mr. Frog Scanlon's compliments, professor," I said, bowing politely to the fake Andrew, "and he hopes there will be no objection to my playing his hand.

A message for you, too, Skimp," I went on, holding the little weasel under the muzzle of a gun. "Frog hopes you will release Mr. Steel—pronto. Must I insist?"

Andrew sat very still, his face white, jaw sagging. Isobel calmly took a cigarette from a box near her and lit it. As for Skimp, he freed Jim without the need of argument.

"What does all this high-handedness mean?" Andrew finally found his voice and demanded.

"It means that the skull now sits in judgment, Kinsley," I answered. "Poor Briggs, in stalling Miss Anne, certainly named it well. You are under arrest for the murder of Andrew Larrimore, which crime occurred near Hanging Rock, Arkansas, about five years ago. There will be further charges, notably those of fraud, false pretense, attempted embezzlement—and the second murder which was committed here tonight. The murder of Briggs."

"Mr. Norton!" Anne cried, getting slowly to her feet. "What in the world do you mean? The gentleman you are arresting is my uncle, Andrew Larrimore! Have you lost your mind?"

"I should like to know the answer to that question myself!" Andrew exclaimed. "Of all the fool stunts I ever heard of—"

"Shut up!" I interrupted. "Isobel," I went on, turning to the woman, "did you read that confession of Briggs' before you locked it in the little casket in the hearth?"

"I knew you had found it, chief," she informed me calmly, "when you mentioned the name of Kinsley. Of course I read it. I stole it from Briggs' trunk and locked it in the hiding place. Briggs, who it seems had learned of the little casket, stole the key from me. That is how he happened to get bumped off—so soon."

Kinsley, to name him properly, got to his feet, rage in his eyes.

"What do you mean, you fool!" he snarled.

"Just this, Frank," she replied wearily. "And you may as well sit down and hold your tongue. I told you when I cut in with you on this job that if you foozled it I would get the best bargain I could—and you've foozled it. Now I'm going to get out from under."

Kinsley, seeing that the game was up, sat down again, his face congested.

"Frank Kinsley has been a crook all his life," Isobel went on in a cold voice. "And I'm his wife. One of them. Frank has been rather absent-minded in marital matters, and I doubt whether he knows himself how many women he has led to the altar. He made Andrew Larrimore's acquaintance and figured to 'make' him in a different way. Then came the letter from Ronald Larrimore's attorney, advising Andrew that he had been made executor of his dead brother's estate and guardian of his daughter. Frank knew Andrew's history, and he determined to usurp his double office of exectuor and guardian—to his own profit. He killed Andrew—which was safe enough in that out of the way place—presented himself with Andrew's papers, and the scheme worked like a charm. Worked until Briggs, a crook himself, got wise.

"Briggs fooled Frank and me about the skull, claiming he did not really have it. After it was too late, and Briggs had smuggled the thing out of hiding early this morning, we got wise. Frank's secret telephone set, connected with the set downstairs, wised him up. He tried to get Norton to come through with the box, failed, then hired that crook, Scanlon, to get it. Scanlon failed.

"The idea in letting Anne go to the Lone Jack was to make the play I later made, get Norton in our hands, force him to give up the skull—and then bump him off. But it didn't work. Norton has been too strong for us.

"Finally, Briggs' actions put Frank into a rage, and when he learned that he had stolen the key in order to get possession of the confession he had written, he laid for him and shot him. We had given Norton up, thinking he had got wise and would not come. I learned, by calling the Lone Jack again, that Norton had gone away in company with a cigarette girl—and I knew that part of the scheme was all smoke. Right then is when I began to feel that we had lost. Anything more you want to know, Mr. Norton?"

"That's all," I told her. "The skull can easily be identified by the silver plate, and Kinsley's guilt is apparent in his imposture here. Even without your evidence, he would go up for life. With it, he'll hang."

At that Frank Kinsley jumped up out of his chair suddenly, and, with a blistering oath, leaped for Isobel, his long fingers groping for her throat.

Steel, alert as always, leaped at the same time he did—and the barrel of his sixgun dropped neatly onto the crown of Kinsley's head. When he came back to consciousness he was on his way to jail.

Isobels testimony, plus the mute evidence of the trepanned skull, put a rope around Frank Kinsley's neck. Whether or not it was because of her evidence or because of her beauty, she went free.

There wasn't much on Scanlon, and he wasn't bothered. He's still running his snoopery. Anne, too tender hearted for her own good, made me let the rat go.

But, does some hombre offer in criticism, Frank Kinsely sowed tares all his life, and reaped tares in the end! What about that statement at the beginning, Norton?

I've proved it. Kinsley sowed tares all his life, and never reaped anything but fruits and flowers. Yeah, that's the kind of crop he reaped clear to the end—*and then he got reaped.*

THE CURTAIN OF FROST

FROST

A Vee Brown Story

by

Carroll John Daly

Author of "The Sixth Bullet," etc.

Clogged were the wheels of the Crime Machine for the D. A. had said: "Bullets are out!" Now, behind a frosted window of mystery, Vee Brown, Killer of Killers, must spring a terror trap—or die.

FOR some time the piano in Vee Brown's studio, behind the closed doors which separated it from the library, was strangely silent. I looked at the well-filled shelves, the expensive first editions and the leather-bound sets—and I wondered again how Vee Brown, with all this luxury, all the money the writing of sentimental songs under the name of Vivian brought him, could still stick to his job as a first-grade detective assigned to the district attorney's office.

Lighting another cigarette I glanced through The Herald Examiner, a rival sheet of The Globe— The Globe, to which I contributed articles regarding Brown's cases as a detective, defending his killing of criminals in his duty to the State and in defense of his own life. Certainly, in a great many cases he had killed men. But they were without exception desperate, wanted, brutal murderers. And each instance had been—Brown's life or theirs. His record as a killer of men was now finding its way into the editorials of the newspapers and so to the homes of the

The snub nose of his automatic was smack against my chest.

honest citizens as well as to the denizens of the underworld, who hated and feared him.

The Globe defended him. Jack Ferris, the city editor, published my stories of Vee Brown in action under the rather lurid heading "In On The Death," yet he was a bit hot under the collar because I would not disclose to him the source of Vee Brown's wealth. But Vee Brown kept his pent house atop one of Park Avenue's most select apartment houses very secret, and I respected his secret and his shame as facetiously he often referred to his writing of sentimental songs.

Now, as I glanced through The Herald Examiner again, I missed the editorial sheet, and as I looked beneath the couch the door of the music room opened and Vee Brown strode in.

"It's unfair, Dean." He held the offending editorial crumpled in his hand. "A warrant signed by a pompous judge, over the seal of the State, is not the fearsome awe-inspiring document the State means it to be—and perhaps thinks it is. It is no protection against the steady hum of bullets from a Tommy-gun. The widows' and orphans' fund of the police department will all too often bear witness to that statement. No, the only protection is a keen eye, a quick hand, and the slightest pressure of a finger upon a gun trigger. This editorial! You'd think I was a man devoid of any human feeling; that I killed for the pleasure of snuffing out a human life, while I am simply a machine employed by the State. A crime machine, that—"

"But just how do you feel, Vee, when you—you kill a man?"

"How? How do I feel?" He twisted up the corner of his mouth into that little crooked smile of his. "Like the singer, perhaps, who has made a sensation, the business man who has put

through a deal in which his competitors have failed, the reporter who has made a scoop for his paper—like any other man who has a natural pride in work well done. Even—" And that sparkle of enthusiasm died suddenly as his hand dove into his jacket pocket. "The new lease for this apartment. It was inevitable that it would become known I live here sooner or later. Your editor knew it. The district attorney knows it now. But that I make my money writing songs, no one but you must know. I have the lease in your name. You were quiet well off, you know, Dean, before your securities shrunk. Now, no one need know the difference." And in that jumpy way of his: "The district attorney is to honor us with a visit. I thought it better to have him come here—here, to your apartment. It will allay all suspicions. The name 'Dean Condon' boldly meets all eyes twenty-one stories below."

"Mortimer Doran coming here! Something big in the wind, then, Brown."

"My biggest case." He jumped a loose cigarette from his vest pocket to his mouth and stuck a match to it. "It's all over the front pages, Dean."

"Lieutenant Eswal Grim!" I fairly gasped the name—and then: "But he's disappeared. They don't know where he is?"

"No, they don't. I dare say I'm the only man in the city who knows where he is—or rather, where he will be tonight."

"And he's guilty—of all these; the framing of the innocent—the protecting of the guilty? It seems too terrible, Vee."

"Guilty as hell—of all these, and many more. The police nursed him too long. They knew as well as I knew. But it was a shock the administration hesitated to take—facts it hesitated to face. No, the investigation was sincere and honest enough in its purpose and District Attorney Mortimer Doran is as straight as a die. Simply the frailty of human nature. We all shun the unpleasant; deny the truth of things we don't wish to believe."

"You have the case? You are to—to," I hesitated over the word 'kill'—"bring him in?" I finally said.

"Yes." He nodded. "And for once, Dean, I believe the human side will enter into the quest of the Crime Machine. It is hardly to be expected that Lieutenant Eswal Grim will be taken alive. And I think," he snapped his jaws, "it will be with considerable satisfaction that I can place a bullet straight between his pig-like little pink eyes. No—don't look shocked, Dean. The man is rotten clean through. There is not one extenuating circumstance. His advancement was obtained through the persecution of the innocent and the protecting of the vicious. The crooked policeman is the citizen's greatest peril. I could shoot him down without a pang of conscience. Now," he shrugged his shoulders, "the district attorney has waited too long. I may have to do just that little thing."

"You know that he's guilty—absolutely guilty?"

"I have known it for months. Long before the investigation started. But knowledge was not evidence. I worked for over a year, secretly gathering evidence about Lieutenant Eswal Grim. To-day I could go on the stand and convict him on a dozen different counts. He knew it and he fled. They waited too long." He paused and listened. There was a ring at the door. "Mortimer Doran, the district attorney." Vee Brown nodded. "I told them not to bother announcing him from downstairs."

I RECOGNIZED him of course. Huge of frame, steady of eye and thick of jowls. Mortimer Doran's picture had too often decorated the front pages not to be known to most every citizen.

"Nice diggin's." He squinted his eyes tightly. "You're in luck, Brown. But I don't know about Mr. Condon, here, if some of the boys got onto your—your hideout. Philanthropic reporter, eh?" He grinned pleasantly. "Gives you board and lodging for exclusive stories on your cases. That explains the big car—and the Jap driver too, eh? Well—I can't say that it troubled me." And suddenly his lips setting, his face hardening and his gray eyes growing sharp: "Lieutenant Grim has slipped through our fingers—entirely."

"Slipped!" Brown twisted his mouth. "Why—an entire police parade could have walked through the opening the police left."

"Yes, perhaps they could. It was a case of not wanting to believe it, I guess. But he carried no large bank accounts. There were nothing but rather loose connections. Coming to a point, I'll admit—but until you spoke out to me yesterday, hardly a thing to pin an indictment on. You—you should have told me sooner."

"I shouldn't have told you at all. There was enough for an indictment, and I'd promised you a conviction when I went on the stand. Yesterday I opened up a bit. Just proof of what you already knew. But it was too much. Somehow Grim found it out—and he's gone."

"But you've promised to get him, Vee." Mortimer Doran was across the room, a huge hand upon one of Brown's slim shoulders. "You're to bring him in to-night, you know. You've never failed me." His voice was anxious. "The papers are rather jumping down on me, you know. You said he was a rat, Vee—and he'll talk."

"I'll bring him in." Brown nodded grimly. "But I can't promise he'll talk. Not now."

"He must." A huge hand closed on Brown's shoulder, and I saw him wince slightly. "He's the key-man to the whole terrible mess. He'll talk when we tell him what we've got on him. He'll talk to save his own skin. No guts, Brown. You said so yourself. Don't grin like that! I—I want Grim alive."

"I'll do my best." Brown nodded.

Mortimer Doran looked at Brown steadily for some time. Then he said: "Your best won't do. I've got to have him alive." And before Brown could speak: "Look here. If you know where he is, out with it. We'll surround his hideout. I'll put every available man on the job. And you'll—you'll get the credit for the arrest."

"You can give the credit to someone else." Brown's black eyes sparkled. "I want only the man. He knows I'm after him now. He knows I'll come for him. And he'll be ready and waiting. Even a rat fights when cornered. You want me to go to my death? It's no use to talk about 'every available man.' If there's a police parade there'll be no Lieutenant Grim. I'll have to take him in my own way."

"I've always given you a free rein, Vee. You've worked alone, independent of instructions. No one to report to. No time—no check in—no routine of any sort. I see you've got the paper there in your hand. They're riding you, Vee. But they're riding me much harder. Killer of Men—killer detective, legalized by a befuddled and incompetent district attorney; and this time, Vee, they'll be right. They'll say you were sent out to get Eswal Grim because you produce a body—not a man. They'll say you were sent out— By God! I believe you want to kill him."

VEE'S head came up; his chin went out. "And why not? People are unfair—the papers are unfair. The police department of the city is the finest, the most honest, and the bravest in the world.

There isn't a minute in the twenty-four hours that they don't take their lives in their hands. Glad to—willing to. And because one betrays his trust, they condemn the whole force. They don't condemn the entire bar association because a lawyer turns crooked. They don't condemn— Oh, hell—sir, Grim is rotten clean through. He hasn't the excuse of the average criminal. Environment—association—lack of opportunity. He hasn't the excuse of the chance murderer. Jealousy—sudden passion—insane vengeance. No—I don't think I ever wanted to kill a man. I hope I don't now. But if he must be killed to be brought to—to account; if he must be eliminated by the great police machine, that protects the citizens, then I'm willing—even glad— to be the cog in that machine which presses the trigger that completes the execution. If he won't be taken alive— and he won't, I—"

"There, there," Mortimer Doran shook Brown's shoulder gently. "Everything you say is true—except one thing. Grim is more important to the force—and the honor of that force—alive. He's just one of a big system. A big, corrupt system that's eating at the vitals of the finest body of men any citizen ever had to protect him. Personally, Grim would be better for me dead. If he will talk—and it's you who has assured me he will—then he will bring the department under severe criticism. That isn't to my interest, is it? But it is to the interest of the people I serve. I'm willing to face it; I want to face it. I want to know and drive out the men who block investigations, accept graft, work hand in hand with the racketeers. There're rackets all over the city—of every sort and description. It's in the police department—the district attorney's office. Well—I want to clear it out. And I don't care where the axe strikes. Those I have considered my friends! Those who will be my staunch supporters at the coming election! If I've got to go out, I want to go out with a clear conscience. I want to be able to look honest men in the face. I want Grim alive, Vee Brown. I must have him alive!"

"I'll do my best." Brown set his lips grimly.

"And I've said that isn't enough." And now I saw the fighting face of Mortimer Doran. "I've pleaded with you—spoken to you man to man. Tried to make you see my picture of it. I've given you your own way in cases because I liked your courage—believed, with you, that the police officer today should meet the new criminal with his own weapons. Gunfire with gunfire. I've respected you because you did not know fear. Now, am I to believe what others have hinted? That your stock in trade is that of an ordinary gunman; that your success is due entirely to your quickness with a gun. Well—despite our understanding; your freedom in your work—yes, and even in the cases you accept and the cases you don't accept, you are still a detective—a detective assigned to the district attorney's office, and you'll take orders from that office. At least, to this extent. You'll bring in Eswal Grim alive. You'll give me your word on that—or," he hesitated a long minute, "you'll turn in your shield. You'll be just another detective who has gone under the hammer of an official shake-up."

"You—you don't mean that, sir." And I think it was the first time I ever saw Vee Brown shaken—at least, visibly shaken.

"I mean every word of it. Now, will you bring in Eswal Grim alive?"

A LONG moment of hesitation, and then: "I'll bring him in alive—if I bring him in at all."

"That won't do—not exactly do. *Will you* bring him in alive?"

"I will bring him in alive, or—or take the bumps myself." For a moment Brown was very serious, then his lips parted. Again that twisted, crooked grimace as he said: "You put it over. I didn't think you could. But I guess— Well, after all I've often said I'm a crime machine. Maybe I've always just looked at it—a man or a body. They've been such clean-cut cases, where the— Hell! Mr. Doran—if ever a man deserved one good killing that man is Eswal Grim."

"Just the same it is for the good of the city. We can't clean up the underworld, Vee, until we clean up our own house. This will be the first—and let us hope, the last step in that cleaning. If Grim talks."

"And he will talk," said Vee Brown. "He's that kind of a skunk."

"It must be rather quiet. I don't want to be hampered by habeas-corpus writs, high-priced criminal lawyers, and—or—"

"A friendly judge." Vee Brown helped him out.

"Exactly!" said Mortimer Doran. "A friendly judge. You might bring him here—to Mr. Condon's place. You've got enough evidence to convince him that we can make it worth his while to talk."

"I can go on the stand and swear to enough to roast him over and over," said Vee Brown almost viciously. Something like an animal deprived of his "kill," I thought. "I'll bring him here by two o'clock—or I won't come back."

"That's the stuff. I'll be back at two. Good night, then." And to me: "Well—Mr. Condon, this time you won't be able to head your article, 'In On The Death!'"

"I wouldn't be too sure about that," said Vee Brown very slowly. But Mortimer Doran preferred to ignore the sinister significance of Brown's final words. The next moment he was gone.

"He was right of course, Dean," Vee said emphatically when we were alone. "It's just a truth that I didn't want to face. The man isn't fit to live," he hesitated a moment and looked down at the open palm of his right hand, "but I don't know if I'm doing it so much for the sake of the citizens I serve as for myself. I want the job, Dean. It means everything to me, and Mortimer Doran has treated me fine. Everything he said was true. He has let me work my own way—even select my own cases. Now—" He looked toward the music room. "Which is my life? Which is myself? Master of Melodies as they call Vivian—Killer of Men as they call Vee Brown? Or are the two inseparable; one the outlet for the other —one impossible without the other?

"But, there! Don't look so glum. Things are not, perhaps, as bad as I paint them. If I must meet the criminal at his own game I must meet him at the whole of that game. I won't argue the point of your not coming with me; I know the futility of that. Sometimes I think that I have proven it to you many times, in death. Tonight I'll try to prove it to you in life. But—" He stopped suddenly and started to hum.

"I have often wondered what a man would do if he had but a few hours left to live, Dean. Now, life is like a flower— and so is love. It buds, it breaks into a glorious bloom, and fades—dies. Or perhaps, after all, it doesn't die—but, like the flower, is preserved between the pages of a book—a book, Dean. Memories that are never forgotten; memories that linger with the years, and—and— Hooey, you think—Dean. Well—perhaps, but there's nothing like it to get under a man's skin. I've got the tune and the sentiment— and, by Jove, the title even—*Love Knows No Winter—Only Spring.* The— But I've got just time to write it. We'll be leaving here at twelve sharp. No gun tonight for you, Dean. I've passed my word that if a man must die, it will be— that it won't be Lieutenant Eswal Grim."

He passed, humming, into the music room. The door slammed, a quick movement of feet—and soft notes upon the piano. A dual personality? Certainly, though Brown insisted on calling it a double emotional identity. And—and he would.

IT WAS almost exactly twelve o'clock when Vee Brown came out of his studio, running his tongue across the flap of a long manila envelope, tucking a small flask in his hip pocket.

"Finished!" He grinned boyishly. "And like everything I just complete—my masterpiece. Let us hope it won't be published posthumously." He took off his house coat, and as he slipped into his jacket I noted the shoulder holster beneath his left armpit, and the heavy handle of the automatic that protruded from it.

"It's bitter cold to go without a vest." He shivered slightly. "But even if I'm not to use a gun it's nice to feel that one is handy. I'd as soon go without my shoes, Dean. That's psychology, I suppose—if we must have a name for the frailty of human nature. And you—" He was on me suddenly, his hands so deft that the gun was out of my jacket pocket before I suspected what he was after. But he simply shook a finger at me.

"I know, Dean. You thought that my word not to kill Grim didn't include you. And I appreciate your idea of protecting me."

"You made it so real. As if your death was imminent—absolute. Well—it wasn't as if we had a chance to take him alive. I didn't understand, of course. You know where he'll be. You can—"

"Of course I can," he interrupted me. "It's just that I feel stifled by official red tape. Just the childlike stubbornness to do things my own way; accept the responsibility of shooting if necessary. One thing only. Suppose Eswal Grim knows that I must—must take him alive?"

"How could he know that?" I was frankly skeptical.

"How could he know that I talked to Doran? But he did know, and was gone almost the very moment the warrant was issued. Come!"

"We'll have to take the car, Dean," Brown said as we climbed into the high-priced sedan, and he dismissed his Jap chauffeur. "Not the full way, of course—but near enough to have the car handy to bring him back with us."

It was bitterly cold, even for early March. Certainly not more than eight or ten above zero.

Ten minutes later we had parked the car on the avenue, walked along the street and entered a rather unprepossessing tenement. Brown thrust open the door, found the stairs in the dim light, mounted them with me at his heels, and on the floor above let himself into a front apartment with a key.

"Follow the light from the street," he said as we went down a narrow hall into the front room. "I rented this place six months ago." He led me to the window. "Across the street, there—the book shop. You will notice that the window is different from those of the shops beside it. You can see clearly into that shop—and if you take these glasses," he handed me a pair of field glasses that he lifted from the floor below the window, "you will see a figure sitting there in the chair by the table light—just before the curtains that lead to the rear room. Very dimly, to be sure—but recognizable, with the glasses, as the owner of the shop. I want you to study him well, Dean. He's about your size and build. Note the way he crosses his legs—the tilt of his head. Not important, you think. But, you see, you are to take his place there tonight."

"But, with glasses anyone could recognize me; if close enough to the window, without them, and—"

"Yes—of course, Dean. But put the glasses on the shop next door—the clothing shop. You see the dummy far back by the shop light. You would recognize it as a dummy, of course. But the features—any distinguishing marks? Nothing but form and bulk are visible."

"But that is because of the frost on the window, while the book-shop window is free from frost, and—"

"And how would you explain that?"

"The man who reads has heat, of course, while the other shops—"

"Exactly." Vee Brown nodded. "But unless it was called to your attention, would you notice that that single window was clear and the others frosted?"

"Why—not unless I looked at the others."

"And suppose you had an interest in the window of that particular book shop and found it frosted, like the other windows—would it strike you odd if you then noticed that the other windows were also frosted?"

"Hardly odd—since the other windows are frosted," I said. "It is a very bitter night. How am I to take that man's place?"

BROWN shook his head. "Ah! That is the advantage the criminal has over the police officer. I am not suggesting it, of course—Dean, but you can see how simple it would be to kneel here at this window, take a rifle equipped with a silencer, allow the fraction of an inch necessary for the deflection of the bullet by the window glass, and place a tiny pellet of lead in that man's forehead. I dare say the taxpayer would be better off for his death too. But, there! I dream of a man-hunter's Utopia. Perhaps, after all, if it were as simple as that the thrill would go out of it. Now—I've watched that book shop for several months. That man reads in that chair certain nights from twelve to two. It is his custom and his habit. Tonight he faces uptown. And when he does, it is a signal for a visitor that things are clear. At least, when he faces downtown Lieutenant Eswal Grim never visits his shop—only when he faces uptown."

"And you think Lieutenant Grim will be there tonight? That he will venture out, with every policeman in the city watching for him?"

"Dangerous for him, certainly," Brown agreed. "But he must come. It is far more dangerous not to come. Eswal Grim must leave the city, of course. He has arranged for his escape for over a year. And the reason, Dean, that the banks do not hold large credits to his account—and that it is useless to watch the safe-deposit vaults, for him to come for his hidden wealth—is because Lieutenant Eswal Grim's ready cash is hidden in that book shop. Greed made him betray his trust, Dean. Greed will bring him out of his hole tonight, to take that money away with him."

"Grim won't suspect you're waiting for him?"

"I think not. I have never gone near the shop—never moved from this window. But I know the lay of it, from a customer who talked to another. And here, Dean, is where you are invaluable. You must watch here, with the glasses. I shall enter by the side door. I am as careful and efficient with locks as any burglar. But only curtains divide a narrow hallway from the front of the shop, where our friend reads. I doubt that he will hear me. I doubt that, if he does, it will disturb him. For when Grim enters that side door, the man in the chair never stirs, until Grim has left the shop again. If Grim looks in and greets him or not, I can't be sure. But it is certain that Grim visits that shop quite often at night, entering and leaving quietly, when—and only when the figure in that chair faces uptown."

"And I'll join you—when?"

"When you no longer can get a clear picture of the watcher in the chair."

Brown did not explain that last rather cryptic remark, for he was gone. I heard the lock of the apartment door snap—then, listen as I would, not a sound as Vee Brown descended the stairs.

He must have gone down the block a bit, for I did not see him cross the street. Nor did I see him enter the little alley beside the shop. But I was watching intently the figure—so still, so— And the word had an unpleasant ring, but it was there just the same—so deathlike, in the chair.

Two, five, ten minutes passed—and it was lucky I was watching closely. The man in the chair hardly seemed to move. Yet I knew that he had dropped the book he was reading between his knees. But he still faced uptown; still sat without a movement, his left leg across his right knee, his elbow slightly on the table— And he jerked erect. No other word will describe that sudden stiffening of his body.

Then I thought I saw Brown. At least, the shadow of another figure seemed to flash for a moment across the window— and was gone. I looked back at the figure in the chair, lowered my glasses, polished the lenses with my handkerchief and raised them again.

The figure was still in the chair, but the features were gone—the face blurred and indistinct.

I rubbed at my own eyes, then remembered Vee Brown's final words—"When you no longer can get a clear picture of the watcher in the chair."

Without the glasses I looked at the window of the book shop now, and noticed that the window pane was no longer clear —but heavily frosted, as were those of the other shops on the block. Natural that, I thought. But why? Before, of course, it had been heat in the book shop but not in the other shops—where the heat was shut off for the night. But why now, when—

But I didn't bother to think that out any longer. I was down the stairs, along the side street, entering the alley. Searching out the side door, finding it unlocked and entering it.

THERE was a narrow hall in the dull light, a door almost straight ahead of me—curtains to the left, which led to the front of the shop. I parted them cautiously and looked in.

Vee Brown spoke quietly. "Quick, Dean—the chair, and let me see what kind of an actor you are. The stage is set. Come quick. There may be plenty of time for talk if you can do it without moving your lips—though I dare say it won't matter now."

I looked at the empty chair by the table, where the owner of the shop had been; sat in it, leaned far back and swung my left leg over my right knee, facing uptown. Then I lifted the book from the floor and leaned back as the previous occupant of that chair had leaned.

Vee Brown was in a dark corner of the room. I squinted over the book and made out dimly his slim, quickly moving figure. He was bending over a long, black—something.

"He won't see him from the window," Vee said. "Nor from that door." He was rolling a human form into the corner. He turned, straightened—and I saw the whiteness of his face in the darkness.

"I miscalculated a bit, Dean. There—to your right, the little room behind—between the curtains. I think that is where our friend, Grim, will go. It can be entered from the hall, without passing through the shop here. I might have chloroformed our friend and left him in the chair. Not that he wouldn't have

looked his part, but the smell of the damn stuff would have given it away."

Brown was out of the room now. I heard the door in the outer hall lock, then another door open—and Brown was in the little room behind. I could see him plainly as I looked out the side of my eyes.

"I'll have to change the curtains a bit." He moved them slightly, there close to my right elbow. "So. Now, unless he deliberately looks in, we're set—and I don't think he'll do that until I surprise him. Did anything happen, Dean? I wasn't clumsy, you understand—but he heard the lock turn and thought it was Grim. But did he change anything?"

"Just put down the book he was reading and jerked up. I've got the book now. And the window, Vee—the sudden frost?"

"Oh, not a new trick, Dean. Perhaps it is new to this generation of gun-toting, stick-up men, who do not take a pride in their work. Just a little quicklime by the window, and some water poured upon it. The steam from it frosts the windows. I don't think it will give us away. It's the last bitter weather of the winter, and the windows will only be the same as the adjoining shops. It's hardly believable that he'll think of it—and if he does, he'll dismiss it when he notices the other shop windows. So you see the little flask I carried held nothing more harmful than water from the kitchen tap."

"And the man?" I wanted to be sure of that silent thing, black and shapeless in the far end of the shop.

"Not dead." Vee Brown must have caught the meaning in my voice. "Though there was nothing in the bargain, about bringing him in alive." And raising his voice as he came through the narrow hall and into the front of the shop again, though out of vision from the street, "And he won't be dead, Dean, unless he is able to work that gag loose, groans, or otherwise conducts himself in an unhealthy manner. But he's small fry, and if he behaves himself there's no reason why I shouldn't cut the ropes and let him go—afterward." All this in a voice meant for the bound man, I thought.

"You mean— But he's in it—he must be in it."

Brown's hoarse whisper came out of the darkness, for my ears alone now.

"And he must know a lot, Dean—be pretty closely connected with things in the underworld to have the confidence of Eswal Grim—and pretty close mouthed too. No, Dean, I won't lock him up. He might make a valuable bureau of information later; tell me secrets of the night in his natural gratitude—and more natural fear—of what I hold over him. Informer! A nasty word that? But a stool pigeon is to the detective of fact all that clues are to the detective of fiction. But the trap is set. We only wait for Mr. Rat, alias Eswal Grim."

"Do you think we'll have to wait long?" I said, after the silence became oppressive.

"Not long, certainly. The book seller was not disturbed by my entrance, so he was expecting someone—and only one. Why—" A moment of silence. Then: "Stiff, Dean. So! He's coming."

DULLY, from the corner of my eyes I saw the muffled figure through the frosted window pane. The misty outline of a white face, with two flashing holes that were eyes. The soft slouch hat, the turned up coat collar, the great blur of a huge body. A nose that for an instant seemed to be pressed against the glass. And the figure stepped back, the white blur turned so that the flashing holes might survey the other windows. Then the blur nodded, and the man was gone.

"I'll wait by the door to the hall, follow him into the room behind. Don't move—

stay so. If he does look through the curtains I'll be close upon him. There!"

A split second of silence—the dull tread of feet, I thought—and the click of a key in the lock. Then the soft closing of a door and the click of a lock again. Rubber on hard wood, the heavy breathing of a man—and, I thought, a draft as the curtains moved slightly, moved just as my eyes involuntarily turned; and for the fraction of a second I saw him.

He was kneeling on the floor before a shelf of books, lifting them out on the floor, feeling quickly in the back, removing a loose board—and then, I thought, a bag. But the side of his face was there, the largeness of an ear, the high cheek bone and the semblance of a heavy jowl. I knew him, of course. It was Lieutenant Eswal Grim.

But he didn't see me—he couldn't have seen me. Just the side of his face was visible before the curtain settled again. Then I heard his breath as he straightened; felt rather than heard his feet beat softly across the wood, upon a rug, to the wood again. And this time the decided draft from moving curtains—the whistling, sharp intake of a man's breath, and the sudden words that rushed from his throat.

"Hello! It's not the professor. And—damn my soul! It's Vee Brown's little playmate."

I never moved. I never shifted my eyes. I scarcely breathed, I guess. Something round, hard and flat and black flashed for a moment into my vision—and the voice of Vee Brown came from that little room—across it, over by the hall door, I thought.

"I wouldn't do that, Grim." Brown's voice was very quiet, his words very slow and without the semblance of a threat or even excitement in them. "I'd drop that gun." And when I turned my head and looked into the quivering lips and blinking eyes of Eswal Grim, and he didn't drop his gun, Vee Brown added: "Vee Brown talking. I'm supposed to take you alive, Grim, but I wouldn't be averse to squeezing a bit of lead into you. An excuse would rather—"

Lieutenant Eswal Grim swung and fired in one quick movement. And Brown took it. Brown, who could draw, shoot—and, yes—kill, in less than one second, stood there with a gun in his hand and took it.

I didn't understand, maybe. But somehow I knew—knew, as Brown staggered, half swung, and seemed to collapse over the table, that in the split second it took him to gun out a man, he had hesitated; had thought perhaps of his promise to Mortimer Doran, and remembered that he was drawing a bead as he always did, straight between the eyes of his man. And in that split second that he might have tried for a different mark, Grim had closed a finger on the trigger of his heavy gun and the force of the bullet at that distance had swung Brown clean around.

Yet, was it possible that Vee Brown, who could snuff out a candle at— But such thoughts were simply a kaleidoscopic picture of the moment. I had somehow whirled from my chair, thrown up a hand as Grim swung—and the next shot from his gun went some place between Brown and myself and into the side of the room. Then I was on him.

HE WAS a big man—a strong man. We swayed for a moment as I gripped frantically, caught his wrist, tried to pull my body to the left, realized I had failed and that the man with phenomenal strength had jerked his arm down, bent it at the elbow, and— The snub nose of his heavy automatic was smack against my chest.

A white face—glaring, but brilliantly conquering eyes. And then, above that face, a white clenched fist, with something black in it. A dull thud as I jerked back, stumbled over a chair, and just before I crashed to the hard wood I saw Lieutenant Grim's knees sag—then he sank to the floor. Vee Brown leaned quickly down, rose almost as quickly again, half hesitated as he looked down at the gun which had dropped from Grim's hand—then straightening and kicking the gun across the floor, sent it spinning into the front room of the shop.

"I was a fool, Dean," Vee Brown said as I came to my feet. "But the temptation to fire would have been too great. Yes, I crashed him with the barrel of my gun. He won't give us any trouble now; the irons are on him. But it was a nasty dig he gave me in the side, and I could have killed him before he half turned if—" Brown leaned heavily on the table a moment. "Just watch that he doesn't get into the other room, for his gun—for he's got a hard head on him and is coming around already. I'll shove a cold, wet handkerchief under my coat—but mostly water on my head, Dean. It burns like ice. Funny—burning like ice. Not scientific, maybe. But then, science can't give a name to something you feel yourself." He turned, swayed, staggered slightly, I thought, as he sought and reached the wash-bowl in the corner.

And at that moment Lieutenant Eswal Grim came to his feet, stood dazedly looking at his manacled wrists and blinking his eyes.

"They're going to roast him, Dean." Brown spoke without turning from the little basin. "The people's money will be spent lavishly. Twelve men will give up their earning power to listen for days to the objections of high-priced lawyers for the defense. Bribed officials will try to pull strings; witnesses will be riddled with bullets from a Thompson machine gun—and then the expense of an appeal. The board at the big house, the final electric bill to juice him out—to say nothing of the few hundred for the executioner who plays the switches for the hot seat. All unnecessary, if I had but closed my finger on a fully loaded gun."

Lieutenant Grim lurched or fell forward, seemed to grasp the table for support, leaned heavily on it. And I saw the gun—for the first time I saw the gun that Brown had left upon the table. But I saw it only after both those eager, manacled hands had reached it and grasped it, and Eswal Grim turned triumphantly, threateningly from Brown to me—the muzzle of that automatic covering both of us.

"Look out, Brown," I shouted as Grim raised both his hands, aimed directly at the middle of Brown's back and tightened the finger of his right hand on the gun trigger.

Brown turned slowly, just as the dull click came.

"It isn't loaded." Brown twisted his lip into that crooked, wistful smile. "I'd have killed him before if it had been. You see, Dean, I wanted to keep my word of bringing him in alive or not coming back. Oh, he knew! Not that the gun wasn't loaded, of course—but that I was to take him alive. He wouldn't have the guts for it." And as Grim collapsed completely into a chair and buried his head in his hands: "And that's that."

Brown crossed slowly to Grim, lifted the gun from his hand, motioned me to get the one in the front room, and said in a tired voice: "The phone, Dean." He gave me the number. "Tell Mortimer Doran that he can come to the apartment any time now. And, Dean," when I had lifted the receiver, "tell him to bring a doctor along. His family physician—not that butcher of a police surgeon."

THE telephone call completed, the loaded gun taken from my hand and shoved into Vee Brown's jacket pocket; his carefulness in pulling his coat collar about his neck, my solicitude about his wound dismissed rather roughly, our walk to the car which I had to drive began. Brown's steady conversation in the back seat—all of death, the electric chair, the horror of the weeks and days and hours preceding the execution, was hard to understand.

But he explained that to me in a low voice as we thrust Lieutenant Eswal Grim into the big living room of our apartment.

"He's a rat," Vee whispered to me. "Twice he begged, offered me money to let him have his gun, to kill himself. He can't face it, Dean—and I've been playing on his fears. He'll be in the humor to talk when Mortimer Doran arrives. And I wouldn't be surprised if he'd open up, turn state's evidence—involve a great many higher officials even, and particularly Benny Nevis, the racketeer we've wanted so long, if he were promised a life sentence instead of the chair. But to kill himself! Yes, he fears life, right now, more than he fears death. He's in a position to know what goes on in those damp, barred rooms below— But that'll be Mortimer Doran. Just tell them to send him up." This last as the phone rang.

Eswal Grim stood uncertainly in the center of the room. Brown had, with feigned indifference, thrown himself upon the long low couch. "Hard night, Dean," he said. But the crooked smile was a pitiable little grimace now. His teeth set tightly below the curved lip; his eyes had lost the misty, filmy look of the book shop and taken on a new brilliancy, and his bloodless face was now a flushed red.

"There. Let Mortimer Doran in, Dean." His face was distorted with pain as he would have motioned with his right hand. "The show is over. The curtain is about to drop."

I don't know why I turned as I reached the living-room door. I don't know why I took that last look at Eswal Grim. But I did—and stood frozen there as the hall bell rang sharply out again. Lieutenant Eswal Grim had lost his hang-dog look. He stood now stiff and straight, with a certain hardness—a determination in his face. But it wasn't that which held me. It was his raised hand, so close to his mouth—the little glass vial that held the liquid—his sharp teeth, that already had drawn the cork and, as I looked, shot that same cork from between his lips to the polished floor.

Then the single movement of his hands —the quick jerk back of his head—my cry of horror—the sudden roar of a gun, and Eswal Grim's sharp shriek of pain. The broken glass vial, the liquid upon the rug, red streaming down Eswal's right hand—finally, the smoking gun in Vee Brown's hand. The queer look on Brown's face, the running feet of Brown's Japanese butler—my hurried words to him to open the door that Mortimer Doran was pounding on.

All that in a few seconds, I guess. All that in a dim half-understanding that it was happening. Then Mortimer Doran, with two other men and a doctor. Brown standing in the center of the room, bowing to Mortimer Doran and saying in a rather cracked voice: "Not dead, you see. Alive, as you wanted him. Slightly damaged as to a finger or two, perhaps— but alive—quite alive. And—and— The curtain, Dean. We have had our final curtain for a bit."

And Brown was right, for it was exactly two weeks later that I stood beside his little white bed in the hospital and heard the first coherent words he had uttered since he made that final bow before the district attorney.

Out of the Night

by
J. Allan Dunn

Author of "Horror House," etc.

The Mad Tabors they were called —and only two remained—last of a long line. Now on them both the Voodoo curse was laid—and out of the jasmine-drenched night had come the Red Bull of the House of Tabor, herald of horror—and death.

The frightful gorge opened and snapped the offering like a trained dog.

CHAPTER ONE

The Guest in the Tower

THE rackety flivver stopped and, while the driver took out his baggage, Dan Merwin had his first survey of Oak Manor.

It was probably one of the oldest buildings in the United States. It had been built originally by Edwin Tabor, one of the noblemen granted vast tracts of land by Charles the Second of England in 1663. The first structure had been submerged by the additions of son and grandson. Now it was a manor built of brick, showing the influence of Queen Anne, Jacobean and even Georgian architectural types. Time had blended it into a mellow whole.

Great liveoaks, older than the house, shadowed it, furnished the avenue of approach from the entrance gates, the great boughs reaching across the wide driveway, Spanish moss pendent from the giant arms. There were lawns and gardens, a profusion of flowers and semi-tropic growth. Spreading from the main structure were the abandoned barracoons where the slaves had lived, brought from Africa to South Carolina to labor in the plantations. Farther afield were the cabins in which their descendants had lived until the Civil War freed them and almost ruined their late owners.

The place was fairly well kept up. There was pride here still that had survived that conflict. Yet the whole aspect was gloomy. There was too much shade, too little sunshine. Vines clambered over the bricks, obscured the windows. Jasmine vines tried to strangle the sturdy trees and their yellow bloom gave fragrance to the air that was stifling, so strong that it almost suggested decay. Wisteria drooped in purple festoons unstirred by wind. It was late February and this was the semi-tropic South, abundant and, to Dan Merwin, down from the North, almost unreal, theatrical.

THERE was silence, solitude. He had expected to see darkies, friendly and smiling, but no one had greeted them, though Merwin was expected.

"Strange things are happening here," Edwin Tabor, the ninth of that name, had written to Alwin Foster, in New York City. "I am growing old, my friend, and know that you are also close to my age. I do not ask you to come but I pray you to send someone, young, active and intelligent. Also with courage, someone of your own choice, to act for me. I do not, above all, for various reasons, wish the ordinary operative or investigator, the so-called detective.

"I am working steadily but slowly on my book, The History of Famous Gems. It might be well if the person who comes will appear as an appraiser of jewels. You know my collection of gems. It is under-stood that I am having them valued in anticipation of making my will. Do not fail me, my friend. It may be that certain dangers that threaten, or seem to threaten, can be averted. It may be that they are inevitable.

"I shall, of course, pay all expenses and a worthy fee. Delay no longer than must be, for the shadows are gathering about Oak Manor and the House of Tabor.

"Yours in all friendship,
Tabor."

Merwin had the original of that letter in his pocket, countersigned by Alwin Foster, his guardian and godfather, together with other credentials. He was at a loose end, accredited with a degree in engineering, and with some practical experience cut short in an age of depression. Foster considered his qualifications measured up to Tabor's requirements and had sent him down to South Carolina on a mission at once mysterious and inviting, with the assurance that Tabor would not ask for aid lightly, close to seventy though he was, but still hale and sane.

With him Merwin had brought apparatus used by gem experts. He had made a swift but comprehensive study of the methods of appraisal and, aware he would not be called upon for any actual valuation, that Tabor undoubtedly had a good idea of the worth of his specimens, he felt that he could make a satisfactory showing as an expert. His work was to be a mask for an investigation of mysteries and threatened dangers which were, however, tied up with the jewels, with the making of Tabor's will. It seemed sure that this will must be a new one. A man of Tabor's age would hardly have put off the drawing up of such a document until now.

Merwin looked with interest at the venerable pile before him. It was getting late in the afternoon and, as the sun descended, its light grew orange, deepening to crimson, casting level shafts and accentuating the shadows. It blazed back from some of the casements, from small, diamond-shaped, leaded panes and mullioned windows, some of them long, arched acutely.

But the upper stories were entirely dark, without a light showing anywhere, and the darkness seemed to descend upon the mansion like a pall. Something ominous seemed to emanate from it that made Merwin's pulses slacken and his body gooseflesh as, suddenly, the daylight was gone. The sun must have been shrouded abruptly by clouds or have sunk behind a hill. The air seemed to grow chilly, the fragrance of the flowers mingled now with that of ivy and the dampness of old brick and stone. The suggestion of decay and death was oppressive. A wind moved through the great garden, swung the mighty boughs with their long trails of moss, like the old banners and war standards in an ancient cathedral. The branches creaked, the leaves and moss rustled softly and the breeze passed with something between a sigh and a moan.

For a moment there was silence. The driver had set down the baggage before the main door and stood quietly as if he too felt the strange spell of the house and the hour. Oak Manor was veiled in the thickening dusk. Merwin switched on the none too powerful lights of the flivver and they cast faltering lemon rays down the drive, across which something slunk, barely visible, save for a pair of glowing orbs. It was like a great cat, but it might have been a prowling lynx. Then the driver pulled at a bell and its jangle sounded faintly inside the house.

BEFORE there was any response a sound came out of the blackness that had gathered about them, a sound that could not be placed, echoed and broken as it doubtless was by the great boles of trees. It might even have come from underground, a deep, blatant bellow, monstrous, hideous in its suggestion. Merwin thought of the kelpies his Scotch nurse had told him of, fearful creatures that rose out of meres, water beasts, half stallion, half dragon, only to be stopped by the branch of the sacred rowan tree, preferably twisted into the shape of a cross. It died away, unrepeated, as lights now showed through the windows of the mansion and the great oaken front door, reinforced with straps of wrought iron, opened and showed a glimpse of a wide and high hall where a fire was leaping and candles gleamed. A maid was moving about, lighting these last in branching silver candelabra with a waxen taper. Merwin caught the glint of the ruddy glow on a suit of armor, on weapons trophied on a paneled wall, antlers, paintings, stairs ascending in double flight to a gallery. He might have stepped through a magic mirror back into the time of two or three centuries ago.

A man came out, almost a giant, a negro whose face, with the light behind him, showed no features but the gleam of eyeballs and the shine of teeth. He was dressed in black alpaca with a low-cut vest as a sign of service.

"This Mistuh Merwin?" he asked. "I'm suah sorry, suh, you find de house all dahk, but Massa Tabor lyin' down, Massa Egbert he ain't come in yit from de fields an' Missy Grace is in her room changin' after she come home from her ridin'. Didn' hahdly 'spect you so soon, suh. De train offen late. Figgehed Lawton gwine to toot his hawn, anyways."

Two younger colored men had come through the hall, neatly dressed in white drill but barefooted. They took the bags.

"The train was on time an' my hawn's broke," said Lawton, the white flivver driver to whom the negro butler had neglected to give any title of respect. "Too bad you all don't keep your fences up an' stop that bull roamin' round loose. Might take a fancy to charge my kyar."

"We don't have no bull on this estate," said the butler. He spoke stiffly, then gave an order to the two with the bags.

"You all tote those up to the Tower Room," he said, "an' staht a fiah. Come inside, Mistuh Merwin. I'm Hosea, Massa Tabor's major, suh. I hope to give you comfort, suh. Lilian Jane, you go see those boys fix that fiah right an' tell Missy Grace our gues' is arrive."

Merwin stepped inside the paneled hall with a feeling of comfort that contrasted sharply with the night outside. It was starless and moonless and darkness had swooped down as if some great bat had spread its opaque, sable wings across the firmament.

Lawton was driving his antiquated flivver along the curves of the drive as if he was anxious to leave the place. His pale headlights picked up the veils of gray moss and made them look like phantoms.

"Did you all hear a bull bellowin'?" Hosea asked Merwin as they stood alone in the great hall. His voice was low and charged with mystery. Merwin saw him more clearly, a black man with gray, close-curling hair, with an aquiline nose, broad shoulders and enormous chest. For a moment he seemed to change. His decorous garb became that of a warrior clad in a kaross of lionskin, bearing shield and spear. The leaping, crackling fire of logs and lightwood in the big stone fireplace became a blaze in the open, round which naked figures leaped to the beat of tomtoms. A wizard made incantations. Hosea was a chieftain waiting on a magic rite, a brave man, a mighty fighter and eater, but afraid.

It was almost incredible to see how thoughts and associations blended with memory to arouse this phantasmagorium.

"I heard something," said Merwin. "It didn't sound exactly like a bull."

"It warn't no ordinary bull, suh. It hain't given to all to heah it. It hain't good to heah it too often. It might be jus' as well, suh, meanin' no offense, if you all don' speak of that bull. Massa Tabor, he don' like to heah talk about—his fences bein' down."

THERE was a light dew of sweat on Hosea's face. His eyes rolled toward the big fireplace. Merwin's glance trailed. There was something more than the matter of fences in Edwin Tabor's objection to mention of a bull.

Then Merwin saw a shield, flat, wooden, above the high mantel. It was an escutcheon, the arms of the Tabors, at least of the resident branch. On a field of tarnished gold there stood a bull in faded scarlet, one leg advanced, as if to paw the ground. The head was turned backward over its massive crest, the tail curved upward. The candles picked out the lettering of the motto. SPES MEA IN VIRTUTE EST. His Latin was good enough to translate. "My hope is in honor."

Then a girl came down the staircase and the sense of magic passed. For Merwin another enchantment had begun but he did not realize it.

He saw a slim figure, not very tall but infinitely gracious, advancing to meet him with a white hand outstretched in greeting. Her hair was close to a shapely head and threw off golden gleams in the candlelight. Her nose was aquiline, her mouth was demure, but the lips were full above a rounded but decisive chin. There was the flash of a jeweled pin, amethyst, he fancied. She gave off the faint perfume of violets.

He did not know what she wore. It was a chintz of some kind, he thought, later. Anklelong, clinging but flouncy, it showed a V of stately neck and the sleeves revealed white arms that held little shadows in the elbows, as if, there were dimples there.

"I am Grace Quincy, Mr. Tabor's secretary," she said. "You, of course, are Daniel Merwin. I am sorry to be late to greet you, but I was late getting back from my ride. Something startled my horse and he tried to bolt. As a matter of fact he did bolt. But here I am and here you are. Mr. Tabor will see you later. He is resting. He has not been very well lately and he takes his meals in his room. You and I and Mr. Tabor's nephew, Egbert, will dine together."

"I am delighted," said Merwin, truthfully, but he did not include Egbert Tabor when he spoke. Then he wondered what it had been that startled the girl's horse. Was it the bellow of a bull, a bull like the one on the escutcheon above the fireplace?

"You will want to go to your room," she said. "It is a tiresome trip. Hosea, will you look after Mr. Merwin."

"Yes, Missy Grace. Lilian Jane she's up theah now."

Someone had come in from a door at the back beneath the gallery. It was a man in riding clothes, booted and spurred, carrying a riding crop to which a long lash was attached, now coiled.

The man was tall and swarthy. His features were arrogant, aggressive, boldly carved and clean shaven. He strode forward with easy power, a frown on his face, tossing aside a broad-brimmed black hat like a sombrero. His was a forceful personality. For the moment he ignored Merwin and the girl, intent upon the thought he had brought with him.

"Hosea, I thought I told you to have this nonsense stopped about hearing a bull. They were talking about it in the quarters as I came through. That boy of mine, Ned, was full of it again. I silenced him. It's up to you to silence the rest. You know it upsets your master."

There was just a trace of Southern accent in his voice. It was more distinctly English, as if its owner had been educated in an overseas university. His mouth was cruel as he spoke and Merwin felt certain that Ned had felt the lash of that malacca-handled riding crop.

Hosea stood up to him for a moment. For a fleeting second the white man's arrogance was matched by that of the negro. There was masterful ancestry in both of them, beyond question. Then Hosea bowed.

"Yes suh, I'll see to it."

Egbert Tabor turned, noticed Merwin. "A ridiculous superstition," he said. "It has cropped up just lately. It upsets the niggers. Spoils them for work. The story is down in Cypress now. It has got to be stopped. How is my uncle, Grace? You're the appraiser, I suppose?" he went on with easy insolence.

"Mr. Tabor is feeling depressed," the girl answered. Her dignity offset the familiarity of his address. "I wish he would see Dr. Tolliver."

Egbert Tabor laughed shortly. "Or Tolliver see him. They're at swords' points, those two, or would be, if this was a hundred years ago. He accused my uncle of using opium. That ended it."

IT WAS hardly good taste, Merwin thought, to talk that way of the old man's condition before a stranger. But Egbert Tabor's manner practically ignored the newcomer save as an intruder tolerated for an old man's whim.

"You'll eat with us," he said to Merwin. "Dinner at seven. We usually change, but it doesn't matter."

The casual assurance that Merwin would not have dinner clothes or expect to dress was almost insulting. It was the attitude of the nobleman who is forced to house a tradesman but does not propose to entertain him or treat him as an equal. For a moment Merwin's eyes blazed, his blood tingled and his fists were clenched involuntarily. Then he relaxed and grinned. He had come largely as a favor to Alwin Foster, though he was not averse to earning a fee. The mission was one of protection to Foster's old and dear friend and already Merwin began to see it would be no ordinary assay.

"If you're too tired to dress I'll change into another lounging suit," he said. "Pray don't let me in any way disturb you."

Egbert Tabor scowled, but Merwin saw the girl's mouth twitch humorously. After all, the man was a Southerner, he was a scion of a family that had lorded it here for generations over whites deported to the Colonies, almost as subservient as the bought slaves from Africa. Hosea was still waiting. Merwin had seen his head go up at the word 'niggers'. The butler, who called himself 'major'—probably an abbreviation of major-domo—stood by the newel post as Merwin passed on up.

The Tower Room seemed as if it must be the principal guest chamber. Evidently his host was not slighting him. There was a fire on a stone hearth; there were tapestries on two walls, portraits of ancient Tabors and their dames on the panels of two more. The 'bull regardant' was carved on the stone of the fireplace, the rugs were large and valuable and the furniture antique and authentic. The bed was canopied, with posts elaborately carved. A Jacobean night table held a lamp and books in a rack; there was a glimpse of a bathroom with tiled floor and walls and a modern tub of porcelain.

They might dispense with electricity at Oak Manor, but they were not lacking in conveniences, even in luxuries. Hosea deftly emptied bags, set things away in wardrobe and drawered chest of stately design and workmanship. Without com-

ment he laid out Merwin's dinner clothes, placed links and studs.

"Shall I help you all to dress, suh?" he asked.

"No, thanks," said Merwin. "I don't rate a body servant, Hosea."

"Then I'll run the hot wateh. De gong sounds at ha'f afteh six, suh. Misteh Tabor expec' he able to see you erbout nine."

Merwin, as he bathed and shaved, realized that the secretary, Miss Quincy, had tactfully worn a dress that might or might not be considered an evening gown. There was a curious mixture of courteous consideration and scorn in this household. He put on a dressing gown and sat in front of the fire in a Queen Anne wing-chair, smoking a half-pipe before he dressed, surveying the portrait of some dead and gone Tabor in body armor. The face, dulled by time and varnish, was not unlike that of Egbert. The sort of man who gives no mercy to a fallen foe, to whom all below his rank were rabble. But the contemplation did not daunt Merwin. He had an excellent sense of humor and a profound belief in his own standing as an American bred and born. Tabor might have come over in some private barque, but the Merwins were on the Mayflower with the rest of the Independents. He doubted whether the Tabors and the rest of the noblemen would have thriven as well if they had landed on Massachusetts' uncordial strand.

Also he held the vision of a gracious girl—and the scent of violets.

The room was hot from the piney fuel and he opened a window with lozenge-shaped panes, brushing aside a vine where trumpeted jasmine blossoms hung. Again he sensed their heavy, charnel-house odor.

A mist was rising; an owl hooted. The night was mysterious, pregnant with omens. He almost expected to hear again the deep bellow of the beast whose presence Egbert Tabor had ridiculed and Hosea denied.

CHAPTER TWO

The Red Bull of Tabor

EDWIN TABOR, owner of Oak Manor, was in his great bed when he received Merwin. He was propped up with pillows, clad in a brocaded gown. Here was an aristocrat, a man noble by nature more than by king's endowment.

His white hair was a little long, his mustache and goatee were white. They seemed less Southern than courtly, attributes of stately times when men wore ruffs and doublets, trunks, hose and jeweled daggers in their belts, long blades by their sides. A courtier, filled with courtesy. His face was pale, his eyes shone somewhat feverishly from deep hollows, there were veins outstanding on his hands.

The chamber was vast. That part of it used as bedroom was raised from the rest and could be curtained off by heavy draperies, now drawn back, the deep folds showing the woven story of olden chivalry.

The rest of it, facing the front of the manor, had a fireplace, shelves lined with books, the equipment of a library in general. Here again was the escutcheon of the scarlet bull on the field of gold and the motto SPES MEA IN VIRTUTE EST.

Hosea was in attendance, quiet, but ready in the shadows, still as a carving.

"You are Daniel Merwin, the protégé of my friend," said Tabor. "It is good of him to send you, and of you to come. One I can trust, from one I have always trusted. He is well?"

"Save for his gout," said Merwin. "I believe they call it neuritis nowadays. He sends you his esteem."

"Ah! His esteem? That is a word un-used these times. I am not so well myself. My heart is uncertain, which should not be in a Tabor. We were always saddlemen until we were eighty, at least. But Time swings his scythe to suit his own ideas of harvest. I'm not mown yet, Merwin, though I may be marked for it. You have dined well, you are comfortable?"

"Excellently so," Merwin answered.

"Good. Hosea, bring me my casket. Do you know anything of jewels, Merwin?"

"Not much, sir. I have tried to qualify as one who can go through the motions of an expert."

"That will be sufficient. That is what we want. A little hocus-pocus while you keep your eyes open. But there is much joy in jewels. I am writing a history of famous gems. Infamous, some of them. They seem to breed envy, bloody strife, greed and sudden death. Women crave them, and also men. Nations have been won and lost for them. There is no great jewel but has a grim record, yet they brighten women's eyes, enhance their beauty. Are you in love, Merwin?"

Merwin found himself flushing. There was lamplight in the room that saved him. But Tabor chuckled as he made denial.

"Not yet, eh? But you will not escape it. Not till Time dulls eyes and senses.
Not till the fervid flame that burns
Within the fane of Eros, faltering, dies.

"Egad! The Tabors have been great lovers. Yet I lie here without wife or child. She lies not far from here, within the boundaries of Oak Manor. Two sons died for France. Once, long ago, Tabors fought in Aquitaine and helped to conquer it. There was a Tabor at the Field of the Cloth of Gold. Time whirls his teetotum. Destiny casts the dice. You have met Egbert? He is styled my nephew. A son of a half-sister. Not the direct breed. The House of Tabor passes."

Hosea had brought the casket. Tabor gave him a key he took from a thin golden chain about his neck, restored it after the casket was unlocked, set before him.

"You must forgive the maunderings of an old man," said Tabor. "We who reach three score and ten, live in the past. Here are the gems you will appraise. There are no famous ones among them, but it has been my fancy to collect perfect specimens of all precious stones. The renowned jewels are set in my book, nearly finished now, with the assistance of my secretary, a jewel herself, Merwin, worthy of a perfect setting. You have met her, also? So."

HE MADE, with his nervous hands, a hollow in the counterpane and spilled out the contents of the casket. They made tiny rainbows as Hosea tilted the shade of a standard lamp. Diamond, emerald, ruby—topaz, amethyst and spinel. Beryl, garnet, turquoise and opal. Alexandrite, cat's-eye, kunzite and tourmaline. A dazzle of color.

Tabor lifted them, spilled them through his thin fingers that suddenly seemed tired.

"Take them away, Hosea," he said. "You shall see them again tomorrow, Merwin. They will be in your charge. I want to talk to you. Give me one of those tablets, if you will. And a little water. It is all on that stand."

The phial was marked *Strychnine: grs 1/20*. Merwin set an arm about Tabor's shoulders and raised him as he swallowed the stimulant. Then he let him lie back while Hosea replaced the jewels, snapped the modern spring lock on the brass-bound casket and replaced it in a drawer that formed the base of a tall highboy.

"That will do, Hosea," said Tabor weakly. "You may come back when I ring."

Merwin was anxious, but Tabor soon gained strength. A faint color came back to his cheeks and lips, light to his eyes.

"Merwin," he said, "you see that shield, that coat of arms upon the wall. The Red Bull of Tabor. Long ago it was given us, when a Tabor was first ennobled. There was a bull-baiting, with dogs against the gallant brute—they did such things in those days. There was a rash princeling, a bull enraged, battling for its life, furious. A Tabor saved the prince and won his golden spurs. Since then the Red Bull has been borne into battle. It saw the Crusades, it fought with the Plantagenets, it hangs in Westminister Abbey over the tombs of my sires. It is the fetich of my race.

"And, through the centuries, the Red Bull has appeared to warn the Tabors of death and disaster, to the head of the house or the heir. I, since the Great War, am the head of the House of Tabor. When that house nears its end the Red Bull will surely manifest itself. You, Merwin, may call it superstition—magic. We scoff at things we do not understand. Eight centuries stand back of this manifestation. Yet I, Edwin Tabor, am not over credulous. But my health fails and before I die, if I have to die, I wish to set my house in order. We Tabors in this country, in the South, are not entirely empoverished. There are still goods and chattels to leave, to those worthy of them. Therefore—Merwin—look—there at the window!"

Hosea had set down the shade on the lamp. There was little illumination in the front part of the room, save for the fire, burning evenly.

Through the windows there showed a fearsome sight. It was enough to curdle a man's blood. Merwin felt the grip of the apparition that glared in, a shining horror.

Eyes lambent green, that seemed to light the tips of long horns that were tipped with blood, that dripped with gore. Distended nostrils from which came jets of smoke. A hint of a scarlet front. And then again that blatant bellow, blasting the night.

TABOR gasped, fell back among his pillows, his fingers clutching at the woven coverlet. Merwin grasped the crimson cord to the old-fashioned bell and jerked it violently before he leaped forward. He tore down the steps that divided the room, snatching out the flat automatic he had in a hip pocket.

Before he reached the window, as Hosea broke into the room followed by Grace Quincy, the shining horror vanished abruptly. There was darkness there and nothing more—

He noted, however, when he flung back the casement, that the strong scent of jasmine had been eclipsed. There was a stench upon the night air, the stench of sulphur, active and virulent, the reek of the stuff with which, they say, all hell is lined.

He turned, baffled. Tabor was lying back. The girl was sponging with alcohol the arm Hosea had bared. She held a hypodermic syringe.

"He's had a twentieth of strychnine," Merwin called to her.

"Hosea told me," she said. "Don't worry. I've had training. I know what to do. It may be a trifle illegal but, if we can't get a doctor, we'll give him this."

Merwin had closed the window. He still had the gun in his hand. He felt a trifle foolish.

Tabor had relaxed again. The girl felt his pulse.

"He'll do," she said. "What did you see?'"

Hosea had gone. Merwin told her.

"I suppose an automatic wouldn't be much good against that sort of thing," he said, "unless it had a silver bullet."

"I'm not so sure," she answered. "It might depend upon how good a shot you are."

The door opened and Egbert entered.

"Hosea says my uncle has had a spell," he said. "I've been in the lower fields, watching the tobacco. There was a fog tonight. We'll have to cover those young plants with cotton."

"He is all right now," Grace Quincy answered. "You see. He won't need a sleeping draught tonight. Mr. Egbert Tabor is an expert agriculturist," she added to Merwin, almost needlessly. "It is he who has made Oak Manor produce a revenue. I'll sit up with your uncle for a while," she concluded.

"I'll do that," said Egbert. "What happened? Has there been any more of that damned nonsense? About the bull?"

"Not that I know of," she replied. "You must ask Mr. Merwin. I'll stay with him. Remember, I'm a trained nurse, or was one. Unless you want to call Dr. Tolliver."

"Tolliver be damned," said Egbert. "Did you see any bull, Merwin?"

"You'll have to ask Hosea," said Merwin evenly. "I didn't see anything. Or hear anything."

He had put away his gun and he smiled at Egbert.

Egbert scowled. He turned to the girl. "You go to bed," he said. "Both of you. I'll sit up with my uncle myself. He's resting all right."

That was true. Tabor was lying quietly but he was breathing in little stertorous puffs and the flesh about his mouth was blue. The girl said nothing. After all, Egbert was in virtual charge. His interest in Oak Manor manifested itself in attending to the crops. There was not very much good land, much of the estate had been sold, but on what remained he raised good crops of tobacco and cotton and also bred excellent horses which he sold as hunters and riding hacks to the exclusive tourist resorts.

He was diligent if dour. He ruled the negroes with an iron hand—a pair of them—but he actually made money which was not really required. Tabor had investments, aside from his jewels, that brought in a good income. Egbert might have loafed instead of being a 'Kin to kant' overseer, with his men from sunrise, when they could see, to sunset, when they could not, often working later himself, if a mare was foaling or a horse ailing. This was kindly of him, his offer to go sleepless to sit up with his uncle, and Merwin gave him credit.

THE mists had gone; there was a half-moon over the oaks; somewhere a mocking bird was playing nightingale. Merwin and the girl stood on a brick loggia, a roofed, open porch of brick, part of the main building, rather than a mere veranda, and watched the moon and listened to the bird.

"I do wish Dr. Tolliver would come over. Of course I'm not a doctor, much less a heart specialist," the girl said. "But I have seen some heart cases and Mr. Tabor's is strange. I can't think it's entirely natural. Just now his heart was beating at a tremendous rate, you could see it pounding his chest as if it would wear itself out. Two months ago he was normal and vigorous. He rode every day, ate well, was animated. Now he gets tremendous fits of mental and physical depression. He was really terribly frightened tonight.

"He isn't the kind to be frightened—of anything. The last time Dr. Tolliver was over here—they used to play chess three nights a week together; had for years—Mr. Tabor was not well. He was jumpy. The doctor insisted upon examining him. He was very thorough and then he said the symptoms were unusual and suggested the use of opium in some form. Mr. Tabor flew into a rage and so did the doctor, finally. They are both fiery Southerners. It ended by Tolliver saying that he would not come unless he was sent for and Mr. Tabor saying it would have to be a message from the dead. But I think the doctor ought to come though it would make Egbert terribly angry, and he is not pleasant in a rage. I hear that he flogged his boy, Ned, horribly. I'm going to see him presently."

"Ned his body servant?" asked Merwin.

The girl hesitated for a moment. "I'll be frank with you," she said. "I know that you are here confidentially on some other mission than merely appraising jewels. Besides, they have been appraised. Mr. Tabor talks to me familiarly sometimes when we work. I knew he did not like certain things that have been happening. In fact I wrote that letter he dictated to Mr. Alwyn Foster. Ned is Egbert's personal servant outside the house. He is very good with horses. And —he looks very much like a Tabor. He is a quadroon."

Merwin did not comment. It meant that Ned's father had been a half-white, that his grandfather had been white. Some Tabor had been injudicious, if indeed such things were so regarded in those days. His children would be octoroons.

"Egbert abuses him, taunts him," the girl went on. "He has done it in front of me and made me feel ashamed for him, sorry for Ned. Ned has flared back once in a while. The part-breeds often feel resentment at being neither black nor white especially on plantations and estates where the negroes are proud of their full blood, their black skins. He told Egbert that he hated all the Tabors, that he wished he had never been born rather than to have their blood in his veins. Egbert beat him for that, later, I know."

"You can't flog colored men these days," said Merwin. "A Legree can be fined or jailed for that."

"You haven't lived down South, like I have, for months, in such a place. The Tabors have owned this land, and much more at one time, for almost three hundred years. Their word has been law and it is not far from it now. I mean that no one would dispute it. No one would prosecute them. And Egbert has just that sort of streak in him that made him throw stones at a frog when he was a boy. I know he did it. Mr. Tabor is severe but just, and all of the servants treat him with respect and affection, except Ned. Hosea is the only one who can handle Ned and Ned hates him, too, but he is afraid of him. Hosea is a Gullah. His father was a chief in Africa."

Merwin caught her by the arm, bare, white and smooth as ivory, soft as a magnolia petal. She looked at him quickly but did not appear to resent it. But, although he was falling in love, and had begun to surmise it, there was nothing personal in that grip. He pointed to where, through the trees and the garden growth a prick of light showed, shining like a fallen star, unevenly. There came to them, out of the night, the beat of a drum, monotonous and insistent while the vagrant breeze that brought it lasted. Then it died.

"Let's take a look at that," he said.

"It's outside the garden," she answered. "If it hadn't been for the drum I might think it some of the hands cooking yams they have taken, or even a chicken or two. We never pay attention to that as long as they keep their pilfering within bounds—but the drum makes it different. It looks like obeah to me."

"I didn't know they practiced it, outside of Haiti," said Merwin.

"They've always practiced it and always will. Love charms, charms and spells for sickness, for women who want children and, in its worst form, to work against an enemy, to make him ill, even to kill him; though that is against the law. But they do it. There is always some old conjuror or some old witch who works on their superstition and makes a living out of them."

"Want to go?"

"Of course," she said. "It's over toward their graveyard. The Tabors are buried on the estate and so have their servants been. Not, of course, in the same cemetery. Come on."

CHAPTER THREE

Voodoo Spell

THEY went silently through the garden growth where massed azaleas were in their best bloom, then passed the boundary of the home place and saw the burying ground. There were scores of low mounds and places where the earth had sunk to mark the dead. There were no crosses, no stones; only rude boards on which had been painted or burned in names and dates. Over almost every grave was a crude shelter, a sort of low hutch, beneath which was a collection of the last things the deceased had handled, mostly household utensils, the earthern ones broken.

They could see the fire more clearly now, hear the *tom-tom-tom* of the drum more plainly. They made a circuit of the graveyard to where cypress trees kneed out of a bayou that came in from a main inlet, a tidal place of brackish water. There were lotus blooms on the surface with other waterflowers. The tide was coming in; the mud beneath the cypresses shone under the moon.

A solitary figure crouched by the fire it occasionally fed. It was that of a man, naked save for a scanty clout, his skin daubed and smeared with red and yellow, white and black, in some crude attempt at design. He was crooning softly, in time to the drum he beat, a gourd covered with skin, laced about with fiber, so arranged to make a handle by which he held it on one knee as he hunkered. Drum and chant were old, perhaps, as the Mountains of the Moon, in far-off Africa.

There were scraps of cloth tied to bushes here and there. At the foot of one cypress were three little images of soft clay. One was black, two had been painted white and a little cotton had been used for hair, black tufts for one white man, white for the other, with a tiny goatee. Here was juju. Here were the images made and named for Hosea, for Tabor and his nephew.

"Oh, whoo-ree- ee-eeree, eyah-ah!"

That was what the monotonous plaint sounded like and the repetition of the spell, the tap of the drum, were working the quadroon into excitation. Merwin knew well enough it was Ned. He hesitated what to do. It was all mumbo-jumbo but he did not like it. It was hate resorting to witchcraft against those he feared. Then the girl caught at him suddenly where they stood back of the cypress on the bank and pointed at the bayou.

A blunt snout was appearing, knobs on a cruel head with gleaming eyes. It was an alligator and it was hauling out. The boy took no notice and the saurian slithered and then waddled out on the mud and stayed there, its flail of a tail curved, serrated, powerful enough to break a man's leg, to sweep him into the water. But the enormous reptile kept quiescent, as if the drum fascinated it; as if the spell had drawn it, conjured it, a wizard's familiar.

Ned reached forward, took the first of the figurines, muttering some giberish of an incantation. It was the black one. He crushed the soft clay shapeless, thrust it into the dead body of a rabbit, tossed it to the alligator whose frightful gorge opened and snapped on the offering, like a trained dog. The next figurine had a thorn thrust into its belly, the last, with the white cotton tufts, had one through its heart. He did not crush these but wrapped them up in separate leaves and hid them in a hollow between the knees of a cypress. Then he rose, his face exultant. He quenched the fire and, carrying his drum, marched straight across the graveyard while the alligator slid back into the ooze.

"It's all mummery," said the girl as they waited a while before starting back to the house. "It doesn't mean anything."

Merwin did not agree with her but he did not say so. There was meaning enough behind the barbaric ritual—the spirit of hate, of murder.

It was late and the moon was sinking. The perfume of the jasmine was overpowering. The girl too disliked it.

"It is like tuber-roses," she said. "It suggests corruption. The negroes make poison out of its roots. They say it cannot be traced after death, that the tissues absorb it. It's in the pharmacopoeia as gelsemium and they use it medically for spasms and neuralgia, and for malarial fevers. Gelsemine is a crystalline alkaloid from the same source, the root of the Carolina jasmine. That is very deadly."

THE house was dark, save for one dim light on the ground floor and another on the second, where Tabor lay and Egbert kept vigil. Merwin parted with the girl in the hall, taking one stairway while she took the other. He wanted to kiss her and he had a vague idea that she would not have minded, might have kissed him back and clung to him for a moment. He knew that under all her brave front she was a frightened girl and he was glad she had not seen the shining horror at the window.

He did not sleep well in his tower room. He remembered tales of barbaric witchcraft, especially how the witch or wizard would use means to make certain their spells worked, if the psychological effect was not sufficient. Ned's desires were plain enough. He wanted Hosea to be eaten by an alligator, he wanted Egbert to suffer torture in his entrails and Tabor, head of the house—the thorn had been thrust into his heart. The negroes used gelsemium root for curing, and they could use it for killing.

He tried to dismiss this. Ned could have no opportunities of administering poison to Tabor, even to Egbert. And he certainly could not have contrived the apparition at the window; whether it was supernatural or not. Merwin scoffed at the latter idea but it persisted in his half-dreams. The thing had been frightful. It had glared in, twenty feet or more from the ground, then suddenly vanished. Had it left any trace? Merwin wanted to find out.

Sunrise found him up, bathing and dressing swiftly, exploring a little. As he had half expected, he discovered, at the top of the winding stairs which led to his room and went upward, a way to the roof. Over the edge of this, on the tower, the creepers had curled like a wave. They had done the same on the main and lower roof. Merwin did not know how to gain access to this and, though he had an idea in his mind, it was only a vague one as to what he might find if he mounted there.

Then he saw a figure coming through an opening trap. It was that of Egbert Tabor, clad in a dressing gown. He had clipping shears in his hand and he started to trim the errant vines. It was a curious thing to do, at that hour, and why Egbert did not employ one of the colored gardeners puzzled Merwin.

Merwin watched for a few moments. Egbert seemed intent upon his task, lifting and examining the tendrils, replacing some of them untouched. Then Merwin made his retreat, not quite sure at the last moment whether Egbert, who had looked up, observed him or not.

It was early for breakfast and he got out his apparatus for valuing jewels, scales, callipers, magnifying lenses and microscope. He had also a camera and drawing and coloring outfits for the registration of unusual shapes and patterns. It all was to explain his presence at Oak Manor but he was wondering if he had not come too late. It seemed almost certain that Tabor's illness, the matter of the red bull and its shining apparition, were allied with the announced making of his will, with the sending for Merwin, the strange things happening.

Egbert was not in the direct line but, if Tabor died intestate, Egbert would inherit as next of kin, over such distant relations as might lay claim to the inheritance in England. The estate had originally been granted by the Crown but those rights had reverted with the War of Independence. Merwin wondered whether Egbert had any idea that when the will was drawn he would be eliminated. He meant to ask Grace Quincy if there was any friction between the two men.

He put a bottle of waterproof black ink into his pocket, together with a brush and strolled through the grounds as if seeking an appetite before breakfast. Two gardeners were already lazily working; the hands were out, in the fields or barns. He saw Egbert on a blooded horse ride off in a gallop, spurring the spirited animal. He would be back for breakfast, which would not be ready for an hour or more.

Smoking a pipe, Merwin walked unnoticed around the burying ground to the cypresses where Ned had made his incantations. The tide was ebbing, there was no sign of the alligator. But he found the two images and discovered that they were not made of clay but of beeswax, and that not thorns but sharp fishbones had been thrust through them.

That was important. Beeswax and bone were both animal products, considered essential in juju for the setting up of malignant vibrations toward the intended victims. Merwin had learned that in reading about Haitian witchcraft. Now he did a little white-man's magic on his own account. He picked off the tiny tuft of white cotton that represented Tabor's goatee, dyed the rest of it and then painted both the figures black over the whiting Ned, or the conjurer he had consulted, had applied.

When Ned looked at them again he would wonder what opposing magic had interfered with his deviltry. It might convince him that the spirits were against his project. It might stop him from proceeding to more active measures. The image of Hosea was in the alligator's belly, but Merwin was inclined to think that Hosea could look out for himself.

HE returned leisurely to the house but hastened as he saw the girl come out on the loggia. He joined her and told her what he had done.

"It may seem childish," he said, "but there is likely to be more going on than just the making and piercing of images. Of course that shining apparition at the window was not supernatural. It had a definite manufacturer. I suppose that a man of Mr. Tabor's intelligence may be influenced by an old family legend, even when he is normal. In his present low condition such an appearance might have been designed deliberately to affect his weak heart, perhaps in the hope that the shock might kill."

"You don't think Ned could have had anything to do with it?"

"I don't know. No doubt he desires evil toward all three. He may well have thrust that bone into the heart of Tabor's figurine because it is common knowledge that Tabor is so affected. His throwing Hosea to the alligator might have been only a childish hope. Certainly Egbert does not seem to have been affected."

The door from house to loggia opened and Hosea stood there. It was not to summon them to breakfast, as they expected. The butler's face showed alarm.

"Massa Tabor want you an' missy to come to his room, right away," he said.

"Has anything happened? Is he worse?" asked the girl.

"He feel bad. Something suah happen," Hosea replied. "You come."

They hurried upstairs, Hosea following. Tabor was huddled up among his pillows, clad in his dressing robe. He looked very ill, very old and infinitely forlorn. The thought came to Merwin that his mind, inclined toward abnormality already by sickness and the coming of the red bull, was unhinged. He was a badly frightened old gentleman, cowering and apprehensive, far from the robust man the girl had pictured him, as Merwin had imagined he might well be from the talk of Alwyn Foster. There had been a tremendous change overnight. His eyes were deep sunken, dull. His hands trembled and his voice quavered.

"See there, on the hearth," he said, "This is the second coming. The third—that will be the last, the end of the House of Tabor."

Mentally weakened or not, there was no question that he was doomed. He was a pitiful sight, the wreck of himself.

Hosea had opened a window but the room had the same odor of brimstone that Merwin had noticed the night before when the shining horror had disappeared.

"When I come in it jus' natcherully smelled like hell," said Hosea simply. "I didn't see that thing in the fiahplace then.

Massa Tabor he git up, gwine to the bathroom, an' he saw it first. He fall back but I kotch him. His eyes close and his heart go like a big drum."

Merwin and the girl were staring at the ashes on the wide hearthstone. They were deep. The fire had burned out during the night and Hosea had been ready to rebuild it if Tabor felt cold, as he was apt to lately.

There, plainly imbedded, was a cloven hoof. The footprint of a bull, though Hosea named it differently.

"That the foot of Satan, suah," he decleared. "Massa Tabor been conjuah. Yes, suh, he been conjuah. That what make him sick, and then the devil begin to walk around. Suppose Doctuh Tolliver cain't come, I like to have Kiku come heah."

"Who's Kiku?" asked Merwin.

Tabor lay exhausted and quiet with his eyes closed. The smell of the brimstone, the sinister sign in the ashes affected all of them, fight against it as they might. It could not be—yet there it was.

"Kiku, he mighty big conjuah man," said Hosea. "I'm gwine to talk to him. I got a notion he might know the way Massa Tabor been lately. He act to me like he been fed conjuah root."

"Conjure root!" Merwin and the girl looked at each other with the same thought. Gelsemium or gelsemine, in solution or in crystals. The root of the yellow wild jasmine that clung to the trees, whose odor suggested corruption.

"You mean you think someone has been putting poison in his food?" demanded Merwin.

"Not his food. No, suh. I done tote that food myself, all the time he been sick. Nobody in kitchen gwine to give Massa Tabor anything bad. Not Massa Tabor. But—" he lowered his voice— looked about him and was suddenly silent.

CHAPTER FOUR

Hoofprint of Hell

EGBERT was standing in the open doorway, in his riding clothes with his crop. His face was like a thundercloud. "What's this about conjure?" he said. "About conjure root? Out with it, Hosea."

The big negro did not wince. "I say someone done conjuah Massa Tabor," he replied. "I say I gwine fin' out."

"Get out," Egbert cried. "What has happened?" he inquired of the girl, ignoring Merwin for the moment. He followed her gesture with his eyes and started at sight of the cloven hoof. He sniffed at the air of the room. "By God!" he said, "this is incredible."

"Tell him to go away," piped a feeble voice from the bed. "I do not want him here. He knows that. I do not want him in my room at night. Tell him to leave."

Egbert strode halfway to the bed and Tabor shrank, trying to hide under the clothes.

"You had better go," suggested Merwin. Egbert swung on him fiercely.

"You mind your own affairs," he retorted. "I saw you spying on the roof of the tower this morning. You had better pack your belongings and get out. You, with your pretense of appraising gems!"

"I am not taking orders from you, sir," said Merwin. "I came here at the request of the owner of this place and shall leave when he wants me to."

Egbert glared at him, swung on his heel and ran down the stairs. They heard him cursing someone below, then the sound of furious galloping.

Grace Quincy had gone to the bed, trying to comfort the whimpering old man. "I don't like to take the responsibility of giving him another hypodermic," she said, "but his pulse is very low. I am afraid another shock would kill him."

Merwin picked up a bottle and looked at the label. It seemed to be a sedative, pinkish in color, marked 'BRO POT'. Bromide of potassium. He put it in his pocket.

"We'll go to Tolliver's," he said. "He can't refuse to come under the circumstances. We can go together."

"No," cried Edwin Tabor feebly. "One of you stay in the house, to keep Egbert away from me. Tolliver can do no good. It is beyond medicine."

"You give me the directions and I'll go. I suppose I can get a horse," said Merwin.

He got a cup of coffee and ate a couple of biscuits while Hosea got Ned to saddle a mare. The boy brought it round. There were weal marks on his face plain by daylight, and his handsome features were sulky.

Merwin found the way easily enough but Tolliver was absent. He trailed him at last to where he was working over the overseer of a plantation who had got a badly crushed arm in some machinery. Tolliver was white haired but active, a benevolent-looking man who showed no sign of resentment.

"I can only give you a minute or two, suh," he said. "I've got a lot to do with that poor devil inside, or he may lose his arm. I heard you were visiting at Oak Manor. I heard also you were there to appraise jewels. There is nothing goes on in a community like this, with colored servants, that is private property."

"Did you hear about the apparition of the bull?" asked Merwin. "I suppose you know the legend."

Tolliver nodded. "I know of both," he said. "I have often talked with Tabor about the legend. I suppose, you suh, scoff at it. But apparitions are curious things. It is quite possible for a person in a low state of vitality, to see things, objects or persons, optically, and yet not register them mentally. The machinery is all there but it is not motivating properly, you see. Then, at a later period, with renewed activity, the machinery may become normal and the belated memory image connect with the mind. Ghosts are seen that way. It is not beyond the bounds of possibility that an idea, handed down through generations, might be seen as a flash. There are a lot of things we don't know about the subjective and objective brain, the transmission of thought."

"I saw it also," said Merwin, "and I smelled that sulphurous stink. Miss Quincy and I, also Hosea and Egbert Tabor, saw the hoofmark on the hearth this morning, and the same stink was present."

"Ha!" cried Tolliver. "I hadn't heard about that hoofmark yet. Tell me. The morphia I gave my patient in there will hold him for a while. Go ahead, suh. A hoofmark?"

Merwin told him everything briefly and swiftly, including Ned's images, Hosea's talk of conjure. He handed over the bottle of sedative. Tolliver sniffed at it, tasted it.

"I'll analyze this," he said grimly. "Since Tabor blew up at my suggestion— it was not an accusation, mind you—that his symptoms suggested the use of opium derivatives, the fool has been doctoring himself. Miss Quincy has helped out, of course. A fine girl who has put up with a lot, including Egbert. He fixed his own bromide. I think Hosea has hit on something. Gelsemium will produce just such symptoms as the opium derivatives. I was a fool not to think of it. I'd get back if I were you, Merwin, as fast as you can. I don't like what Ned was doing. The boy is a menace and it would be much better if Hosea stayed away from that witch-doctor Kiku. I'll come to the house and make my peace with Tabor as soon as possible."

MERWIN galloped back in a hurry. He wondered what Tolliver had meant by the hint that Grace Quincy had had to put up with a lot from Egbert. They were decidedly cool to each other now.

He saw Egbert's horse in the drive, the sulky Ned holding it by the bridle. Merwin went in to the breakfast room. He was hungry and meant to see if Hosea could not get him something to supplement his scanty meal, as soon as he had assured Grace Quincy of the success of his mission. Hosea was not there, did not appear to the bell.

Off the breakfast room was a sort of study that Merwin expected to use for his bluff at appraising. He heard voices there. One was the girl's, the other Egbert's. Merwin would not have listened, save for the sudden change in pitch of both. It was an altercation, hastening to a climax.

Then the girl screamed, a cry that was quickly smothered. As Merwin made for the door he heard a bolt slide, a scuffle. Egbert's voice was clear.

"Despise me, eh? Well I'm sick of your stand-off manners. I would have married you; now, by all that's unholy, I'll make you wish I had!"

Merwin flung himself at the door. It was a stout one; the bolt held. He backed up and tried it again and again, desperate in the dread of what was happening. Once more the girl called out, despairingly, and the bolt gave way.

If Merwin had been carrying his gun there would have been murder committed then and there. Egbert had the girl almost subdued, handling her with a savagery that she could not long resist. She sank almost helpless on a lounge as Merwin leaped at Egbert, set a knee in his back and tugged so hard at his collar that the coat ripped as Egbert, partly choked, twisted about and struck viciously at Merwin.

"You interfering hound," he said. "I'll teach you your lesson!"

He was strong, heavier than Merwin, maddened by a blazing fury and the fight was fast and furious. Merwin smashed Egbert twice in the face, once on the jaw, but Egbert bored in, trying to clinch, to wrestle, fighting like a fiend, fast and foul. Twice Merwin loosened grips that showed the other knew how to wrestle. Once he was thrown, Merwin knew it would be the end of him. If he was not kicked to death he would be crippled for life, left only the maimed remnant of a man. There was no doubt about Egbert's intentions, nor his belief that he would conquer. It showed in his grin, marred where Merwin had split his lips.

He got Merwin off his feet, started to adjust a strangle hammerlock. And Merwin got his chance. A trainer had shown him something of jidu—Chinese equivalent of jiu-jitsu. He got his thumbs at the base of Egbert's throat, with his fingers clenched in the collar of his shirt. He sank the thumb tips back of the windpipe, back of the gullet, vised them in. To pull back was as fatal as to come forward and relax the throat muscles. He had him. Egbert's eyes began to start from their sockets, his tongue protruded, his face grew purple and the strength suddenly went out of him. He slid to the ground, choking, moaning harshly.

"He won't swallow with comfort for a few days," said Merwin to the girl. "After this I'll pack my gun all the time. I'll shoot him down like a mad dog. Did he hurt you? If he did, I'm through with him even now."

"He didn't do me any harm," she answered. She had caught up a drape from the lounge and wore it like a shawl to cover the damage done to her blouse. "Let's go," she said. "I think he's mad—one of the mad Tabors.

"Once he wanted to marry me," she went on, loathing in her tones, as they left the discomfited and defeated Egbert still unable to rise. "I believe he had an idea that Mr. Tabor might leave me his property and wanted to be sure of it. He is just a beast when he's angry or excited. I knew his uncle did not like the way he handled the servants. And Egbert was furious about being criticized. Is the doctor coming?"

BY MUTUAL impulse they went to the loggia to breathe more freely. The girl had not thanked him for his rescue and he was glad of it. She had accepted him as her protector and he meant to be. It was no time to talk of it, but he knew that they understood each other. He started to tell her what Tolliver had said about the conjuring when they heard a distant wailing, the lamentations of many voices in chorus, half chant, half individual, ineffably mournful. It grew nearer and the girl clutched his arm.

"Someone is dead," she said. "I've heard that before, when there has been a death in the quarters. I wonder where Hosea is."

"He might have gone to see that wizard, Kiku," suggested Merwin. "Here they come," he added.

Four men were carrying a hurdle taken from the fields. The burden they carried was too long for the improvised stretcher. It was covered with cloth used for tenting the tobacco plants and the cotton was hideously stained. Behind the four bearers was a procession of field hands. Others joined it, from the garden, the kitchen, all taking up the death wail, tossing up their arms, the women covering their faces with their aprons òr their outer skirts.

Catching up with them as they swung into the main drive in front of the house, came Tolliver on a horse streaked with foam and sweat, that showed with what urgency he had come when he was able. He checked the carriers, lifted the cloth.

Then he spurred his mount to meet Merwin and the girl.

"You'd better go in, Miss Grace," he said. "You can't help. It's Hosea! Take him round to the back, boys," he added. "You can come, Merwin, if you wish. You go on up to my old friend, Miss Quincy, and don't leave him until I come. Don't let anyone go into the room until I arrive. I won't be long."

Egbert came out of the front door, feeling his throat, his voice a feeble croak as he wanted to know what had happened. One of the bearers answered.

"Tom heah, done found Hosea over by Kiku's cabin. He done been tromped and gored to death. By a *bull!* And there ain't no bull round hyah."

Again the wailing broke out, with groans and lamentations. Egbert staggered back inside, though it was more from weakness than shock, Merwin fancied. The hold of jidu was a terrible one and he had put all he had into its execution. The girl passed through the loggia door to Tabor's chamber and Merwin went with Tolliver, who had dismounted.

"What was wrong with Egbert?" asked Tolliver.

"He was insulting Miss Quincy and I mixed with him," Merwin told him. "I got a Chinese strangle hold on him before he got away with me."

"By God, it's too bad you didn't finish the job, suh! It's a family matter, but you've broken through conventionalities, suh, in regard to the Tabor family. This chap Egbert, comes of a strain in which there is undoubted insanity that may hold over for two or three generations but is bound to prevail. He is, of course, a relation of Edwin Tabor, but Edwin's direct line is free from that sort of thing, unless you call the belief in the red bull madness. Egbert's great-great-grandfather was a pirate. They were common enough in those days and more than one of them, like Blackbeard, was mad. They delighted to torture, to kill, to loot and rape, to make their victims walk the plank. It was that Tabor who ripped open a man's stomach while he was still alive, because he had swallowed a valuable ring, rather than let the pirates have it. Things are more civilized now, perhaps; but I know that my old friend Edwin never intended to let Egbert inherit Oak Manor. The line would end with him, he said, after his two sons had died in France. Well, we'll have a look at this poor chap, Hosea. It is curious he should be found near Kiku's. Looks like more conjure. Perhaps it is, of a sort."

CHAPTER FIVE

The Shining Horror

MERWIN was content with one glance at the mangled body. Tolliver made a more thorough investigation.

"He seems to have been gored, viciously, in the abdomen, the throat, and through the ribs. Undoubtedly some kind of curving, tapering weapon, like the horn of a bull. I'm not quite satisfied, though. I am not inclined to give a certificate and I am acting coroner. I shall notify the sheriff and have the body taken away by the Cypress undertaker for an autopsy. There are only two bulls within a dozen miles, to my knowledge. We'll look them up. And we'll look up Kiku, too."

"It might be a good idea to see where Ned is," suggested Merwin.

"I saw him just now. He hasn't run away. I doubt if Ned is guilty of anything greater than a grudge and a hope that his witchery will work. But he didn't get it from Kiku. Kiku would not work charms against a white man, certainly not a Tabor. No, suh, Ned's grandmother was a kind of obeah woman. There are plenty of them about. Ned was trying out what he had learned from her before she

died. Though she, like Kiku, would not have tried to bewitch a Tabor. For one thing, according to her belief, she couldn't do it because they had Tabor blood in them."

Tabor seemed a little stronger, more self reliant when Tolliver and Merwin entered. The girl was there on watch and guard.

"Ah, Tolliver," said Tabor. "I'm a sick man—but it's not opium."

"I never said it was, my friend. I only said it looked like it. I apologize for having done that. At least I'll apologize if you'll let me go over you properly. I've known you too long not to know there is nothing organically wrong. You're good for twenty years yet, more than that, and I'm going to see you get them. What's all this nonsense about your making a will? Are you throwing the race?"

"Making my will has nothing to do with the way I feel, Tolliver. I never made one because I thought my sons would succeed to the natural inheritance. Then I put it off, it was a painful idea, until—until I knew that was coming."

He pointed feebly toward the coat of arms on the wall.

"I heard it, Tolliver. Then—I saw it. At the window. It left its spoor on the hearth. The bull, the Red Bull of Tabor. And I have been ailing. I have no strength."

"We'll give you back strength, Edwin. Our young friend Merwin here, and myself, are not so sure that bull is genuine. Now sit up and let me go over you."

"Where's Hosea?" he asked. "He hasn't been near me since morning, since he saw that hoofprint. He called it the foot of Satan."

"I took the liberty of borrowing Hosea," said Tolliver with a warning look at Merwin and Grace Quincy. "I wanted to send in for some medicine. My own man is sick."

"Use him as long as you want to,"

said Tabor. "I too must apologize to you, my friend."

Merwin left with Tolliver when the auscultation was over. Grace Quincy was left installed as nurse.

"I'm giving him digitalis," said Tolliver, "but I don't know just what to prescribe until I've had that bromide analyzed. His pulse is bad and his diastolic rhythm weak, but I'm positive there is nothing radically wrong. The mucles are not actually weak. Poor Hosea was right when he said he had been conjured, unless I'm mistaken."

"And saying so cost him his life," said Merwin.

"You're going too fast, suh. We've got to look into the matter of those bulls, and into the exact cause of Hosea's death first. But you are wise to be careful. I'll be back some time, perhaps not until after dark. I'm leaving things to you, suh. Don't let him know about Hosea. Any shock in his condition might be fatal."

Merwin went to his room when Tolliver had ridden off. He got his gun and set it in his hip pocket. Then he went on a trip to the roof of the main building where he had seen Egbert trim the vines. He was not worrying about Egbert. He felt he had his number, but he meant to use the automatic pistol if he had to. He intended to keep Egbert in mind, if not in sight, but, for the moment, he was glad Egbert was not visible. Probably he was trying to alleviate his almost disrupted throat somewhere.

Merwin did not find much on the roof beyond the fact of the trimmed vines. Nothing definite, but sufficient to nourish an idea of his.

The maid served luncheon, then took a meal upstairs, knocked on the door of Egbert's room and was cursed at and sent away.

Tolliver had peremptorily hushed the lament for the sake of Tabor and the place was quiet. But no work was being carried out. Death hovered there though a wagon came and took Hosea's riven corpse away.

DARKNESS came. Egbert was still in seclusion. Merwin had knocked gently on the door of Tabor's room three times and got assurance that all was as well as might be expected. At last Egbert came stalking out of his chamber, passing through the hall, up the staircase. He paid no attention to Merwin, in front of the fireplace, waiting for Tolliver, but Merwin trailed him until he heard Egbert's footsteps pass Tabor's room, go on to the topmost floor. Grace Quincy had Tabor's door bolted, anyway. She had not let even Merwin in until she recognized his voice.

Then Tolliver came, his face grave, greeting Merwin. He sat in front of the fire, smoking a long thin cigarro.

"There was gelsemine in that bromide," he said. "I don't know where it came from, but it isn't hard to distil, or even brew. And, while Hosea was pierced by a horn, or something like a horn, he was killed by a bullet. I've got it. It was in his heart. The horn thrust through his ribs was made to cover up that shot. I had my suspicions the way the wounds had bled, especially the rib wound. It looks serious, Merwin. The sheriff is coming out later. We've got to be careful to keep things from Tabor, but now I know what has been destroying him I can soon build him up. And—"

There was the sound of a door opening and the girl's voice, calling urgently. "Dan—quickly—please!"

Side by side Tolliver and Merwin made the stairs. Tabor was on the floor in a crumpled heap.

"He had to get up," she said. "Then it came, at the window. It was horrible, ghastly. He fell."

Tolliver had fetched upstairs the case he had brought with him. He knelt beside the prostrate man whose face looked waxen. Grace Quincy, pale but efficient, was helping him as Merwin made for the roof, gun in hand.

He reached the hall where the trap led to the roof, a ladder in place beneath it. The trap was open.

Merwin climbed it like a boarding pilot, got to the roof, seeing, as he thrust through head and shoulders, a dark figure carrying a big bundle toward the trap. It was Egbert. He seemed to recognize Merwin and leaped toward him with a maniacal laugh. The folds of the stuff he bore in both his arms spread wide, muffling Merwin. The open trap was close behind him and he fired through the stuff, squeezing the trigger rapidly. The weight of Egbert behind the cloth was swiftly gone. Merwin flung off the folds. His gunfire had started the stuff to burn.

He saw Egbert staggering backward. A shot had got him in his leg, close to the knee. He stepped on one of the long tendrils of the vines he had trimmed to cover up where he had bruised them in his performance with the shining horror, slipped, tripped as his leg gave way. Then with a yell, with arms upflung, he fell backward from the roof.

MERWIN looked down for a moment. Figures were hurrying round from the back, lanterns swinging.

He gathered up the sable fabric, put out its smouldering patches, grimly admired its ingenuity as he found the bull's head of papier-maché, the sort of expensive mask used at carnivals. There was a battery for the shining eyes, a contrivance for smoke to fume from the open nostrils. The whole mask had been treated with phosphorescent paint; red pigment was wet on the horns.

It had been lowered from the roof, stiffened by wire, the black cloth a perfect background for illusion. There was a flap that could be let fall over the head and cause it instantly to vanish.

Merwin carried it down, stowed it, and returned to Tabor's room. Tolliver met him at the door.

"What was it?"

"I've laid the ghost," said Merwin, and told him. "How about Tabor?"

"I administered adrenalin. He responded well. He's got lots of life to enjoy yet."

When the sheriff comes," said Merwin, "we'll search Egbert's quarters. I've an idea we'll find gelsemine and the means of making it, not to mention the gun that fired the bullet you took from Hosea, and some sort of hardwood weapon shaped like a horn."

"Suh," said Tolliver, "I would not wager you the value of a doubtful dime against your conclusions. It was fortunate that you came to Oak Manor. Egbert should have hung, if he did not happen to be a Tabor. As it is, unless you insist upon all details being aired, seeing that Tabor should not be excited, that I am the coroner, it might be best not to stress things too much. Egbert fell off the roof, by accident. A bull gored Hosea. It is true both the bulls near here are accounted for, but, after all, why rile a clear pool?"

"It is nothing to me," said Merwin, "how you settle the matter. We can't bring Hosea back to life. We don't want to bring back Egbert. I don't want to interfere with your quaint local, Southern customs, doctor."

Merwin took Grace Quincy down to the garden. The jasmine did not seem so strong tonight. But a mocking bird sang lustily.

"When you called downstairs tonight," he said, "you called me Dan."

"Did I, Dan? Have you any objections?"

The mocking bird kept singing, though it had lost an audience.

PHANTOM FINGERS

A Cardigan Story

by
Frederick Nebel

Author of "And There Was Murder," etc.

Three times those livid prints had been found on dead men's throats— three times the mysterious widow had made her kill. And now, a grim avenger, Detective Cardigan sets out to rip away those mourning weeds that veil murder.

Cardigan saw it was not the man whose picture had been on the handbill.

CHAPTER ONE

Mr. Bartles of 303

PAT SEAWARD was locking the office door from the outside and Cardigan was halfway toward the elevators when the telephone rang. Pat looked after Cardigan, called: "Phone, chief. Should I let it slide?"

"Yeah, let it slide."

"Well, maybe I'd better answer it."

"O. K. Answer it."

Cardigan stopped and leaned against the wall, his faded fedora battered down over one eye, shaggy gobs of hair sticking out around his ears.

Pat reappeared. "For you, chief."

Cardigan growled: "I thought my day was done," and went slowly, heavy-footed, toward the office.

Pat sang, lightly: "When day is done and evening shadows—"

"All right, brat, all right. Let that slide too."

"Arf! Arf!"

He entered the outer office, swept up the telephone. "Hello, . . . Yes, this is Cardigan. . . . Just a minute." He put the phone on the desk, leaned down, collected pencil and pad. "Spell it, please. . . . Yeah, I've got it. . . . *Uhunh—* Westminster." He looked up at Pat, looked down at the pad again, wrote scattered notes. "Well, it's five-thirty now. . . . Well, if it's important I could. . . . *Uhunh.* O. K., then. . . . I get you. Sure. . . . Good-by."

He depressed the hook with his right hand, hefted the receiver in his left for a moment and then slapped it into the hook. He tore a sheet off the pad, regarded it, regarded Pat quizzically.

"This is funny," he said. "A guy named Bartles out in the Western Arms is having a jane call on him at six and wants a private detective out there to sit through the interview. Details—" he stroked his jaw—"when I get there."

"So what?"

"He's sick a-bed."

"Maybe he wants you to hold his hand or something."

Cardigan folded the slip of paper, tucked it into a vest pocket, grabbed Pat by the arm and hustled her out. "For two cents I'd slap you down. Get along, you."

"But first I must lock the *casa, señor.*"

Cardigan went on to the elevators, caught a down-bound car and held it while Pat came skipping down the corridor. Below in the lobby Cardigan said: "If you promise to shut up I'll drop you at your hotel."

"Promise," she said, with a flash of long eyelashes.

They rode west on Olive, turned right at Twelfth and stopped in front of the Hotel Andromeda. Cardigan got out, handed out Pat and said: "Dinner at eight and omit the mascara."

"Oh, you big, strong silent man!"

"Scram!"

Chuckling, he climbed back into the cab, gave a number on Westminster. The cab went up Locust past double-decker busses. At Channing it swung into Lindell and went over the hump past the big Masonic building. The rush of air through the open windows was cold and Cardigan held his hat between his hands and let the wind tousel his shaggy crop of black hair. The cab made a right turn into Vandeventer, caught a green light at McPherson and took the next left into Westminster.

The Western Arms was not pretentious, but it raised six stories of red brick which the chemical cleaners had recently gone over. It had a green lawn out front and a narrow cement terrace with six wicker armchairs in a row. The lobby was clean, cool and deserted. There was no desk— no elevator.

Cardigan climbed three flights of stairs, walked toward the front of the building until he came to a door marked 303. This door was made of horizontal blinds and when he opened it there was another, regular door of dark wood. He knocked on this, then turned the knob, opened it.

"Mr. Bartles."

The living room was dark because the blinds were half drawn. Bartles had said over the phone that he should walk right in. Cardigan, having closed the door, said again: "Mr. Bartles."

The living room was stuffy. Objects began to make themselves apparent as Cardigan's eyes became accustomed to the dim room. He went toward a partly open door, but turned back when he saw it led to a bathroom. He espied another door across the room and walked toward it, wearing a wrinkled frown.

The door was open and Cardigan saw first the foot of a brass bed and next the shape of a body beneath a white coverlet.

"Mr. Bartles."

Westminster was a quiet street and there was no sound of traffic. A clock was ticking in the room. The shades were drawn all the way down. The shape on the bed remained motionless.

Cardigan took a few steps into the room, moved nearer to the side of the bed. His hand went out and he turned on a small reading lamp that stood on a table beside the bed.

He muttered: "Oh," quietly.

His hand shot in beneath a blue pajama coat, remained there while his eyes regarded a twisted, discolored face. He stood up again and put his fists on his hips. There was a slip of paper lying on the little bed-table. On it had been scrawled hastily the name of his agency, the address, and then across one corner his own name.

"*Um,*" he muttered.

HE DID not disturb the paper. His lips felt dry and he moistened them with his tongue. He looked at the alarm clock on the table. It was ten to six.

There was a green ash tray with the stub of a cigarette resting in one of three niches. Cardigan bent closer. There was a bit of red color on the end of the cigarette that had been between two lips. Rouge. . . .

Cardigan looked at the clock again. Beside it was a telephone. He picked up the telephone and said: "Police Headquarters." He glanced around the dim room with thoughtful eyes. "Headquarters? . . . This is Cardigan, the Cosmos head. Say, there's a guy dead in apartment 303 at number — Westminster. . . . Where am I? In the apartment. . . . Oh, I just walked in. I had a date. . . . Bartles. . . . Well, strangulation. . . . Sure, I'll stay here."

He hung up and put the phone back on the table, gently.

Bartles was a small man—skinny. Even alive he must have been a dry and twisted clinker of a man, standing perhaps five feet five, weighing perhaps a hundred and ten. His fingers were like bones. His chest was bony. His body didn't make much of a lump in the big brass bed. Pitiful body, all wasted and bone-ridden.

"*Um,*" said Cardigan with a vast, heavy sigh.

He turned on more lights. He opened a closet door and looked at clothes hanging there. A black alpaca suit—a tan linen suit—a dark blue suit of serge, of fair but not excellent quality—a soiled shirt hanging on a hook. On the floor of the closet—a suitcase of worn, cracked leather and a smaller handbag—a drab gray overcoat. Marks on the clothing showed where labels had been ripped out. Shoes on the floor—a black pair and a tan pair, both pairs old with soles curving upward.

Cardigan went back to the bed-table, rapped the sides. He found a small drawer, opened it and found a worn pinseal wallet. Bills were packed neatly into one of the folds: five hundred and twenty dollars. Otherwise the wallet contained nothing. He returned it to the drawer, bent down to look at a pair of worn slippers.

Beneath the head of the bed, where wall met floor, he saw an automatic pistol. He reached under and got it. It was a 30 caliber Luger. He smelled the muzzle, put the gun down beside the telephone.

He stood looking abstractedly at the door leading to the living room, then strode toward it and entered the room, looking for a light switch. He heard a scraping sound. In a split second the dim form of a man crowded him and Cardigan felt the hard muzzle of a gun pressing against his stomach.

An instant later there was a man behind him. Wedged between two guns, Cardigan let his hand slide away from his hip.

"Git 'em up!" muttered the big man facing Cardigan.

When Cardigan's hands rose the man behind him took the gun off his hip and said: "Got his gat."

The big man had on a tremendous overcoat, the collar turned up. A floppy hat he wore was yanked down far over his eyes. His face was nothing more than a shadow which emitted harsh, deep-voiced sounds.

"Now them other things, bo—them other things," he grated.

"Them what?" Cardigan said.

"*Ah-r-r!*" rasped the man behind, jabbing his gun hard against the small of Cardigan's back. "Lay off that, lay off that!"

The big man menaced: "You hear, bo —you hear!"

"You birds cripples? Search me."

"Arnie," the big man growled, "frisk him. If he moves I let him have it."

CARDIGAN felt small, nervous hands ransack his pockets. He peered hard and tried to make out the features of the man he faced. It was impossible. Darkness had fallen rapidly. The room was quite dark now. Way behind him was the bar of light coming from the bedroom.

"Remember, Arnie—six o' them."

Arnie gave up. "They ain't on him. He musta bunked them."

The big man muttered in a deep, passionate voice: "Bo, we ain't foolin'! We want 'em! Six o' them!"

"You frisked me, didn't you?"

"We frisked you and they wasn't there! You killed Bartles for them—"

"If I had them they'd be on me, wouldn't they?"

The big man grated: "I ain't askin' you for questions, bo! By God, I mean what I say! You got 'em. You gotta have 'em! Six, bo—six. And they don't take up much room and they're worth enough

as I'd blow your belly out to get 'em. You hear me! I ain't lettin' eighty thousand in emeralds git away from us! There's been too much double-crossin' goin' on and— Listen, bo, maybe you ain't got me right. I'm a killer."

The wail of a siren came up from the street. The big man stiffened.

"What the hell's that?" he growled.

The small man cat-footed to a window. "Cops!" he gasped, whirling.

"Stoppin' here?"

"Out front!"

The big man seemed to bulge in his overcoat. The small man was a shadow scampering to the door.

"On the lam, 'Beef'!" he hissed.

The big man towered, swayed. Suddenly he swore. His gun whipped up, chopped down. It ran against Cardigan's head. Cardigan muttered: "*Unh*," staggered back a step, reached out a hand blindly, felt the wall and held himself up with a great effort.

The big man followed the small man through the door.

Cardigan felt his way along the wall, snapped on the light switch. He looked at himself in a mirror, took off his hat, punched out the dent the blow had left, replaced the hat on his head. He saw his gun lying on a divan where the small man had tossed it. He recovered it and put it back in his pocket. He looked at himself again in the mirror. There was no blood. Only a throbbing pain on the top of his head.

Making a face, he stood with clenched fists and muttered a stream of oaths in a low, vindictive voice. Then he stopped swearing and rolled a thought off his tongue: "Six emeralds . . . eighty thousand bucks." Savageness had fled from his eyes and his eyes narrowed and a tightness came to his lips.

Flying glances hit and stopped on a low, thin-legged desk. He lunged to it, sent fingers probing rapidly into pigeon-holes. Dusty pigeon-holes. Nothing there. He yanked open a drawer and found two pint bottles of Bourbon lying side by side. Nothing else.

He turned and went lunging into the bathroom, searched the cabinet over the wash-basin. He let out a short oath as pain beat harder through his head. Finally he left the bathroom with long, swift strides, as if he were headed for a definite point. He stopped in the middle of the floor and looked exasperated.

A small portable gramophone stood on a low end-table by the divan. He went to it, picked it up, shook it. *Body and Soul* fell off, rolled across the floor. Cardigan put the gramophone down, straightened, listened.

He went back into the bedroom, took his handkerchief and unscrewed the brass knobs on the bed-posts. He shook the knobs and listened and then screwed them back on. The pain throbbed harder again and he closed his eyes and winced and when the pain lessened he cursed and tramped back into the living room.

His eye dropped on the record that had rolled off the gramophone. He picked it up and carried it back to the end-table. He looked round and round the room intently, looked for something he might have overlooked.

"Six emeralds," he muttered. "Eighty thousand bucks."

He dropped to the divan, stretched out his legs, lit a cigarette. He heard the clatter of heels coming up the stairway. The door opened and a man stood there.

"Hello, Cardigan."

"Hello, Fitz."

CHAPTER TWO

Green Ice

SOME uniformed cops remained in the hall. Some came into the apartment and looked around. Lieutenant Fitz, plainclothes, followed Cardigan's gesture and went into the bedroom. Dumpy Sergeant Conkey made eyes at Cardigan, grinned, made mysterious gestures with pudgy hands. He grinned eternally. He looked over his shoulder at Cardigan as he followed Fitz into the bedroom. His moon face beamed like an idiot's.

"Hey, Cardigan." That was Fitz—lantern-jawed, lean-boned, somber-eyed.

Cardigan went across the room and leaned in the connecting doorway.

"When 'd you find him?" Fitz rapped impersonally.

"Ten to six."

"How come?"

"When I was leaving the office the phone rang and this guy asked me to come right out. Said a jane was calling on him and he wanted me here. Said he'd explain when I got here. I thought I might pick up twenty-five bucks—and it was on my way home."

"What's his name?"

"Bartles. He'd told me to walk right in. He said he was sick in bed. So I walked in. Found him—this way. The gun there was lying on the floor, so don't throw a fit if you find my print on it. I picked it up. It hadn't been fired recently. There's a wallet in the table drawer containing five hundred and twenty bucks."

"Couldn't you leave things alone?" Fitz snapped.

"You know how it is."

Fitz took out the wallet, counted the money. He examined the gun. It was fully loaded. Fitz looked at the dead man. He chewed on his lip and his eyes scowled. Conkey pried into the closet, tossed out the clothes. The coroner's man came in and made a superficial examination while carrying on a spirited conversation with Fitz about the stock market.

A cop marched a baffled-looking man

into the bedroom and the man almost took a header when he saw the body.

Fitz scowled. "Who 're you?"

"He's the manager or something here," the cop said.

Fitz pointed. "This guy's dead. He was choked to death between five-thirty and ten to six. How long's he lived here?"

"Only—a week. He paid a month in advance."

"Know anything about him?"

"No, sir. I didn't see him from the day he took it."

"Took what?"

"Why—the—this apartment."

Fitz settled on his heels, tossed off shortly: "Get in anybody living in apartments around and above and below this one. And you come back too."

Conkey was happily tearing apart the clothing on the floor.

Fitz jabbed Cardigan with a frank stare. "Are you sure this guy didn't tell you anything else?"

"Sure."

Fitz dropped his voice, dropped a glance toward the body. "Happen to know him?"

"Never saw him before."

"Why do you suppose he wanted you here?"

Cardigan shrugged. "You've got me, Fitz. I guess he was afraid of the dame."

"He didn't give her name?"

"No."

Conkey said cheerfully, "No labels in these duds, Fitz. There was though, once." He got up and went over and looked down at the twisted face. "Nope. I don't know him, either. Hey, here's a watch under his pillow."

He held up a big gold watch by a chain. He pried open the back of it and something fell out and fluttered to the floor. Conkey bent down and retrieved the picture of a girl. Patiently it had been sheared down, rounded, to fit the back of the watch.

"Not bad-looking," Conkey said. "Huh, Fitz?" He held it up and Fitz scowled at it.

CARDIGAN went into the room and looked innocently over Fitz's shoulder. Fitz glanced around at him.

"What makes you interested, Cardigan?"

"Conkey said she was good-looking."

Conkey said, beaming: "That picture ain't been in there long. It's new. You can see it's new." His mouth was wide open, grinning. His big pop-eyes sparkled.

There were voices in the living room and a cop said that some people had come in with the manager. Fitz strode briskly from the bedroom, struck at each new face with a swift, bitter glance.

He said: "There was a murder committed here between five-thirty and ten to six. Anbody hear anything?"

No one had. Fitz seemed angry. He whirled suddenly and drove a kick to the seat of a man who was training a camera through the bedroom doorway. The man turned around, grinned and tipped his hat.

"Sorry, lieutenant."

"Get the hell out!" Fitz bit off.

The news photographer went out with mincing steps.

Fitz turned back to the group. "Well, then, did anybody see anybody in the halls, or hear anybody about that time going up or down? Speak! Don't look scared, dammit—I'm not going to bite you!"

"Well," ventured a spinsterish little lady and paused to make a gentle curtsey.

"Well, madam?" said Fitz stonily.

"Well, I live directly beneath this apartment. I was coming in at about twenty to six. It was rather dark in the hall. So I had a time finding the keyhole and when I finally found it I saw a woman come down from this floor and go on down toward the lobby."

"What'd she look like?"

"Well, sir, the only thing I know was she was wearing mourning. There was half a veil hanging from her hat, and she was kind of tall, I would say. I mind I listened, rather fascinated, to the way her steps were going down the stairs—slow and measured kind of. I felt sorry for her, sir."

"You didn't see her face?"

"No, sir."

Fitz snapped: "Anybody else see this woman?"

There were negative movements of heads.

"You may go," Fitz clipped.

When they had gone Fitz said to the cop stationed at the door: "Close it—and if that photographer shows up again kick him in the face."

Cardigan buttoned his topcoat. "You know where to find me, Fitz, in case you want me."

Fitz chewed on his lip. "What do you think of this?"

"I'd say, offhand, that there's a killing widow loose in town."

Fitz said: "Mind if we look you over?"

Cardigan chuckled good-naturedly and held his arms out. Fitz searched his pockets, read the notation Cardigan had made in his office. Cardigan kept smiling down at Fitz's bony face. Fitz stepped back and eyed him levelly.

"O. K. I just wanted to make sure. It's funny as hell, the way this happened, the way you happened to be the first on the scene."

Conkey was grinning, showing most of his teeth clamped on a cigar. Cardigan looked from Conkey back to Fitz, chuckled briefly deep in his throat and strode to the door. He opened it and passed into the hall and went down the stairs slowly.

Halfway down, a fierce breath gushed out of his mouth and he raised a hand to his head, dropped the hand hopelessly. He covered the remainder of the steps with a savage, reckless gait; reached the cement terrace and stood for a moment in the blustering wind, looking up and down the dark street. He lit a cigarette and sloped to the sidewalk, caught a taxi at Vandeventer.

PAT leaned back against the door and laughed softly, gently—eyes twinkling. Cardigan glowered from the mohair divan in his apartment and said over a glass of rye and White Rock: "Clown around now, clown around."

"But you do look a perfect scream, chief."

There was a turkish towel rapped around his head. In the hidden folds of the towel was a quantity of chipped ice, to freeze away the pain. He looked quaintly oriental.

"Run into something?" Pat asked.

Back of the droll humor in her eyes was a spark of concern. Another woman might have exclaimed, run to him with tender hands. But Pat knew her men, knew, particularly, Cardigan. He was a hard party, hated to be fussed over.

"Maybe," he said, took a swallow, added: "Pardon me if I don't get up and kiss your little hand, madame. I might get the ice down my neck. . . . Well, some big bruiser—I couldn't figure him out—he took a swing at me."

He gave her the details. She sat on the edge of the divan, looked at empty dinner dishes on a card-table, and listened. Occasionally she said: "*M-m-m!*" or "My!" or used her lips or eyebrows to register surprise, concern.

"So that," Cardigan said, "is why we didn't dine and dance tonight. I walked into something all right."

"But don't you think you should have told Fitz about those two men?"

"Sure I should have. I should do a lot of things. But I didn't. Besides, those two guys didn't kill Bartles. Besides—" his eyelids lowered—"there's eighty thousand dollars worth of green ice floating around this man's town. Stolen, you can bet. Well, they pay rewards for stolen jools, Calamity Jane. And papa needs new shoes and a vacation from this lousy business and maybe he could salvage some of his stocks."

"Sure. But the home office might get peeved."

Cardigan said: "This is private business."

"O. K.," Pat said, shrugged. "You'd have your own way anyhow. And with that—" she indicated his head—"you're off to a swell start, I might add cattily."

"Maybe I'd give you a bauble or a gadget or something."

"Greeks bearing gifts. . ."

Cardigan chuckled lazily. "Good little woiking goil."

"Another forward pass like that and I'll smack you!"

Cardigan finished his drink, spread himself in a rousing grunt of satisfaction, and said: "Mind you, kid, keep what I've told you under your hat. There's a few guys in the office who'd break their necks to tattle-tale to the home office in the hopes of getting my job. The business is getting too big. Too many operatives. Too much—envy."

Pat made a little jaw. "I certainly know one—" She stopped short and sat silently.

"Huh?"

"Nothing."

"Tell papa."

"I'll mention no names."

Admiration lay drowsily in his eyes. "You're a natural, Pat," he said. "You're sure a natural."

POP-EYED Miss Gilligan was all of a-twitter when Cardigan pushed into the office next morning.

"Oh, Mr. Cardigan, you f-figured in a m-murder again, oh!"

Cardigan mocked the magisterial. "Please don't put it that way, Miss Gilligan."

"Did the p-poor man suf-suffer?"

Miss Gilligan was not ordinarily a stammerer, but headlines invariably knocked her askew. She was a good-hearted, unlovely, faithful secretary.

"Any wires?" Cardigan said.

"N-no, sir."

He entered his private office, taking off his big overcoat, hung it with his battered hat on a costumer in the corner. Morris Katz came and stood in the doorway leading to the operatives' room. He was tall, dark, with sliding hazel eyes, polished ebony hair, and arresting clothes.

"Greetings or condolences?" he droned languidly.

Cardigan said: "Good morning, Katz," and sat down at his desk.

"Who was this Bartles?"

"Bartles—that's all."

"What's all this crap in the papers about a mysterious widow?"

Cardigan said: "Just what it says," and became absorbed in the morning mail. His back was to Katz. His hair, so black, thick and bushy, hid the bump on his head.

Katz remained leaning in the doorway, a striking figure of a man in his dark, polished hardness. The agency used him a lot at formal dances, dinner parties and big social and political functions.

"Was there really a widow?"

"There was a widow," Cardigan said, "in the building at the time. A woman in mourning."

"Talkative, aren't you, this morning?"

Cardigan turned down a letter. "Aren't you on that Willis job, Katz?"

"Sort of."

"Then get the hell on it. There's no special privileges around here."

"I get you. Only concerning the *femme*, huh?"

Cardigan rose, turned and crossed the room and regarded Katz with candid malevolence. "Watch that tongue of yours."

Katz showed even white teeth in a crooked brazen smile. "You wouldn't be getting tough, would you?"

"I happen to be running this shebang. Get on the job."

Katz shrugged, dropped his sliding eyes and went back into the big room. He came out wearing a tan polo coat and a secret little smirk. He walked quietly on soft leather soles. From the back he had an athlete's build. Vanishing, he left an aromatic odor of Turkish tobacco.

At ten Miss Gilligan announced that Sergeant Conkey was calling, and a moment later Conkey's round face appeared in the doorway—beaming as usual, with eyebrows halfway up his forehead, eyes bursting with bright wonder, and mouth grinning and pushing up fat cheeks into bloated red balls. He came toward the desk in a hunch like a bear's, palms pressed to his sides; then he shot one hand outward as if executing a rare trick in magic.

"Good morning to you, Cardigan!"

Always a little baffled by this man's hocus-pocus, Cardigan shook hands casually and said, "To you, sergeant."

"Ah!" Conkey exclaimed as if receiving a great favor. His voice was no voice at all but a rushing hoarse whisper which he somehow managed to freight with wonder and mystery.

Cardigan hooked a heel on an open drawer of his desk and watched Conkey sit down opposite.

CHAPTER THREE

Big Man—Little Man

CONKEY said: "Fitz thought I ought to drop in and see if anything turned up since last night." Eyes shimmered, mouth grinned in eager anticipation.

"Not a thing, Conkey."

Conkey aimed a finger joyously at Cardigan. "Who do think Bartles was?" He raised his hand, put thumb against second finger and held the forefinger rigidly straight.

"Dunno, Conkey."

Conkey snapped his fingers. "No sooner was his picture in the papers this morning than a gent named Hardin calls up from Cleverly Hotel and says Bartles looked like one of four guys that held up his jewelry store in Indianapolis two months ago. We get Hardin over at the morgue and he says Bartles not only looks like the guy but is the guy."

"There's a break for you," Cardigan said.

Conkey exclaimed: "Ain't it!"

"Sure is."

Conkey rubbed his hands together slowly and put shining, merry eyes on Cardigan. "And so a guy who lives in a house back of the Western Arms calls up and says about six last night he was putting his car in his garage. He seen two guys come out the basement door o' the Western Arms. One's little and one's big. Big, little—see? And these guys stand for a couple minutes and then go away. So, reading in the paper this morning about the murder, he calls up."

"That's interesting."

"Ain't it!" His eyes bubbled. "Fitz was wondering, since you got there before six, Fitz was wondering didn't you maybe scare away two guys."

Cardigan leaned back, clasped hands behind his head. "If I did, I didn't see them."

Conkey looked almost ridiculously coy. "Fitz thought maybe you saw them but didn't link it up with anything."

"No."

Conkey darted out a finger. "That's what I said! I told Fitz that if you saw them, you'd sure as hell tell us; you wouldn't let a thing like that slip your mind. That's what I told Fitz. I said, 'Hell, Fitz, Cardigan wouldn't forget a thing like that.' That's what I said."

The way he leaned forward, with mouth and eyes eager, gave the impression that he was hard of hearing and trying to read lips.

"How about that widow?" Cardigan asked.

"Great possibility! 'Sure,' Allison from The Globe-Herald said, 'Make it a widow. Better headlines, better story. Go ahead, you guys, make it a widow.' But finding now this Mr. Hardin from Indianapolis and the guy that says he saw—"

A door banged. The inner connecting door burst open and Pat came in, flushed and out of breath. The presence of another in the office besides Cardigan whipped her up short. She appeared like a flame suddenly blown tall and thin and congealed and her teeth bit into her lip and the red color of her face deepened. Something struggled valiantly in her eyes and her lips started to twitch as she felt she had to say something and didn't quite know what.

So she said, breathless: "How—how is your hurt head this morning?"

The fleeting look on Cardigan's face gave the impression that he felt like a man with a bridge suddenly giving way beneath him.

But he said. "Swell . . . Now I don't want to have you busting in here late every day, but if you keep on running to work like that something'll happen to you."

She gasped: "I—I'm sorry."

Cardigan became gruffly formal. "That's O. K. Don't let it happen again. And don't try to wash things up by asking about my health. I'm busy. Please . . ." He nodded toward the big operatives' room.

She made a meek little bow and disappeared.

Cardigan, frowning, moved about some objects on his desk and said: "Women, women, Conkey—especially in this kind of a business."

All of Conkey's face was toned down to a shallow, softly radiating expression of mirth and bafflement. He looked at the door Pat had closed behind her. He looked at the ceiling, at the wall, at various objects in the room. Then his face went blank—like a light snuffed out—and an instant later was beaming again, joyous and cheerful and buoyant.

"Hope you weren't hurt too bad, Cardigan."

Cardigan said: "When people build doorways high enough for guys like me, I guess I'll stop cracking the old dome."

Conkey bounced to his feet like a heavy rubber ball, put his palms on his sides and then shot his right hand forward. "Well, been a pleasant little call, Cardigan."

"Any time, sergeant," Cardigan said, rising and shaking hands.

"You know Fitz, always shooting me around to bother folks. Hope I ain't bothered you. Fitz is all right, but you know Fitz. Come around for pinochle sometimes, Cardigan."

He swivelled like a squat turret and went out with a heavy, bounding tread, humming an air of *Pagliacci*. He left behind him in that room a weird admixture of carnival mirth, side-show cunning, that left Cardigan high and dry as to what it was all about.

Cardigan clipped a short, exasperated oath between teeth that clicked. He turned and looked at the closed door leading to the big room. He went to the other door and opened it and saw Miss Gilligan in violent combat with the typewriter. He closed the door, crossed the room and sat on the desk.

"Pat," he called.

MUCH of the flush had gone from her face when she reappeared. There was evidence that she had touched up with puff and lipstick. A black hat with a pert little brim was raked becomingly over one ear.

"So I pulled a boner," she said.

"Outside of that, what did you pull?" He flipped open a plain cedarwood box. "Smoke?"

"Never before breakfast and toothbrush."

"Been out all night?"

She dropped to a chair and wagged her head. "And was it a night, milord—was it a night! Look at my shoes. I walked."

"Serves you right."

"What a big help you are to come home to. I feel as if I want to put my head on your shoulder and weep—and tell all."

"Cut out the clowning."

She settled back and looked gravely at him. "When I left you last night I walked out of your apartment house and heard footsteps coming down the front walk back of me. When I turned a chap took me by the arm. I said, 'Pul-lease!' and he said, quite to the point: 'You got a date, sister.' I said: 'With you?' He said: 'No. With this gat in my pocket— if you try any shenanigans.' So I went along with him and we were joined by a big fellow and then we all hopped in a car and I was blindfolded and we drove off. Miles. At least it felt like miles."

Cardigan didn't exclaim. He kept regarding her with intense, narrowed eyes.

She said: "I was hustled into a house, into a room. The blindfold was removed —and there I was! In a beastly room, all smelly and simply frightful. And there were the two chaps, the big one and the little one. I was so mad I forgot to be frightened.

"It seems they'd tailed you to your apartment when you left the scene of the murder. The little one hid in the linen room obliquely across from your door. The other one waited at the car. The little one had hoped you'd come out again. Instead, I went in—he saw me—and he saw me come out half an hour later and took it into his head that I was your moll and tailed me. What I get for knowing folks like you."

"They hurt you?"

She pulled up a sleeve, showed some black and blue marks. "Only these—some very crude arm-twisting—and I'll tell you I'll bet I kicked holes in their shins."

"The mutts," he growled.

"So they swore high up and low down that you killed Bartles, that I was your moll and that they'd kill you if I didn't tell all. Whereupon I said: 'First you'll have to find him.' Well, that brought the house down and brought on the arm-twisting. A little later—it really hurt— I passed out."

Cardigan smacked fist into palm.

"But wait," Pat said. "When I came to, the room was deserted. The door was locked. I was up three stories, couldn't jump. I tried the lock with a hairpin. No go. I turned up the mattress, forced one of the little circular springs from the bed-spring, twisted it to a shape I wanted and tried the lock again. It took me ten minutes to open the door and I used the back of my little nail file to take four screws from the snap lock on the hall door. And so out."

A glimmer of admiration in Cardigan's eyes was followed by: "Swell, kid— swell!"

"I got the number of the house and

when I got to the first corner I got the name of the street. 205 Ellsworth. By this time dawn was breaking. There were no taxies, no street cars. So I began walking and then I got sick and sat down in a doorway and like a fool I began crying. An old Italian woman opened the door and she made me come in and gave me a drink and I was dizzy and sick and went to sleep. So when I woke up I walked again and found a street car and got off when I saw the first taxi and took it and here I am."

Cardigan grumbled: "Poor kid," and regarding her gravely, his thatchlike eyebrows shadowing his eyes.

"That was Sergeant Conkey, wasn't it?" she asked.

"Yeah."

"I'm sorry, chief."

"Forget it. Only Conkey has something up his sleeve. He put on a fine act here. He gets me, that guy does. I always expect him to pull rabbits or something out of his hat. They know who Bartles is— or was. It was a jewel-store stick-up in Indianapolis."

"Really!"

Cardigan nodded and went dejectedly to the window where he stood, spread-legged, staring down into Olive Street. A scowl began to overshadow his face, his lips tightened and then curled in a wintry, sardonic smile.

Conkey and Morris Katz were standing on the corner, talking.

CARDIGAN lunched in the Clevely Coffee Shop, then climbed into a taxi and said: "Ellsworth and Hale," and settled back with a dappled cigar. The sky was overcast, the air muggy and motionless. Sounds reechoed with a dull, heavy clarity, as in a fog. Street cars slambanged over switches and trucks came up like thunder out of side streets. Neon lights scrawled red script in the gloom.

Far over on the South Side Hale Street crossed Ellsworth and Cardigan got out and stood on the corner watching the taxi disappear. A block north an old brewery reared forlornly. Squat, dumpy houses crowded each other in a galaxy of colors, heights and stages of decay.

Cardigan turned down Ellsworth. The street was shoddy, quiet. A rusty garbage can, overturned and empty, gave the impression that everybody in the street had packed up and gone away. 205 Ellsworth was a narrow frame house with a door flush with the cracked sidewalk. The windows of its three stories were shattered.

Cardigan used a gloved hand to try the knob and miraculously the door swung open. Something scraped on the floor. It was the black snap lock that Pat had unscrewed. Cardigan closed the door and stood for a moment in the dim, musty hallway. Presently he groped his way till he found the staircase. He climbed slowly, a step at a time, and paused on the first landing. Hearing no sound, he moved and found the second staircase and climbed to the top.

There was a door slightly ajar. He drew his gun and swung the door open. Light filtered in from a dirty window. The room was empty. The mattress of a bed had been removed to the floor. Obviously this was the room in which Pat had been detained. He retired quietly and moved down the hall. In another room, a larger one, he found six five-gallon crocks of mash. In another room he found a still. A third room was empty of anything but dust.

He went down the staircase to the second floor and stood for a moment in perplexed indecision. Then he moved and his groping hand found a door, groped until it found a knob which he turned slowly. The door gave. A glow of wan daylight hung outside the horizontal blinds of dark shutters but did not penetrate the room.

His knee struck something and there was a slight metallic squeak. A bed-spring. He pulled a match from his pocket, struck it on a thumb nail and watched the glow spread to a wide-eyed face on the bed. He blew the match out abruptly and breathed quickly once or twice. He moved and swung his arm in an arc above his head, over and over, until a chain rattled against glass. He pulled the chain and light flooded the room.

There were two beds in the room. On each bed lay a dead man. One was big, burly, the contour of his head and shoulders was similar to that of the big man who had cracked him in Bartles' apartment. The smaller man's mouth was slack showing broken teeth. On each man's throat were fingermarks.

Cardigan's heavy brown features froze in a grimace that lasted a long minute. He put his hands in his overcoat pockets and stood looking vaguely around the room. Presently he crossed to an old roll-top desk. There was a sheet of paper on which figures had been scrawled, added at the bottom making a total of $243.50. In a pigeon-hole was a batch of papers: advertisements of various kinds of malt, flavoring, a Burlington time-table, a clipping from a magazine setting forth the advantages of Wildflower Hair Tonic and another advertising a full set of false teeth—former price twenty-five dollars, reduced to nineteen-fifty. A pamphlet entitled, *How to Win the Girl of Your Dreams,* a speakeasy address in Columbus, Ohio, a magazine picture of Clara Bow, a pink handbill, slightly yellow, advertising *The Vagabond Road Show,* on the lower half of which were photographs of a man and a girl: Vantura & Arline, Famous Acrobats.

"*Um,*" mumbled Cardigan.

Arline was the same girl whose picture

Conkey had found in the back of Bartles' watch.

Cardigan folded the handbill and stuffed it into his pocket, returned the other papers to the pigeon-hole. He pivoted and regarded the two dead men on the bed. He took slow steps across the room and stopped short when he heard a sound from the hallway. His right hand plunged into his pocket, came out gripping his gun.

He watched the half-open door. He saw a hand holding a gun come into the shaft of light that escaped the room. He moved to one side and his jaw hardened.

"Hello, chief," Katz said and lowered his gun.

CHAPTER FOUR

Katz Cuts In—And Out

CARDIGAN went to the doorway and stood looking stonily at Katz. Katz put his hands in his pocket and stood rocking easily on his heels and waving the skirt of his long tan polo coat.

"Thought you might need help, chief."

Cardigan put away his gun and lifted his hard brown jaw, opened the door wide and said: "How's your stomach, Katz?"

Katz saw the dead men on the bed and drew a secret little smirk across his lips, leaving his handsome white teeth bared.

"Dead, I take it."

"Smart, you are," C a r d i g a n said. "Smart-alecky."

Katz acknowledged this with a raised eyebrow, sauntered into the room, looked idly at each of the dead men and then glanced negligently about the room. He walked to a chair, sat down and hung a long leg over one knee.

"Cute," he said.

Cardigan muttered: "What's on your mind?"

"Fifty per cent."

"I thought maybe you'd want eighty."

"No use being sarcastic, Cardigan."

Cardigan snapped: "You dirty cake-eater, you can go to hell!"

"Can I?" droned Katz, smiling. "You wouldn't be talking out of turn, would you?" He folded his arms, revealing a strap-watch held to his wrist by gold links. "You can't waltz me around, chief. There's dough in this and I'm going to horn in for a cozy slice of it."

"Yeah . . . and where's the dough?"

"That, mastermind, I leave to you."

"I see. I go around taking the chances, maybe get it, maybe not—and if I do, you get fifty-fifty."

"Precisely."

"What a belly laugh I get out o' that!" Cardigan put his hands on his stomach, then took them away, made fists and jammed the fists into his pockets. His face became overshadowed and lowering and a dull, malignant fire glowed in his eyes. "You heard me, you cheap tinhorn. You heard me. Ixnay. Nix." He opened one fist and sliced his hand through the air. "Nix!"

Katz stood up, tall and lean and smoothly hard, his satin-dark jaw gleaming. His voice droned: "You thick Irish tramp, if you have to report this to the cops, they'll wonder how come you happened to find these guys. Just as how come you found Bartles. They'll know these mugs."

"Who," Cardigan intoned dully, "says I have to report this to the cops?"

Katz tapped his own chest. "I do—me. I do unless I get a fifty per cent rake-off. By God, there's dough in this and you're not going to hog it!"

"This is not an agency job, Katz. The agency has to stay out of it. I stumbled into this and I'm not asking anybody to take chances with me. It's a rough go. There've been three murders inside of twenty-four hours and—"

"I'm not taking chances, Cardigan—not me. I'm standing by, marking time. You're taking the chances. I'm not even going to get my feet wet. I'm going to watch you."

Cardigan said, scarce above a whisper: "What a sweet stinking rat you turned out to be. Well—" his voice banged suddenly—"to hell with you!"

"To hell with me—and I wise the cops. They'll find these stiffs before the day's out—but I'll wise them beforehand who found them."

"I said—to hell with you."

Katz warned: "Conkey's no fool. I told Conkey I'd keep an eye on you."

"You heard what I said."

Katz inhaled, walked to the desk and picked up the telephone. He held it before him reluctant to raise the receiver. "Think it over, Cardigan. Think fast. We can get a big rake-off out of this. There's fifteen per cent of eighty thousand for the guy that gets those emeralds. Half an' half of that, Cardigan—"

"Half and half of hell! What I said stands!"

"Thick, stubborn and Irish, eh?"

"Thick, stubborn and Irish," Cardigan said.

Katz said: "O. K.," and took off the receiver.

IRRITABLE, moody-eyed, Fitz entered the room with quick, short steps, looked at the bodies on the bed and went to the closer of the two. Conkey bounded heavily through the doorway, threw his stomach out, sneezed violently. Fitz half turned and scowled irritably.

"Pepper," Conkey said, and winked.

Fitz rasped matter-of-factly: "Same thing as Bartles. Choked."

Uniformed policemen circulated and the coroner's man came in jauntily, said: "*Tsk! Tsk!*" and pranced over beside Fitz.

Fitz stood up and his face jerked into tight, sarcastic lines. "It's beginning to be a source of wonder to me, Cardigan, how the living hell you manage to be first on the scene of every murder in this town."

Conkey exclaimed: "'S marvelous, ain't it!" and beamed.

"Shut up," Fitz clipped shortly.

The coroner's man said: "Simple strangulation. No! I think chloroform was used first. Indeed! But not—not on the other fellow. You know—what's his name—Bottles."

"Bartles," Conkey said.

"Oh, yes—oh, yes—Bartley."

"Well?" snapped Fitz, looking hard and bitter at Cardigan.

Cardigan stirred. "Well, here it is: Miss Seaward, my operative, was kidnaped last night when she left my apartment. I didn't know it until she turned up in my office this morning. She said two men had waylaid her, blindfolded her and taken her away. She was beaten; she fainted. When she came to she pried her way out of the room on the top floor, pried her way out of the hall door below—at about dawn. She was sick and didn't get back to the office until late. She remembered the address. I came out here to get tough and found these bodies. Katz, here, thinking I was going into danger, covered me."

"How long did it take you to make up that story?" Fitz asked.

"About a minute—since you came in here."

"Don't be funny."

"I'm not. What the hell do you want me to do, break down and get dramatic?"

Conkey chirped, gleefully: "These are the guys all right! Arnie Oldham and George Beef Cunarko! That's three! Then there's the jane and a guy named Doke. Bless my soul—"

"All right, all right," Fitz cut in irritably.

A cop poked in, said: "There's mash and a still upstairs."

Conkey dived down between the two beds like a hippo and came up, staggering but beaming, and holding a charred cigarette. "See! Rouge on it, too! Holy Moses, I'd hate to have a jane like that!"

Fitz took the butt from him, examined it beneath the light, then tucked it away in his wallet and bent exasperated eyes on Cardigan.

"This crime links up with the Bartles one. It's queer as hell how you happened to be on both."

"I explained, didn't I?"

"What did they kidnap the woman for?"

"She didn't stay long enough to find out. I imagine they wanted her as hostage, hoping to get out of me some information. Maybe they thought Bartles had engaged me already and I knew a lot. Something like that, anyhow."

Conkey exploded in an uproar of mirth. "How's the hurt on your head, Cardigan?"

"Swell."

Conkey pawed g l e e f u l l y at Fitz's sleeve and bubbled: "Yeah, Cardigan's got a hurt on his head. He said—ho! ho!—it was a door! Bless my soul!"

Katz looked askance at Cardigan and Fitz crossed the room and stopped very close to Cardigan.

Fitz said crisply: "I don't like monkeyshines, Cardigan."

"I never liked them myself—"

"Cut it!"

Cardigan knew good metal when he saw it. He knew Fitz. This lean, moody, rasp-voiced man was nobody's fool.

Cardigan said: "I told you what, Fitz. Whether you take it or leave it there's nothing you can do about it. Maybe you think I know who murdered Bartles and these two guys. I don't. I swear by God that—right now—I don't know. Conkey —bless my soul—thinks a bump on my head means something. And what about that? . . . I came here to bust two guys who gave Miss Seaward a rough deal. I found them dead."

Fitz looked at Katz. "What about you?"

"I covered him up."

Cardigan glanced quizzically at Katz and Conkey rocked hugely on his heels and pawed happily at his jowls.

The coroner's man said: "These men have been dead about twelve hours or so."

Fitz, swallowing, looked bitterly at Cardigan and said: "I'd like to do something to you, Cardigan."

"Only call your shots, Fitz. That badge you wear don't make you God."

"You can't lone-wolf it in this man's town."

"When I can't," Cardigan said, "tell me."

"I'm telling you now!"

Cardigan smiled. "You ought to know by this time, Fitz, that I'm no pushover."

HE BUTTONED his coat, yanked his hat lower and strode to the door. He plunged down the stairs and walked up Ellsworth. When he was nearing Hale he heard footfalls and saw Katz following. He stopped at the corner and kept baleful eyes on Katz while the latter drew nearer.

"You smell, Katz. You play both ends against the middle—you and me against Conkey and Fitz, or you and Conkey against Fitz."

"Any means toward an end. Dough in my pocket is as good as it is in yours."

"Only it won't ever be in yours."

"So says you."

"You don't rate, Katz. You're small change and you're all spent. If I catch you on my tail again I'll cave in those pretty teeth of yours."

He pivoted and strode off.

When he barged into his office carrying three newspapers, Miss Gilligan fluttered.

"Oh, I'm g-glad you're back safe."

"What now?"

"Oh, I just had a f-feeling."

He grinned, said: "That's a nice dress you have on," and went on into his private office.

Pat said: "I found out finally that that Maloney girl has been robbing the till at that restaurant for three months to support a drunken brother."

"O. K.," Cardigan said. "Write the report out in full and I'll sign it and shoot it to our client. . . . Well, there's been another murder—two."

"Where?"

"Where you spent the night."

"Oh-oh."

"The two guys who kidnaped you. And Katz—well, Katz is trying to bust into big time. The dirty louse tried to bargain with me and I told him where to get off."

"How were they killed?"

Cardigan held up his hands and looked at her.

She said: "Doesn't this put you in a tough spot?"

"Kind of—but I like it. Go ahead and make that report up. I'm busy."

She left the room, regarding him over her shoulder. He began turning sheets of one paper, scanning the columns closely. He finished with it and started on the second, turning sheet after sheet until finally his forefinger settled on an advertisement. He took shears from a drawer, made two slices upward, one across, lifting a column a foot long. He cut off ten inches of this, retained the smaller portion, leaned back and studied it reflectively, then slipped it into his vest pocket.

For five minutes he sat motionless, his fingers interlocked, stormy shadows moving in his eyes. Then he slapped a palm on the desk and called: "Miss Gilligan!"

She appeared in the doorway with a notebook.

"Take a letter."

"Oh, yes, sir."

"Address it to me, the Cosmos Agency, and so forth, dear sir. All right. 'Dear Sir: I hereby tender my resignation, under the above date. Trusting you will accept, I remain.' That's all. Draw a check to Morris Katz for—" he figured on a pad "—twenty-seven-fifty. I'll sign it."

"That's all?"

"That's all."

When Katz sauntered in, an hour later, Cardigan pointed and said, offhand: "Sign that."

Katz leaned on his arms, read the letter, looked at Cardigan. "Funny, aren't you?"

"Sign it or I'll fire you."

"Like hell I'll sign it."

Cardigan reached over, removed the clip which attached the check to the letter and slapped the check down. "O. K. Have it your way. You're fired."

"Now just a minute, big boy—"

"Shut up!" Cardigan rose ominously, pointed to the check. "Take that and get to hell out of my office before I throw you out!"

"Why you lousy Irish—"

Cardigan's fist arced briefly, hit Katz on the jaw, drove him reeling across the room. Katz struck the connecting door. The square glass panel fell out with a crash and Miss Gilligan yelped from the outer office. As Katz rose Cardigan crowded him.

"Now get, you poaching, two-timing punk."

Katz straightened, brushed glass splinters from his sleeve, adjusted his hat. His eyes glittered and his lips were drawn tightly across his teeth.

"O. K.," he breathed, turned, went out.

Cardigan said: "Miss Gilligan, write out a new check and deduct two-fifty for the glass panel Mr. Katz broke."

"Y-y-yes, sir."

"And mail to his hotel."

Pat, standing in the other door, said: "You weren't by any chance steamed up, were you?"

"Was I!"

CHAPTER FIVE

The Killing Widow

A WARM autumn rain fell, more like a mist, making a shimmering halo around street lights. Auto lights drove long beams down wet macadam and rubber tires made a sucking, swishing sound. People scurried like leaves before a fall wind.

Halfway down a narrow, gloomy street electric bulbs blinked their announcement on and off.

B
U
R
L
E
S
Q
U
E

The usual crowd hung around the lobby: down-at-the heel clerks, red-faced laborers, very young men and very old, sly-eyed men and self-conscious men.

Cardigan pushed through, ignored the ticket window, said to the man at the inner entrance: "I want to see Finkleberg."

"Way up and—"

"I know."

He climbed two flights of stairs and went down a narrow corridor toward a door marked 'Manager.' He knocked and pushed in. A fat, white, flabby-eared man sat reflecting over a cigar.

"Hello, Barney."

"Hello, Cardigan. How's business?"

"Jake."

"With me it's lousy. Don't sit down, the chair's dusty."

Cardigan grinned. "Say, Barney, O. K. if I go backstage tonight?"

Barney smirked. "I didn't think you went in for them dames."

"I'm funny that way."

"But don't say I didn't warn you."

Cardigan said: "What kind of a show is this?"

"Terrible! *Ach, du lieber!* The comedians; the gels are like elephants only not so goot; and the only thing worth admission is a couple of ackerbats . . . I'll phone back you're the King of England."

Cardigan went downstairs to the foyer, walked down a side aisle, back of a box and climbed three steps to a narrow door. Backstage the property manager shook hands limply and wandered away mournfully.

Faded girls stood in groups and chattered. A magician stood alone and aloof like a man in a trance. Two comedians kept calling each other vile names. A singer got temperamental with the orchestra leader and kicked him, and the orchestra leader made a pass at her and was stopped by a blackface. A director appeared and swore violently and the chorus got into formation.

The show started.

Then Cardigan saw the girl—tall, slim, muscular. The man with her was quite as tall, but pale. He was not the man whose picture Cardigan had seen on the handbill. They did their turn about half an hour after the show started. The stage was dark but a spotlight followed them. It was marvelous the way the girl tossed the man about. She had strong arms. The audience cheered and the pair did an encore, took two more bows and then went backstage where they stood with arms folded. They did not mingle with the others. The girl never smiled; she was almost pretty.

Cardigan hung around till the show was almost over, then slipped out the stage entrance and waited. Ten minutes later the crowd surged out. The lights went out. Then the first of the performers appeared; in a few minutes, the girl. Her partner was with her and the girl did not wear mourning.

Cardigan followed. A couple of blocks farther on the pair stopped, conversed in low tones. The man turned right and disappeared and the girl kept on. The street was dark and deserted. Cardigan's legs moved faster, and soon he was close behind the girl, then abreast of her.

"Keep walking, sister."

She looked sidewise, startled.

"Keep walking. There's a gun in my pocket."

She looked straight ahead and kept walking.

Cardigan said: "To your hotel, to your room."

"What is this?" she breathed hoarsely.

"Keep walking and keep shut and take the stairway when we reach your hotel. One move and it will be too bad."

A block farther on she turned into the lobby of a run-down hotel. Cardigan held her arm and walked very close to her. She kept looking straight ahead and they climbed a staircase together. Climbed four flights and went down a hallway where floorboards creaked. Past a red fire-exit light to a brown door with cracked paint on it.

The girl took a key from her purse. He watched her hand and saw how white and smooth and strong it looked. She inserted the key in the lock and Cardigan got close behind her.

"I don't get you," she said.

"You will."

She opened the door and there was a light burning in the room. She stamped her foot.

A man stirred on a bed, blinked open his eyes, muttered: *"Huh?"*

Cardigan gave the woman a push in the back and sent her staggering. He covered the man on the bed. The man's eyes gaped and he rose to his elbows. He was dressed in pants and an athletic undershirt. He was slim but muscles rippled in his arms.

"What the hell!"

The woman stood stockstill, white-faced. Not a muscle twitched. She seemed cool as ice.

Cardigan closed the door.

The man was wide awake now. "Who's this?"

"How should I know?" the woman said tonelessly.

"I'm bad news," Cardigan said. "You," he snapped, as the woman moved, "stay where you are!"

It was awkward for the man on the bed to rest on his elbows so he lay back again, the head of the bed propping his head forward. His face was white naturally, the skin seemed transparent over the framework and the eyes were large and moist.

"Now, then," Cardigan said, dangling manacles. "You, Arline, raise your right hand." He got behind her, watching the man on the bed, and clipped one of the bracelets on her wrist. He prodded her to the head of the bed and said: "Now stick that arm between two of those vertical bars. O. K. Now you, mister, clamp that empty bracelet to your right wrist."

"Say—"

"Clamp it!"

Cardigan watched the bracelet enclose the wrist, then made sure that the manacles were locked. He stepped back and regarded the man and the woman. Neither could move from the bed. He went to the door and locked it and pulled down the window shades.

The man on the bed snarled: "Say—"

"Shut up."

Cardigan crossed to a closet, began tossing out clothes and presently appeared holding a black hat with veil attached and a dress of deep mourning.

"Bartles, Oldham and Cunarko," he said significantly and flung the widow's weeds on a chair. "You have nice strong hands, Arline. Who was Vantura?"

"My husb—" She stopped and tightened her hueless lips.

"So—your husband. Once of the team of Arline and Vantura of The Vagabond Road Show. Died—when?"

The man on the bed said: "What is this, what is this?" in a snarly, petulant voice.

Cardigan pointed. "And you . . . Doke?"

The woman gasped; the man's face blanched.

Cardigan said heavily, and yet playfully: "Just before Bartles was murdered a woman in mourning was seen leaving the house where he lived. In the back of his watch police found a picture of you—Arline."

"Me!"

"Little you. In the house where Oldham and Cunarko were found murdered was also found an old handbill showing pictures of you and your late team-mate —and husband. Two and two equals— something. Emeralds. Lifted in Indianapolis two months ago. At the scene of each murder was found a smoked cigarette with lip rouge on it. I'm pleased to meet the killing widow."

He put his gun in his pocket, crossed to a bureau and pulled out all the drawers. He rifled clothes, boxes. He ransacked all the clothes he had taken from the closet. He lit into a wardrobe trunk and turned it into a shambles. He opened and searched a valise and two handbags.

STANDING finally amid the chaos he said: "Maybe you get the idea that I want those emeralds."

The man cried: "You're crazy! Who are you?"

"I'm not crazy and I'm a private shamus to you. And I want those emeralds. They were stolen from Bartles. He was murdered. Cunarko and Oldham were murdered because they had a share in the loot. You don't turn them over and I'll sic the cops on you. Turn 'em over and I'll spring one of you but I've got to have one to chuck to the cops. Come on—start figuring. You, Arline, did the job but maybe Doke here is a big-hearted guy and will take the rap. Come, Doke, how's to?"

"I'll take no rap! You can go to hell!"

"No? O. K. Then it's the jane. Act fast. Come on. Where the hell are those emeralds?"

The man's mouth began working.

He choked: "In the bathroom—buried in a jar of cold cream."

Cardigan went around the foot of the bed, into the bathroom. When he reappeared he held six emeralds, smeared with cold cream, in his hand.

The man cried: "Come on, you! Come on, lemme go now!"

"You can't," the woman told Cardigan. "Because I have an alibi. I was rehearsing the afternoon Bartles was killed. Thirty people can prove it. Doke killed Bartles and Oldham and Cunarko. He wore my weeds. Bartles trusted me but nobody else, but I didn't think a hell of a lot of him. He was supposed to have an 'in' with a good fence but the guy was out of town. The other guys got the idea he was trying to frame them because he didn't turn the deal. But he was waiting. Doke here was most impatient of all. Bartles went down with the grippe and got scared and wouldn't let any of them in. Doke's a ventriloquist. He telephoned Bartles, imitated my voice and wanted to see Bartles about his grippe. Bartles always had a crush on me but not me on him. Doke knew it. So Bartles fell for it and Doke dressed in my weeds while I was out and went. I'd stopped wearing them three days before that but Bartles didn't know it. So Doke went and did him in.

"I threw a fit when I heard of it but Doke promised me fifty-fifty and I was tired of this two-a-day and fell for that. So then he finished off Oldham and Cunarko. I had no hand in it."

Cardigan said: "But Bartles made a phone call to me."

"That was Doke trying to make it seem more certain that a woman did it. You can't spring him, mister. And you're not going to spring me, either. I'll take it on the button but I can get in the clear. I'll stay right here. So will Doke—the rat!"

"Listen, you!" Doke cried to Cardigan. "Lemme go! You gotta lemme go!"

Cardigan said, bluntly: "I can't. And if I'm ratting on you it's the first time I've ever ratted on any guy. But I don't think I'm ratting. You'll have to fight it out with the court between you—"

Winded and moaning, Doke relaxed.

Cardigan went to the telephone and said, when police headquarters answered: "Send a couple of dicks over to the Rice Hotel, room 509 . . . Cardigan . . . The guy that killed Bartles and Cunarko and Oldham."

"O God!" Doke moaned.

"Oh, hell," the woman said, "shut up!"

Cardigan made another call. "Hello, Pat . . . Cut out yawning . . . Baubles and gadgets and things . . . Yeah, happy ending. Tell you tomorrow. Goomby."

Coming Next Month—Another Great Cardigan Adventure by Frederick Nebel

MURDER Digs its GRAVE

"Hand it over," he snarled. "And don't move or I'll kill you!"

by
Maxwell Hawkins

Author of "The Corpse in Row 2," etc.

Deep down beneath that old vegetable cellar there lay a mouldering corpse. And close beside it, in the cobwebbed gloom, a secret silent witness lurked—waiting to rise and confront the murderer with his horrid crime.

A SINGLE electric light globe cast feeble eerie beams on the cob-webbed joists and dust-filled bins of the vegetable cellar.

As Sim Dorsey, his colorless lips compressed into a hard line, patted the dirt floor carefully with a spade, his stooping figure made a weird shadow that danced across the ground and melted into the gloom beyond the bins.

Occasionally he stopped to cock a listening ear toward the upper part of the house. At such times his shifty eyes moved stealthily back and forth beneath his heavy brows. Once he glided to the narrow window, set close to the ceiling, in order to make sure that the piece of sacking which covered it was firmly fastened.

Placing the spade against the wall, he stomped about on the slightly elevated mound until he had reduced it to the level of the rest of the ground. Again he worked with the spade, spreading the dirt around evenly. Afterward he dragged the whole floor with a heavy gunny sack.

At one time the sack had held potatoes. Now it was filled with the clay soil that had recently occupied the space where his wife's body lay.

At last Dorsey paused and, resting the spade on a bin, dusted his hands softly together. He surveyed the result of his work with a critical eye and smiled—a harsh ghastly smile. He was satisfied.

No one would suspect that the long-unused vegetable room had been converted into a secret burial place.

He lugged the heavy gunny sack into the furnace room which adjoined. Returning, he obliterated all traces of footprints. Then he pulled out his handkerchief and wiped the handle and shank of the spade. He was taking no chance of having any tell-tale impressions of his fingers left behind to accuse him.

When he had closed and locked the thick door of the strange crypt, after first turning out the light, Dorsey stood for a few minutes deep in thought beside the furnace. Finally he picked up the bag of dirt and carried it to the kitchen above.

He dumped the contents patiently into the sink and let the water carry the soil down the drain. That was better, he decided, than to have a pile of fresh dirt in the small rear yard. It might excite suspicion, even be traced to its source. And packing the sack above the streets in search of another place would be risky.

Dorsey was cool and deliberate in all his actions. There was no hurry now. No one, he felt certain, would be apt to call at this late hour in the evening, and presently he could start searching the old fashioned two-story frame dwelling until he found what he was after.

It had not been part of his original plan to kill Jenny. But now that it was done, he suffered no remorse. She had no business defying him, he told himself. No business trying to keep the money from him.

Even that wouldn't have provoked him to violence, if she hadn't threatened to have her brother Nate deal with him when he attempted to force her to disclose the hiding place.

At the thought of Nate Todd, Dorsey's sagging jowls quivered and he frowned till his low-growing hair seemed almost to meet his thick brows.

Sim Dorsey had married Jenny only because of the money she had inherited from her first husband. By constant argument and suggestion he finally had prevailed on her to convert all her resources into cash. He cited the numerous bank failures, declared that investments were risky during the depression, that the only safe form in which to have her wealth was currency.

Under his urging, she had turned over five thousand dollars to him. But there she had stopped. The rest—more than twenty-five thousand—she had doggedly refused to give up.

That twenty-five thousand dollars, Sim Dorsey was convinced, was hidden somewhere in the house.

"I'll find it," he muttered to himself as he climbed the steep and creaking stairs to the second floor. "She's stuck it away like a woman would, and I'll get my hands on it pretty quick."

He began his search in their bedroom. Methodically he went through the closet, the drawers in the old walnut dresser and bureau. He slit the mattress open and his groping fingers sought vainly for the feel of banknotes within.

If Jenny Dorsey had concealed her money in that room, she had taken the secret of the hiding place with her into her shallow grave two floors below.

Sim was undaunted by his first failure. He was as thorough and systematic as he was greedy and heartless. Sooner or later, he assured himself, he'd come across the money. Then he'd leave this house forever. By the time a search was started for Jenny, he'd be far away. It might even be years before her body was unearthed. In the meantime—

He turned swiftly. Then he grew rigid, his eyes peering furtively from beneath his brows toward the door.

From below came the sound of the doorbell. It was ringing with impatient insistence.

DORSEY hesitated. He looked quickly at his watch, and saw that the hands pointed to ten o'clock. They seldom had visitors at the house; no acquaintances who would be apt to drop in so late in the evening, anyway.

The crafty husband had long ago alienated his wife's former friends. He had offended them deliberately as part of his scheme to isolate her from anyone who might side with her against him.

Again the bell. This time in a steady, commanding ring.

With a black scowl, Dorsey walked down the stairs and across the short stretch of hallway to the heavy twin doors with frosted glass. Placing his face close to them, he called out gruffly.

"Who is it?"

"It's me—Nate! I want to see Jenny!"

An expression of alarm flitted over Dorsey's square face. He would have liked to tell Nate Todd to go on away, that they had retired for the night—anything to get rid of him. But he was afraid to.

Sim Dorsey hated the man who was standing outside. He hated him because the brother had tried with all his might to keep Jenny from marrying Dorsey. He hated him, too, because the younger man showed in every move his distrust and dislike of the dour Sim.

"What do you want to see her for at this time of night?" he demanded petulantly.

"I'll tell her!" Nate's voice came back sharply. "Open up! What's wrong with you, anyway?"

Reluctantly and with much fumbling of the bolt, Dorsey opened the door. Nate Todd, his keen blue eyes resting momentarily on the other man with a glance of contempt, stepped into the hallway.

"Where's Jenny?"

"She—she ain't here."

Todd caught the note of hesitation. "Not here? Where's she gone?"

As he asked the question, he walked into the living room and snapped on the light. He sat down on the edge of the horse-hair sofa.

Dorsey remained standing. He was unprepared for this visit. A man by nature plodding methodical, he was a slow thinker. For a few seconds he turned the matter of Jenny's whereabouts over in his mind.

"She went in to Pittsburgh today," he said finally.

"Pittsburgh, huh?" Todd showed surprise. He placed a hand on his hip and looked shrewdly at his brother-in-law. The movement pushed back his coat and revealed a shiny badge.

The sight of the emblem was a disagreeable reminder to Dorsey that his wife's brother was a member of the police department. Detective Sergeant Todd. At that moment, the suggestion of police authority sent an icy chill through the jowled murderer's veins. With an effort he refrained from trembling visibly.

"Yes, she went there this afternoon," Dorsey nodded. "I'm going to drive over tomorrow and meet her and bring her back."

He lied more smoothly now that he had hit upon his line of falsehood.

"What'd you want to see Jenny for at this time of night?"

Todd didn't answer at once. Instead, he let his glance rest in poorly concealed enmity on the other man's face with its bulbous nose.

"Well," the detective said finally, "it was about her money."

Dorsey's beetle brows lifted. "What about her money?"

"Nothing, except that I was talking to Keller at the Merchants National Bank. He told me Jenny had turned all her stocks and bonds into cash and had closed her account. Said she'd decided it was risky keeping money in banks these panicky times. Keller claims he tried to make her understand that her alarm was foolish, but she wouldn't listen to him."

"It's her money after all," Dorsey muttered.

THE detective betrayed signs of annoyance. "I'm not saying it isn't. She has converted everything into cash then, has she?"

"Everything but this house. We decided it was the safest way."

"We? So you were the one who urged her to do it?" Todd said thoughtfully.

"Why not? I'm her husband, ain't I?" the older man snapped.

"Unfortunately, yes," Todd nodded. "But I just wanted to warn Jenny."

"She don't need your warning. We don't need anything from you."

The detective ignored the remark.

"There's been a number of cases lately where folks have withdrawn their savings from the banks—and been robbed of them. I just thought someone might get wind of the fact that Jenny had a lot of cash here and try to get it."

Dorsey cast a suspicious look at Todd, but his ruddy face was bland and guileless.

"You can rest easy. That's why Jenny went to Pittsburgh. She's putting our money in one of the big banks there until —until we can buy some government bonds with it."

The detective stood up. "If that's true, everything's all right," he said, walking toward the front door.

Dorsey followed close behind him. "Course it's true. You don't think I'd be lying to you."

"I'm not so sure," the younger man said dryly. "Tell Jenny I'll see her tomorrow night."

"We won't be back till day after."

"I'll drop in then," Todd said.

Dorsey shut the door behind his caller with almost feverish haste. When he had slipped the bolts, he drew a soiled handerchief from his pocket and mopped his brow.

"Damn him," the killer muttered. "He'd better not try butting into this."

But the threat lacked conviction. Sim Dorsey was afraid of his detective brother-in-law.

He made his way quickly to the living room and turned off the light. Pushing the blind aside a couple of inches, he looked out. He had a clear view up and down the street, although not visible himself to anyone outside.

In the rays of the street lights, he could distinguish the wiry figure of Todd moving down the sidewalk. At the corner the detective paused, then slowly crossed the roadway. Even though the trees were leafless, it was shadowy over there and Dorsey fancied that his recent visitor had headed back on the far side of the street.

Panic seized him. He drew hurriedly away from the window and stood in the darkness of the living room for a few minutes. He could feel his pulse pounding, and his hands opened and closed in nervous agitation. Suddenly he turned and ran up the stairs.

For the moment the thought of the twenty-five thousand dollars hidden in that silent house faded from his mind. He was convinced that the detective had become suspicious, perhaps even surmised that Jenny had been murdered. And much as Sim Dorsey loved money, he valued his own worthless skin more.

His hands trembling, he packed a suitcase with a few necessary articles of clothing. But even in his anxiety for his own safety, his methodical habits stood by him.

In the living room Dorsey stopped and switched on the desk lamp. He ran quickly through the documents and papers in the tall secretary, making certain that there was nothing left that would incriminate him or put the police on his trail. A packet of old letters caught his eye. He picked them up and looked at the handwriting. Then he stuffed them in his pocket.

A few minutes later he had sneaked across the little plot of ground in the rear of the house to the garage. A driveway ran from it to the street, but a second set of doors opened into the alley. As silently as possible he opened them and pushed out the small coupé.

The alleyway sloped, and he was able to shove the car a considerable distance. Climbing in, he started the motor and headed away from the house of death as fast as the coupé would travel.

THE next morning Sim Dorsey sat hunched over the scarred table in his room in a cheap hotel on a side street in Pittsburgh. There was no sound except the steady scratching of his pen as he covered sheet after sheet of paper.

Frequently he examined a letter, written in a round feminine handwriting, which was spread out before him. Invariably this would be followed by a frowning shake of his head and Dorsey would consign his writing efforts to the waste basket, half filled with discarded and torn pages.

At last, however, he completed a sheet of writing that seemed to meet with his approval. He rose from his chair and walked to the window, where in the bright light he compared the letter he had just finished with the one from which he had copied the handwriting style.

A satisfied smile curled his colorless lips.

Dear Brother Nate:

Sim and I have made up our minds to take a little vacation and drive to Florida. I haven't had a real vacation in thirty years so think that now I can afford it I ought to have one.

Most of my money has been put in the bank here in Pittsburgh. It is a big one and ought to be a safe place to have my account. Sim locked the house up before he left and will you please keep an eye on it for us while we're away.

Sorry I didn't get to see you before we left but we just decided on the trip suddenly. Will write you later.

Your loving sister,

Jenny.

"That'll do," Dorsey murmured, when he had finished reading. "Nobody'd ever know Jenny didn't write it herself."

The letter dropped in the mail box, he breathed a sigh of relief. It would forestall any search or pursuit for some time, he was certain. And later he could write others which would cover his tracks even further.

Two hours later Sim Dorsey was sitting in the chair car of a train that was whirling him westward away from the chill autumn weather. He stared out the window at the unrolling landscape without seeing it. His thoughts were back in the old-fashioned frame house that hid the corpse of his wife—and the twenty-five thousand dollars that had brought about her death.

Now that he was safely on his way, he regretted the panic which had sent him rushing from the house without first finding the money. His hatred and fear of Nate Todd, he realized, had shaken his usual crafty self-control. In broad daylight the whole situation took on a different aspect from the one it had had in the gloomy old dwelling in the silent hours of the night.

Silently Dorsey cursed himself for his attack of nerves.

But it was too late now. The very thing that was his greatest safeguard—the forged letter—prevented him from going back. If he were caught burglarizing the house when he was supposed to be on his way to Florida there was no explanation he could make that wouldn't arouse suspicion.

Twenty-five thousand dollars! Dorsey's greedy black eyes seemed to sink out of sight beneath his brows at the thought. His hand went involuntarily to his inside coat pocket. The feel of the fat wallet there brought a grim smile to his face. With the proceeds from the sale of the coupé he had more than five thousand dollars.

And he'd get the rest of that money, he promised himself. But he'd get it by cunning.

Across the prairies of the Middle West, through the bleak sear mountains of Wyoming and Utah, over the hot sands of the Mojave Desert, Dorsey wrestled with his problem.

As he made his way from the Pullman with unseemly haste in order to avoid tipping the porter at Los Angeles, Sim Dorsey's expression was that of a man who is pleased with himself.

He indulged in the luxury of a taxicab and ordered the driver to take him to an inexpensive hotel. The cab moved recklessly through traffic, but to Dorsey it seemed to crawl along. He was impatient to begin his plan, a plan with twenty-five thousand dollars as the stake.

THE first couple of days he was in Los Angeles, Dorsey was busy making inquiries. They put him in touch with three men of widely different occupations. Yet each was able to contribute something to the scheme his sly mind had hatched during the long overland trip.

The first man was the celebrated Dr. Adolph Heinrich, Viennese plastic surgeon, who had kept many a Hollywood actress on the screen long after she would have been a back number if nature had taken its course. And for a thousand dollars Dr. Heinrich agreed to alter Dorsey's jowled face with its pear-shaped nose.

Then, "Professor" Tim Sullivan, physical culture expert, assured the killer from the East that for a cash consideration he could change his walk and his posture, as well as add numerous pounds to his weight.

And another self-styled professor, one Tomaso Alberni, was certain that Dorsey's voice under his capable training would be so changed as to be unrecognizable to anyone who had known him previously. Prof. Alberni pointed to an imposing list of film folk who had won fame in the talkies because of his method of voice culture.

These three experts in their respective lines began to remodel Sim Dorsey's physical make-up without the faintest notion that they were preparing a murderer for a return to the scene of his crime. He agreed to their terms and volunteered no information. Both these circumstances were entirely satisfactory to the doctor and the two professors.

Several times in the course of the next six months Dorsey sent letters to Nate Todd, forgeries purporting to come from Jenny. He explained that they had decided to prolong their vacation and had driven out to the West Coast. And Nate's replies renewed his feeling of security and seemed to augur well for the success of his scheme.

Then came a day when Dorsey stood in front of his mirror and surveyed himself critically. He admitted that his money and time had been well spent.

His hanging jowls were no more and his once bulbous nose had been trimmed to a Barrymore perfection. Even his hair line, which had almost met his eyebrows, had been raised. Electrolysis had killed the hair, leaving his forehead high and white.

He paraded back and forth and the face that looked back at him was smiling. His carriage had become erect and his manner was brisk. And his voice, he knew, had achieved a modulated and precise tone far different from its former strident one.

Dorsey sat down and once more wrote to Detective Sergeant Nate Todd in his well practiced imitation of Jenny's script.

Dear Brother Nate:

Sim and I are enjoying California so much that we have decided to stay here indefinitely so I'm writing you please to try and rent our house. You still have the keys from when you lived with me and a sign in the window ought to bring some prospective tenants.

We figure that you should be able to get about sixty dollars a month for it furnished. As soon as we have a permanent address I'll send it to you. Until then you can continue to write care general delivery but if you rent the house keep the rent money till I write for it.

Your loving sister,

Jenny.

Two days after he had mailed the letter, Sim Dorsey climbed aboard the eastbound limited.

DESK SERGEANT Bill Butler looked up with mild curiosity at the well-dressed man of middle age who had entered police headquarters and was approaching the railed-off section over which he presided.

"I'm looking for Mr. Nathaniel Todd. Is he in?" The stranger's voice was modulated and he spoke the words with a soft and careful inflection.

Desk Sergeant Butler shook his head. "He's not here right now, but I'm expecting him any minute. Anything I can do for you?"

The newcomer hesitated for a moment. "No, I guess not," he said finally. "If Mr. Todd is coming in soon, I'll wait for him, if you don't mind."

"Help yourself to a seat," Butler invited, waving his arm toward the two benches against the opposite wall. Then he turned back to the sporting section he had been reading when the entrance of the stranger interrupted him.

"Thanks."

Sim Dorsey sat down on one of the benches and, removing his soft hat, brought out a silk handkerchief and dabbed it at his brow. The desk sergeant, as he turned a page of his paper, let his glance rest on him for a few seconds.

"Hot day, isn't it?" Butler remarked.

The other man nodded and replaced the handkerchief in his breast pocket. Butler saw that although his face was tanned, the upper part of his forehead was a pallid hue, almost startling in its contrast.

"It certainly is," Dorsey replied. "Do you have very hot summers around here?"

His well-manicured hand patted his short mustache and then the symmetrical eyebrows which crowned his restless eyes.

"Kind of likes his own looks," Butler thought. "Gets hotter than hinges," he said. "You a stranger in the city?"

"Yes. But I expect to be here for some time."

They were interrupted by the arrival of Nate Todd.

"Here's Sergeant Todd," Butler said. "This gentleman wants to see you, Nate," he added to the detective.

The man on the bench stood up, replacing his hat and holding out his hand.

"My name's Gorham—George Gorham," he said in his careful accents.

The detective shook the proffered hand. "Glad to meet you," he said, his shrewd blue eyes darting a swift appraising glance over the other man.

Dorsey was conscious of a tightening in his throat. It was the crucial moment. If Nate Todd saw through the changes that had been made in his appearance it would be all over. But apparently the detective saw only a well-dressed, middle-aged stranger, and Sim Dorsey breathed inwardly with relief.

"I noticed a house for rent over on Maple Street," he explained. His voice was firm now that he felt sure he was unrecognized. "Your name was on the for-rent sign."

"Yes, that's my sister's place. She's moved away from here. At least temporarily."

"Well, I'm moving into the city temporarily, and maybe permanently," Dorsey replied with an attempt at jocularity. He felt a sense of elation, triumph almost. His plans were working out and Nate Todd, detective sergeant, was proving to be easily outwitted.

"I thought if I could rent a satisfactory furnished house, I might bring my wife and kids on from Chicago," Dorsey added.

"I guess the best thing for you to do would be to take a look at the place," Todd suggested.

"If it isn't too much trouble for you."

"Not a bit. I'm anxious to show it to possible tenants. We can run over there in my car in just a few minutes."

As they drove to the Maple Street address, Dorsey volunteered considerable fictitious information about himself. He was entirely confident now. He was considering opening a chain of electrical supply houses in the city. he explained, and planned to spend a couple of months making a survey of the possibilities. Later on, if he carried out his plan, he'd naturally have to live here.

When they reached the house on Maple Street, the detective ran the car up the narrow driveway and brought it to a stop near the rear of the structure.

"We might as well go in the back door," he said, pulling a bunch of keys from his pocket. "It's closer."

THEY crossed the small yard and Todd unlocked the door. As they stepped into the kitchen, dim behind drawn shades, a whiff of musty air struck them. The interior of the house had the unpleasant stuffy smell peculiar to dwellings that have been closed a long time and without occupants.

Dorsey's thoughts carried him to that

dark basement room below, in spite of himself, and he gave an involuntary shudder. But Todd, who had gone to the window and was throwing up the blinds and opening it, failed to notice his companion's expression.

"No one's been living here for more than six months," the detective explained apologetically. "I'd been planning to have a woman come in and clean up. But I only learned a couple of days ago that my sister wanted to rent it, and I haven't got around to hiring anyone."

"I understand the situation," Dorsey replied in his cool precise tone. "Shall we take a look at the rest of the house?"

They moved from room to room, Todd raising the window shades as they progressed, and setting forth the advantages of the place as best he could.

As the late afternoon sun streamed in the windows, however, it revealed the interior in a decidedly unfavorable aspect. Dust lay heavy on the furniture and floors. Even the door knobs, when the detective grasped them, were frosted with it, and his hands were soon black.

"It certainly is dirty," he said. "But I'll see to it that everything is spick and span right away. Get a woman over here."

Dorsey started to speak and then changed his mind. What he wanted most of all was to have the house to himself— to search for the money. But after all, he decided, he'd have plenty of time and there was no use in taking a chance of making Nate Todd suspicious by objecting to a cleaning woman.

Back once more in the kitchen, the detective went to the sink and began to clean the grime from his hands, talking to the other man as he swished the water on them.

"There's a first-rate basement, too, which I haven't shown you. We can go down there now, but the electricity's off and I'm afraid it will be pretty dark."

"Don't trouble. I'll take your word for it," Dorsey said quickly. Then he added: "What rent are you asking?"

"Sixty a month."

"I'll take it at that price," Dorsey nodded. He pulled a wallet from his pocket and removed several bills from it. "Here's the first month's rent."

"Just put it on the table. I'll give you a receipt as soon as I dry my hands. We can't get the gas and electricity turned on until tomorrow. You can move in then if that will be all right."

"Well—" Dorsey hesitated. He was disappointed, but again his sense of caution kept him from insisting on moving right in. It was out of character for him to want to inhabit the house, dirty as it was and without lights.

Todd finished drying his hands on his handkerchief. "Here are the keys. I'll attend to the cleaning, lights and gas the first thing in the morning, if you'll be here then."

"I'll be here," Dorsey assured him, putting the house keys in his pocket. "But you don't have to bother about all those things. I can take care of them myself."

"Wouldn't think of letting you!" the detective exclaimed. "I owe it to my sister to see that everything is in good shape for her tenant."

Dorsey shrugged. "Suit yourself," he said with a resigned smile.

Todd reached over to turn off the water tap at the sink. "Well, I'll be doggoned!"

"What's the matter?"

"Here's something else wrong. The sink's stopped up." He walked to the window and closed it. "But don't worry I'll have the plumber around to fix it."

A quick frown flashed across Dorsey's white forehead. Things were not going just the way he wished—too many people coming in to delay his search. But he closed his lips tightly and merely nodded.

"Any place I can drive you to?" Todd

asked, as he backed his car from the driveway beside the house.

His companion thought a few seconds. "Well, you might drop me at the Union Station, if it isn't too far out of your way. I'll pick up my bags there and then go on to a hotel."

FROM a position well back from the kitchen window where he wouldn't be seen, Dorsey watched Todd run his car up the driveway and halt it near the rear of the house. It was the next morning. Dorsey himself had been at the place only a little more than half an hour, although he already had admitted one visitor. The man from the electric company.

Sergeant Todd was accompanied by a stocky red-haired individual in a grimy suit of overalls. As the car jerked to a stop, the latter picked up a leather tool kit from the floor boards and followed the detective to the kitchen door.

Dorsey could hear them conversing outside as there came a knock on the door.

"There's nothing like delivering a plumber on the job in style," Todd was saying. "Then he doesn't have any excuse for going back for his tools."

The sound of a chuckle came to the ears of the man waiting inside the house.

"That's a worn-out joke. We don't forget anything nowadays," the red-haired man replied.

"Not even a good bill when you're through. But try to go easy on me. This is only a little job."

Dorsey as yet had made no move to open the door. Instinctively he disliked to admit the brother of the woman he had so brutally murdered. But another and more imperative knock spurred him to action and with reluctant hands he slid the bolt and swung the door wide.

"I've brought the plumber around with me," Todd announced cheerfully. "Mr. Cawker this is Mr. Gorham. He's renting Jenny's house."

The two men entered. Dorsey acknowledged the introduction with a nod and said to the detective: "Thanks. But there was no rush."

"Like to get things like this attended to as soon as possible," Todd replied heartily. "There's the sink, Cawker. Get busy on it!" He turned back to Dorsey. "The electric company man been here yet?"

"About half an hour ago."

The plumber dropped his kit of tools on the floor near the sink with a bang and began work.

"Anything at all you find you need to put the house in perfect condition, just let me know about it," Todd said to Dorsey. "And by the way, the cleaning woman promised to be here before noon."

"I don't think there will be many things come up," the other replied. "I—ah—er—am not a cranky tenant."

Cawker, wrench in hand, emerged from beneath the sink. "Sergeant, this thing's plugged up somewheres down below," he said. "The trap here is all clear. How do I get to the basement?"

Dorsey pricked up his ears.

The detective walked across the kitchen and opened a door. Then he reached through and switched on a light that illuminated the furnace room beneath.

"Right down this way!"

The plumber added a hammer to the wrench he already was carrying and started down. Halfway, however, he suddenly turned and called back.

"Say, sergeant, you'd better come along! This may turn out to be a pretty tough job. If it takes a lotta time, it'll be expensive and you'd better know what you're in for. Then you can't kick about my bill," he added, grinning.

The detective laughed and followed Cawker down the steps. Dorsey remained motionless for a few hesitant seconds. He could feel his pulse speed up. And although his expression remained unchanged, through his mind flashed a picture of the dark vegetable cellar.

With a catlike tread he crossed the kitchen. From below he could hear voices. Descending the first few steps, he could see Nate Todd's sturdy shoulders and in front of him the shorter figure of the plumber. Both men were staring at the ceiling.

"This is the one!" Cawker exclaimed, reaching up with his hammer and tapping a pipe that ran along a joist of the floor above.

They moved slowly across the furnace room tracing the course of the drain. From time to time, the plumber reached up and hit it a sharp rap, listening to the sound with an expert air. At the far side of the room, he gave his head a thoughtful shake.

"Don't believe the stoppage is anywhere along here. Must be beyond the wall." His glance rested on a door. "Another room beyond, ain't there?"

"That's an old vegetable cellar," Todd replied.

DORSEY glided noiselessly down the remaining steps. He stood watching the two men with slightly narrowed eyes and every nerve taut. The detective unlocked the door and stepped in. A second later came the dim glow of the carbon lamp and Cawker also disappeared through the door.

As Dorsey tip-toed after them to a point where he could see what was taking place inside the other room, a breath of stale dank air wafted against his cheek. He repressed a shudder and, every sense at nervous tension, kept his eyes fixed on the scene before him.

"Fella can't hardly breath in here," the plumber grumbled. "That's the pipe. She runs right down this wall and into the ground." He struck it a ringing blow, after which he looked around the shadowy room.

"That's a hell of a light!" he exclaimed. "I'd better go back for my flash."

"Wait a minute!" the detective suggested. "Maybe this will help."

He picked his way across the vegetable cellar and ripped the sacking from the narrow window. As the outside light filtered through the grime and cobwebs on the glass up close to the ceiling, the gloom was partially dissipated. Cawker gave a nod of approval.

"That makes it all right."

For a while, the plumber stood studying the pipe. Then he said: "In my opinion, the drain's all clear to this spot. I figure out it joins a big drain underground here and right at the elbow is where she's plugged. This sure is out-of-date plumbing," he added dolefully.

"What will you have to do?" Todd asked.

"Dig, I suppose," Cawker answered without enthusiasm. "Well, here's a shovel, anyway."

Dorsey's heart stood still. In a few minutes it seemed inevitable that Jenny's body would be found and all his carefully laid plans be ruined. With her murder discovered, the house would be overrun with police and he'd be forced to abandon his scheme to stay in it and hunt for the money.

But immediately this thought was replaced with a more terrifying one. There would be a hue and cry for him—Dorsey! The letters would turn the search to California. Heinrich and the others would be sure to recognize the description and—

A movement on the part of Cawker distracted him. The plumber was tracing a line across the dirt floor with the edge of the spade.

"This is where that pipe runs underground, if you ask me," he said.

Dorsey relaxed his taut nerves and breathed a silent prayer of thanks. The course Cawker had lined out would miss the spot where Jenny lay buried by at least a foot and a half. He thought back to that gruesome night six months before. Yes, he was right. He'd dug the hole parallel to those other bins. He moved closer until he was standing in the doorway.

"Well, here goes!" the plumber exclaimed and, spitting on his hands, sank the spade into the ground. He tossed the upturned earth to one side and dug in again.

SMILING softly to himself, Dorsey started to retrace his steps, when a sudden exclamation of surprise from Cawker halted him.

"By golly! Look at this, will you!"

Todd stepped to the plumber's side just as the latter straightened up, a square object in his hand. The detective took it curiously and Dorsey saw that it was a dirt-covered, metal, fishing-tackle box.

"Just banged my shovel into it," Cawker explained.

Todd pulled the wooden pin from the staple that held the box closed and raised the lid. A gasp of amazement broke from his lips. Dorsey's eyes widened and his mouth fell open.

It was stuffed to overflowing with packets of banknotes.

Jenny's twenty-five thousand dollars! Dorsey bit his lips. So she'd buried it in the cellar where he later buried her. Now he'd never get his hands on it.

Instantly his shifting eyes sparkled greedily, dangerously. And, to himself, he cursed the luck that he was unarmed.

The detective was bending over the box of money, apparently too surprised to say anything. The plumber, too, was gazing at it as if stupefied.

Suddenly Dorsey noticed a bulge in the detective's hip pocket. A second later he had glided into the vegetable cellar and in another second he was pressing Todd's own pistol into the small of the latter's back.

"Don't move or I'll kill you!" he snarled out. "And hand that money over!"

With a swift movement, Dorsey snatched the box and backed toward the door, holding the pistol before him. He slammed the heavy door and turned the key. Then he wheeled and ran full speed up the stairs to the kitchen, where he also locked the door at the head of the steps.

For a split second he was undecided. Then, shoving the metal box under his coat and slipping the gun into his pocket, he stepped out into the back yard.

At the corner of the house, the detective's car which was parked in the driveway, caught his eye. A few quick steps and he was alongside it next to the building. He put one foot on the running board and his hand grasped the handle of the door.

But before Dorsey could climb in, his ankles were seized in an iron grip and he was yanked violently toward the foundation of the house. He gave a startled cry and struggled to keep his balance. The money box slipped from his grasp and crashed to the cement of the driveway.

His face struck heavily against the side of the car. Then dazed and frightened he was dragged through the low cellar window and back into the vegetable cellar he had left only a minute before.

Todd, his blue eyes blazing, snapped the handcuffs on Dorsey's wrists as the murderer lay groveling in the dirt.

"Thought you'd get away with that! You dirty thief!" the detective rasped out. He turned to Cawker.

"Go ahead and fix that drain! I'll take the rat to the station and come back later!"

THERE was a haggard expression on Nate Todd's face as he stood before Butler's desk late that day. He had just come from the cell block where he had locked up Dorsey after a long session in the back room.

"And that's exactly what he did, Bill," the detective said. "After he'd killed poor Jenny, he went to California and had his whole appearance changed. He spilled the entire story."

The desk sergeant nodded thoughtfully. "How'd you squeeze the confession from him."

"Well, I was a little rough, I guess, for one thing," Todd admitted.

"Nobody'd ever blame you for that."

The detective smiled sadly. "Don't believe they would. But what really brought him around to admitting he was Dorsey was this. When I first met him, quite a long time ago—before Jenny married him, I didn't like his looks. I tried to persuade her not to marry him and even took his fingerprints on the sly in hopes I could get some kind of record on him."

"What'd you find out?"

"Not a thing. But I kept his prints. Of course, I thought at first today that Gorham, as he called himself, was just an ordinary crook. But I printed him and when Cawker spaded around that cellar looking for a plugged pipe and found—" He broke off with a faint choke in his voice.

"It was too bad," Butler said sympathetically.

"I was dead certain Dorsey killed her. Naturally I checked Gorham's prints with his. They were the same. And when I put that up to him, he told everything."

"He'll get the hot seat," the desk sergeant murmured.

"He will!" Todd said grimly. Then he added: "It's a strange thing, Bill, but when Sim Dorsey buried Jenny in that cellar, he was digging his own grave, too. It was the dirt he shoveled out that stopped up the drain!"

From the Wings

HAVE you ever stood in a theatre just back of the edge of the proscenium arch and watched the performers go through the action of a play out on the stage? It's a mighty interesting experience and gives one the impression that he is really seeing the wheels go round from the inside. The prompter usually occupies this vantage point and from it he can cue both the speech and action of the characters as they need help or correction in their work.

These last few pages of each issue of DIME DETECTIVE MAGAZINE are the nearest approach we have to the theatrical prompter's box. We want you to feel at home in them—and that shouldn't be hard—for unlike the theatre there are no canvas flats which mustn't be leaned against, no tables loaded with properties which mustn't be tipped over.

Cue us just as much as you want to about whatever you think needs change or readjustment in the magazine. And you don't have to whisper your corrections either. No one is going to be annoyed if you speak right up and tell us where we get off.

DIME DETECTIVE MAGAZINE is bound to give a smooth performance when the curtain goes up on the 20th of each month. But it is a whole month between first nights and while we're in the dress-rehearsal process we want you readers out there in the wings to play prompter and director too. Give us an idea of how you think the show is shaping up so that we can roll 'em in the aisles when the play starts. We haven't caught any of the audience sitting on their hands during past performances and we're not going to let that sort of thing begin.

OSCAR SCHISGALL, whose hair-raising story, *The Death Scream*, opened this issue of the magazine, is as interesting a personality as any one of the characters who fill his yarns. It's high time you met him. Let's let him introduce himself. Mr. Schisgall speaking.

Usually, when I'm asked to write about myself, I roll up my sleeves and attack the typewriter with a full 376-page autobiography as my goal. But I know the readers of Dime Detective Magazine are eager to get back to the stories that precede this confession, so I'll cut my 376 pages down to as brief a summary as possible.

I was born. It happened at the beginning of the century over in Belgium, but I was whisked to these shores before I could toddle over Belgian cobblestones. Here, in New York, I grew up and finally became an Old Grad of New York University. One day, at the age of 18, I saw a movie in which the hero, a writer, sat on the veranda of his chateau, sipping lemonade and gazing out at his yacht. Life, eh, what? So I became a writer. Unfortunately, the editors didn't think so.

For three years I continued to write story after story—all kinds but all pretty bad—but now and then one of them would bring a check. To eke out this precarious existence, I sold sand, clocks, meat slicing machines, real estate, and once even got by as a paid public speaker! But the stories suddenly started to sell. I quit everything else to write. And since then I've had published about 400 of them—shorts, novelettes, serials, plus a book and a couple of other books now in preparation.

I have one (1) wife and one (1) son. For "material" we usually go vagabonding. In fact, we've spent several years wandering through every odd corner of Europe. And through quite a few queer nooks of this blessed country. My outdoor hobbies are tennis and golf—plenty of each. My indoor hobbies are chess and chess. Also chess. My—but my wife has just glanced over my shoulder, and she says I've talked enough about myself. So, with a pleasantly modest bow, let me ring down the curtain.

Thank you, Mr. Schisgall! We would have liked to see a picture of you hovering over that chess board doing tricks with the queen's pawn. How about digging one up for us one of these days?

WILLIAM REUSSWIG is another of our steady contributors who is doing much to make DIME DETECTIVE MAGAZINE the ace of action-mystery-adventure yarn books. A graduate of Amherst College, where he captained the football team in his senior year, he still thinks in terms of the gridiron and would rather reminisce about the prowess of the team in those "good old days" than talk over next month's magazine cover. The final results, however, after we've locked him up with a pencil and some sketch paper, always make us congratulate ourselves that he decided to turn illustrator instead of seeking to emulate Benny Friedman and cash in on his athletic prowess.

He received his training at the Art Student's League and the Grand Central Art School, both in New York, and has done covers for many magazines as well

William Reusswig

as much advertising art work. When he has any free time he spends it working on a model of the frigate, Constitution, which he has carved in wood. He has been at it for four years now and when we saw it the other evening it looked like it was about finished but we were assured that it won't be completed for years. Mr. Reusswig says he has hardly begun on the intricate detail work of getting the ropes (pardon us—yards) in place. We have a spot on our mantel where it would look swell just as it is. That's not a hint—just our flare for interior decoration expressing itself.

Mr. Reusswig shares a studio with his better half who signs her work Martha Sawyers. You have probably seen it on the portrait covers of movie magazines and in the Herald-Tribune. We had our own ideas about this arrangement in the studio but are assured that it isn't for the purpose of permitting mutual chaperonage when the model's stand is occupied. It's a workshop and nothing more.

Besides the covers he does for DIME DETECTIVE Mr. Reusswig is particularly adept in his portrayal of Western scenes and characters. In fact he says he prefers doing that type to any other. In order that his pictures appear authentic and true to life the artist has collected a vast quantity of genuine Western cowboy equipment—weapons, saddlery, and various and sundry articles of costume such as sombreros, chaps, high-heeled riding boots, holsters and all the rest of the garb which goes to accoutre the men who ride the range. Insistence on the accuracy of detail in such things plays an important part in making the artist's work interesting as well as veritable. You may be sure, when looking at one of Mr. Reusswig's covers, that—as well as being an artistic piece of work—it is also correct in its detail. As a rule it takes him anywhere from two to four days to complete a cover. Watch for his next one.

J. ALLAN DUNN etc.

It just came into the office with the paint still damp—and it's something to write home about! Tell us if we exaggerated after you've given it the once-over.

AND here is the long-awaited picture of J. Allan Dunn. That master concocter of thrilling mystery yarns assures us that his companion is not the Red Bull of Tabor or even one of its progeny. We have our own ideas though and feel reasonably safe in saying that we know now how Mr. Dunn gets the material for his stories—at least one of them! We had asked him for a snap of himself at the tiller of his yacht—you know he is an ardent sailor and navigator—and this was the result. Maybe it's a sea-going bovine. And while we're on the subject of Mr. Dunn it's a good time to remind you that *The Fire Fiend* in April DIME DETECTIVE MAGAZINE is even more breath taking than *Out of the Night*. You won't want to miss it! Mr. Reusswig has done a cover illustration for it which is as exciting as the story itself. Taking them both together a sure-fire thrill combination is on the docket for April.

STATEMENT OF THE OWNERSHIP, MANAGEMENT, CIRCULATION, ETC., REQUIRED BY THE ACT OF CONGRESS OF AUGUST 24, 1912,
Of DIME DETECTIVE MAGAZINE, published Monthly at Chicago, Illinois, for April 1, 1932.

State of...................
County of.............., ss.

Before me, a notary public in and for the State and county aforesaid, personally appeared Harold S. Goldsmith, who, having been duly sworn according to law, deposes and says that he is the business manager of the DIME DETECTIVE MAGAZINE and that the following is, to the best of his knowledge and belief, a true statement of the ownership, management (and if a daily paper, the circulation), etc., of the aforesaid publication for the date shown in the above caption, required by the Act of August 24, 1912, embodied in section 411, Postal Laws and Regulations, printed on the reverse of this form, to wit:

1. That the names and addresses of the publisher, editor, managing editor, and business managers are: Publisher, Popular Publications, Inc., 205 East 42nd St., New York City, N. Y.; Editor, Harry Steeger, 205 East 42nd St., New York City, N. Y.; Business Manager, Harold S. Goldsmith, 205 East 42nd St., New York, N. Y.

2. That the owner is: (If owned by a corporation, its name and address must be stated and also immediately thereunder the names and addresses of stockholders owning or holding one per cent or more of total amount of stock. If not owned by a corporation, the names and addresses of the individual owners must be given. If owned by a firm, company, or other unincorporated concern, its name and address, as well as those of each individual member, must be given.)

Popular Publications, Inc., 205 East 42nd St., New York City, N. Y.; Harry Steeger, 205 East 42nd St., New York, N. Y.; Harold S. Goldsmith, 205 East 42nd St., New York, N. Y.

3. That the known bondholders, mortgagees, and other security holders owning or holding 1 per cent or more of total amount of bonds, mortgages, or other securities are: (If there are none, so state.) None.

4. That the two paragraphs next above, giving the names of the owners, stockholders, and security holders, if any, contain not only the list of stockholders and security holders as they appear upon the books of the company but also, in cases where the stockholder or security holder appears upon the books of the company as trustee or in any other fiduciary relation, the name of the person or corporation for whom such trustee is acting, is given; also that the said two paragraphs contain statements embracing affiant's full knowledge and belief as to the circumstances and conditions under which stockholders and security holders who do not appear upon the books of the company as trustees, hold stock and securities in a capacity other than that of a bona fide owner; and this affiant has no reason to believe that any other person, association, or corporation has any interest direct or indirect in the said stock, bonds, or other securities than as so stated by him.

5. That the average number of copies of each issue of this publication sold or distributed, through the mails or otherwise, to paid subscribers during the six months preceding the date shown above is (This information is required from daily publications only.)

HAROLD S. GOLDSMITH,

Sworn to and subscribed before me this 25th day of January, 1932.
[SEAL.]

MARY A. JENKINS,
(My commission expires March 30, 1932.)

I Walked Twice Across the Continent to Shake Hands with George F. Jowett

By Ed Quigley

henever I saw a well-muscled strong-man do his stuff my heart always ache with desire. Above all things in the world I to be strong and to have a big chest, broad shoulders and r of powerfully muscled arms.

this particular occasion I sat upon a rail fence on my r's farm and I felt unusually downhearted. A piece of paper across the road, and as it clung to the fence post I saw nted upon it the figure of a powerfully developed man. Eagerly ped from my seat and grabbed it, and for hours I gazed upon magnificent form with devouring eyes. Coming back to reali- is what plunged me into my unusual state of downheartedness. ed myself, "What chance have I, a tall, lanky youth, of ever ing as powerfully developed and as strong as the man in the re? Here I am on an Oklahoma farm with no chance of seeing lking with such a man to learn the secret of getting strong."

han an inspiration came to me. I would write to him—better I would go to see him. I had no money but in the enthusiasm decision that did not worry me. I felt that I must see him. ad once been a weakling and knew what it was to have an erable ache in the heart to be strong. He would understand, positive. I started out on my long hike from Oklahoma to ylvania with all my worldly possessions wrapped up in a small ie—a clean shirt, tooth brush, and a one dollar bill.

walked and hitch-hiked all the way east, only stopping at lace long enough to work until I got the price of a pair of new . I had worn the old shoes out in my long trek. Finally the tame when I reached the city of Scranton where this famous te-teacher is located. It was raining hard but my heart beat anticipation only to be doomed with disappointment. The I had hiked across the continent to see was out of town, but s told that if I cared to go on to Philadelphia a wire would nt him to wait for me. Gee! I was tickled to death. I got th ride all the way through and bright and early presented myself Philadelphia address. Never will I forget my first sight of that Such shoulders! They seemed to overflow the chair in which t. His neck was powerful and supple—his chest broad and —and such arms! I thought they would burst the sleeves. but that was a happy day for me. He was wonderful. He d me down with valuable advice about my training.

left Philadelphia on my hike back to Oklahoma with a new in my heart. When I got home I started right away to put practice all he had told me. Day by day I could see my les grow, and my strength increased at a wonderful rate. By following year I was marvelously improved, and I determined nother hike across the continent to see my famous friend, ideal teacher. He was delighted with my physical improvement. He me he knew I would make good because a fellow who really a thing bad enough will go out and get it in spite of all.

Gee, fellows, I wish you could all see the wonderful muscles I built for myself and the great strength that each muscle has. I wish you could have the same grand experience I had, but you can if you want. It is simply a matter of wanting a well developed body and starting out right to get it.

I walked four times across the continent to see this great teacher and it was the best thing that I ever did. Some day I am going to be famous and every bit as strong as my ideal is. He said it was quite possible. I can't help but win, and with the wonderful start I now have with my well developed body I am going to lick the world. So can you. It makes no difference whether you live on a farm or in the city. The whole thing is to determine you want a well developed body with muscles of steel and you will get them. You can have health, strength, success and a body you will be proud of.

I'm positive George F. Jowett can help you! He will prove it to you! He has prepared six special courses listed in the coupon. Each specializes in moulding a definite part of the body. He doesn't ask you to enroll or sign for his full course now. Just try a test course now. Each test course is a complete course covering the subject it is written about. You'll be amazed at the results in 30 days. You'll be dazzled in 90 days. Pick out your course—rush coupon with only 25c, or if you want all six attach $1.00 to the coupon and get them all.